Echoes of the Fallen

Robin T. Popp

Larkspur Lane Publishing, L.L.C.

Also by Robin T. Popp

TEXAS AFTER DARK SERIES
Death at the Double R
The Ghost Whisperer's Gambit

NIGHT SLAYER SERIES
Out of the Night
Seduced by the Night
Tempted in the Night
Lord of the Night

THE IMMORTALS SERIES
Immortals: The Darkening
Immortals: The Haunting
Immortals: The Reckoning
Beyond the Mist

SUN SERIES
Too Close to the Sun

Contents

Chapter One

"I COULD USE SOME help here!"

Jack Marsden's hands danced skillfully across the controls, his eyes fixed on the hurtling chunks of jagged meteorites that lay ahead as he navigated his ship, the *Black Jack*, with a deadly grace through the meteor field.

"Avoid the big ones," Lena Alvarez, his chief engineer, sounded annoyingly calm. She was in the rear of the ship, double-checking their engine status after colliding with two meteors off the port side.

"Not helpful." Sweat trickled down his brow as he deftly wove through the maze of obstacles, his heart pounding in his chest. He tightened his grip on the control stick. "Get up here. Now!"

Lena appeared a moment later, her purple-hued hair shimmering in the dim light of the cockpit. She slid into the seat beside him and leaned forward, her large black eyes scanning the trajectory of the meteorites.

"You planning to thread that gap? Bold! Suicidal, but bold."

Without missing a beat, Jack yanked the control stick to the port side, sending the ship spinning in a graceful arc between two massive boulders rushing towards them. The ship groaned under the strain, its engines whining with exertion.

"We've got a splitter coming in from port—veer starboard now!" Her voice was laced with urgency.

The *Black Jack* shuddered violently as a stray rock grazed its port side, causing sparks to fly from the damaged hull. Alarms blared throughout the ship, competing with the pounding of his pulse in his ears. Jack did his best to ignore the chaos and focus solely on navigating them to safety.

"I can see the edge of the field." Lena's voice cut through the tension in the cockpit. "We're almost there! Just a few more meteors to dodge."

With a last burst of speed, Jack veered sharply to starboard, narrowly avoiding a meteor large enough to have pulverized the *Black Jack* into space dust, and then the ship surged forward, breaking free from the gravitational grip of the meteor field.

They were finally out of immediate danger, but the ship's engines had taken a beating. Smoke billowed from the vents as warning lights flashed on the console.

Lena surveyed the damage with a trained eye, her hands moving swiftly across the control panel. "We're alive, but I'll need to make repairs before we can go any further."

Jack nodded, his gaze still fixed on the stretch of open space that now lay before them as he killed the engines and let the ship drift. "Let me know if I can help."

"Just don't let us run into anything." She made her way to the back of the ship.

Left alone in the dimly lit cockpit, Jack stroked the ship's console. "Good ol' girl," he mumbled affectionately. That meteor field had come out of nowhere, catching them off guard, but once again, despite her age, the *Black Jack* had responded instantly to his commands.

He prayed she continued to hold together for a while longer. He'd had the ship a long time, and they shared a lot of memories. Looking around, he thought the scruffy interior mirrored himself—worn but resilient, a testament to their shared history. Panels hung loose, revealing a tangle of wires held together by hope and ingenuity, while the exterior surfaces bore scratches and dents that told stories of past battles and too many narrow escapes.

A flickering light above the cockpit cast erratic shadows across the control console until he slammed his palm against the panel and the light steadied. The faint smell of engine oil and last night's flash-meal lingered in the air, adding to the sense of familiarity that made the *Black Jack* feel like an extension of himself.

While he waited for Lena to report back on the damage to the ship, he reached into the pocket of his worn leather jacket and withdrew the small holovault communique. Not for the first time, he played the message.

Immediately, the holographic image of Michael Mattix flickered to life, his face weary and determined. His voice, soft yet urgent, filled the cockpit.

Jack, if you're seeing this, it means things went way wrong and I'm dead. Michael's holographic form flickered, his voice heavy with emotion. *I got involved in something big. I thought I could handle it, but somehow I screwed up and now it might be too late.* He paused, running a hand through his disheveled hair. *I can't give you the details. It's too risky, and I won't put you in that kind of danger. Just know whatever you hear about me, about what I've done ... it's not the whole truth. There's so much more going on here than anyone realizes.*

Michael's holographic image flickered again as he continued, his tone filled with urgency. *After our parents died, it was just me and Alexis. I swore I'd take care of her. If I can't be there to watch over her, I need you to do it for me. Please. She'll want to know what happened to me, but looking for the answers could get her killed, too. Please don't let that happen.*

Then his image faded, leaving Jack alone with the echo of Michael's last words.

In his mind, another image shimmered to life, a young woman with long, dark hair and striking features. Alexis. Michael's little sister, as she'd appeared the last time he saw her in person—a teenager whose beauty was just beginning to blossom.

Where was she now? It had taken six months for the holovault communique to find him in the Outer Fringe. The first thing he'd done was try to reach Michael in his home city of Galathea on Veridian Prime, only to learn his friend had died shortly after sending the communique. When Jack had tried to reach Alexis, he'd learned that she had disappeared shortly after Michael's death, and no one had heard from her since.

"The damage wasn't as bad as I thought," Lena said, coming back to the cockpit and interrupting his thoughts. "It should last us until we reach Centuri-5." She laid in the course and set the ship on auto-pilot. When she finished, she turned to him, studying his face. "Hey, you look like shit. Were you playing Michael's message again?"

"Yeah." He forced a wry smile as he put the holovault communique back into his pocket.

Lena, once again, took the seat next to his; her petite frame and pale skin belied her physical strength and vibrant personality. "Want to talk about it?"

She knew him so well; and she knew he needed to talk through it out loud, because doing so helped him clear his thoughts.

"None of it makes sense." He didn't bother to hide his frustration. "Michael and I met in the military. My parents were dead, so he took me to his home when we were on leave. His parents became my parents; his younger sister, Alexis, became ..." he paused and cleared his throat. "No, I can't truthfully say I thought of her like a sister, but she was special." He smiled now, remembering the nights he and Alexis stayed up late watching old movies, usually after Michael went to bed. Then, feeling Lena's gaze on him, he continued. "I lost touch with Michael after he returned to Veridian Prime and I went to Lortron-9. Then I get his communique—"

"And learn he was killed while committing a felony."

Jack shook his head. "See, that's exactly what I'm talking about. I know what the police report says, but it doesn't add up. The Michael I knew would never get mixed up in something like stealing Luminite crystals. I mean, come on—Luminite? Ever since the

Solaris Dominus government found those things in the Elysian Rift, on that old Wraith planet, they've locked the whole mining operation down tight. The process is so heavily regulated, you can't even move the stuff on the black market. So what's the point in stealing it?"

"People change."

He shook his head. "Not Michael. He was a regular Star Scout. He would never break the law. That's why I need to talk to Alexis. To find out what really happened to him."

"Except now she's disappeared, too."

"Exactly, and I'm worried she might be in trouble."

"Or maybe she needed time alone," she suggested. "It's possible, you know. Everybody grieves differently."

Grudgingly, he conceded her point. "Maybe so, but I still want to find her."

"So, no hits from your spyware?"

"None, yet." She was referring to the computer code he'd embedded, without permission, into the key computer systems of every planet and space station they'd visited in the past three months during their travels. The code was part of a program that used government and private security facial recognition software and would alert him to any sightings of Alexis. Of course, the program's accuracy was only as good as the image he'd provided, and he'd had to use an older pilot's license image, which he'd found after hacking the records of the Solaris Dominus Department of Space Vehicles, also known as the DSV. "It's like she vanished into thin air." Frustration simmered beneath his calm exterior.

"We'll find her," Lena vowed.

Her support meant a lot to him, and he couldn't help but marvel over the freak circumstances under which they'd met. She'd come into his life at the perfect time—just when he and his former flying partner, Adrian Sun, had parted ways. He'd needed work done on the ship's engines and she had come highly recommended. Instead of taking money for her work, she'd negotiated for a ride off-planet. He'd agreed and now, two years later, they were close friends, flying together, hunting bounties, and taking odd assignments. In the early stages of their association, they'd tried being lovers, but had quickly agreed they were better off keeping their relationship platonic.

"Alright." Jack forced himself back to the present. "Let's get back to work. We have a delivery to make at Centuri-5 and while we're there, you can make the necessary repairs to the engines. After that, we have our pick of jobs. There's a family on HydroTerra that will pay for safe passage to Solorix-5, a wealthy client on Veridian Prime who has a yen for Tolaxian brandy, and a reward for the return of some stolen trinkets, which we might find on Purgo-Max. You have a preference?"

Lena sighed. "Transporting the family sounds boring and transporting Tolaxian brandy into the Solaris Dominus galaxy is illegal."

Jack smiled. "That never stopped us before." At her scowl, he continued. "Retrieving stolen trinkets it is."

Thirty-six hours later, after making their delivery and completing the ship's repairs, they set a course for Purgo-Max and were just sitting down to another flash-meal when an alarm pierced the quiet hum of the *Black Jack*'s engines. Jack raised his hand to check the screen of the comm-device strapped around his wrist.

At first, the flashing notification didn't register. Then his heart started thudding against his chest as a sense of urgency swept over him.

His gaze flicked to Lena. "Change of plans." He tried to suppress his excitement. "We're heading for the Outer Fringe. Alexis has been spotted."

Lena nodded, understanding the gravity of the situation. "Alright, let's get moving before she disappears again."

Their movements were quick and efficient as they sprang into action. Jack felt a surge of adrenaline course through him as he prepared to take the controls, his mind racing with thoughts of Alexis. How much like her DSV picture did she look? What had she been doing these past several years? Would she be able to tell him anything about Michael's death? And most important, how would she react to seeing him after all these years?

Chapter Two

THE PULSATING MUSIC INSIDE the bar at the Outer Fringe space station throbbed through her veins as Alexis Mattix deftly navigated the maze of tables, chairs, and patrons. Her fingers gripped the edge of the tray laden with exotic drinks, each in a kaleidoscope of colors as diverse as the beings that filled the room.

She reached the table she was heading for and slid between the chairs of two seated, boisterous aliens, catching a whiff of something sweet mixed with the scent of sweat and alcohol.

"Here you go." She placed the drinks on the table with practiced precision as her gaze flitted from one patron to the next, studying faces but not finding the one she sought.

"Thanks, love," drawled one customer, tendrils of smoke escaping his gaping maw as he puffed on a cigar. Alexis gave him a smile and a nod. It was part of her act, but inside, she recoiled at his obvious interest in her.

If her brother was here, she'd give him hell for putting her through this charade, but that was the problem. Michael was dead, and she needed to be here if she had any hope of discovering the truth behind his death.

As she turned and headed to the next table, her mind drifted back to her meeting with Dominic two days prior.

They had rendezvoused on the lower level of the space station, a place where the air was thick with the acrid scent of illegal substances and people minded their own business.

Dominic, a sallow-faced human with a nervous tic in his left eye, had slid into the dark alcove beside her.

"What'd you find out?"

"I've been asking around." He'd kept his voice low, obviously not wanting to be overheard. *"None of the usual suspects are involved in the Luminite crystal thefts."*

Alexis had leaned closer, puzzled. "What do you mean?"

"The smuggling rings, the black-market dealers ... they're not touching the stuff. It's too hot, too risky. Whoever's behind this is operating outside the usual channels."

A sense of unease had settled in her gut. If the established criminal networks weren't responsible, then who was? "Do you have any leads at all?"

Dominic had nodded. "One. I just got back from Elysian-5. While I was there, I was having a drink at the Trader's Edge Catina and there was this Raniform sitting in the booth behind me. I overheard him bragging to his buddies. Said he was part of a crew transporting a massive haul of Luminite crystals."

A chill ran down Alexis's spine. If what Dominic said was true, this was no ordinary theft. The sheer scale of it was staggering. "Did he mention anything specific? Any details about the job?"

Dominic shook his head, his expression turning apologetic. "Nah, he was pretty tight-lipped about that. Probably didn't want to risk pissing off his employer by running his mouth too much. But I did hear him say they were headed to Solaris Dominus."

Alexis had felt her first rush of optimism. No ship could fly from Elysian-5 to Solaris Dominus without stopping at the Outer Fringe space station. If she could find this Raniform and talk to him herself—

"I don't suppose you can describe this Raniform?"

He'd smiled then and nodded. "I'll do you one better. I got a name. Graxx." Then he'd provided her with a full description.

"Can you tell me anything else about him?"
"He has a fondness for Starlight.*"*

That had been two days ago.

A sudden burst of laughter from a nearby table pulled her attention momentarily away from her thoughts as she continued her delicate dance through the crowded room, balancing her tray of drinks until she reached the next group.

"Three Sunbursts and a Durango Delight for you." She placed their drinks down with a flourish before scanning the room once again. Her informant had been positive Graxx would appear tonight, but so far, he was a no-show.

Focus. Heart pounding in time with the music, she deftly maneuvered her tray back to the bar, the empty glasses she'd collected along the way clinking together in a melodic cacophony.

Kylix, the bartender, currently manifesting in his male-form, caught her eye and beckoned her over with a charming smile. Setting the tray on the counter, she moved closer and leaned against the cool metal surface, enjoying the brief reprieve from the pulsing energy of the crowded room.

"Working hard tonight?" His green eyes sparkled with curiosity as he greeted her. His long brown hair framed his handsome face, a fine mustache and beard accentuating his strong jawline. As always, though, it was the intricate tattoo framing his left eye that held her attention.

"Always." She gave him a wry grin before listing off the drink orders.

Kylix nodded acknowledgement of the order, gazing at her quizzically. "I'm still trying to figure out what a nice girl like you is doing in a place like this?"

"Just passing through," she said evasively, returning his smile. She liked Kylix but he was an enigma, unlike any species she had encountered before.

"Of course." His quiet tone suggested that he knew better than to push her further. As he turned to fill her latest drink orders, Alexis reflected on the events that had brought her to this point.

She had been searching for answers ever since that fateful call from Michael, asking her not to worry because he had to go off-grid for a while. It wasn't the first time he'd called with such a message, but it had been the last.

Then her boss at the time, Police Chief Townsend, had called her to say Michael was dead; he'd been killed during the commission of a felony. Specifically, the police shot him while he was attempting to steal the heavily-regulated Luminite crystals.

Alexis, a newly appointed police detective, didn't want to believe her brother was a criminal, but the evidence against him seemed irrefutable. What had made him resort to breaking the law? She couldn't shake the guilt that came with thinking that, had she been a better sister, she might have prevented it; he might still be alive if she'd been there to help him when he fell on bad times.

Of course, she'd visited Michael's place of work, using the address he'd given her years ago, only to discover the place didn't actually exist—in fact, had never existed. Michael had lied to her and, being too absorbed in her own life, she'd never clued in.

Some detective I am. She'd quit her job shortly thereafter to go in search of the truth.

Just then, Kylix placed drinks on her tray and, giving him a smile of thanks, she headed back out into the dimly lit room, her gaze constantly searching the shadows for—yet not finding—a face with a scar bisecting one eye and a cruel twist of the lips.

"Four Galaxian Ales coming up," she announced, reaching the table that had ordered the drinks. The cool condensation on the glasses left a trail of moisture on her fingers as she handed them off.

"Thanks, Alexis," one alien slurred, his many eyes rolling in their sockets. "You're outta this world!"

"Keep the compliments coming, and maybe I'll bring you an extra round on the house," she countered playfully. Turning back, another patron, his eyes glazed over from one too many drinks, signaled for her attention.

"Could you bring us another round?"

"Of course," she replied. "Coming right up."

As she glided through the crowded bar, thoughts of Dominic, Michael, and Graxx swirled together like the alien brews she served.

"Two more Veridian Tonics and a Solar Wind," she told Kylix when she reached the bar.

As he began mixing the drinks, she marveled at the various species mingling together in the establishment, their differences momentarily forgotten in the shared pursuit of revelry. When she'd first arrived at the space station, she'd convinced Kylix to give her a job here, knowing that, eventually, everyone who came to the Outer Fringe eventually ended up in The Abyss. Now, however, the scents of alcohol and sweat intertwining with the heady beat of the music was a reminder that she'd been at the space station too long. If Graxx didn't show soon, she'd have to go to Plan B in her search for the truth.

Or was it Plan C? Hell, it could be Plan D or E, at this point. She couldn't keep track.

"Here you go." Kylix slid the vibrant concoctions toward her. She nodded her thanks as she placed the drinks on her tray and headed back to the waiting patrons.

As she set the drinks down on the table, a sudden buzzing sounded from her wrist comm-device. Glancing down, she saw the message flashing across the screen: "Performance time." She took a deep breath and headed back to the bar.

"Break a leg," Kylix whispered as she dropped off her tray. His knowing smile stirred an odd mix of comfort and unease in her.

Nodding her thanks, she wove her way through the tables toward the dimly lit backstage area.

Once there, she quickly got ready for stage. First, she pulled on a skull cap and stepped into the body-tint chamber. When she stepped out again, her skin was a delicate shade of aquamarine. It took only a second for the tint to fully dry. While it did, she slipped a green Winkskin into each eye to turn them green. Then she applied the full white eyelashes. Next, she donned a shimmering, form-fitting ensemble in the same color of aquamarine as her skin, giving her the appearance of being nude. The cool fabric clung to her body, accentuating every curve and muscle. Last, she pulled a wig of fuchsia pink hair over her head and aquamarine heels on her feet. Then, she examined herself in the mirror, mentally steeling herself for the performance ahead.

As the pulsating music grew louder, Alexis stepped onto the stage, into the spotlight that cast her in a hypnotic glow. Slowly, she began to dance, her movements fluid and seductive. As every face in the room turned to watch, she scanned them in return. She wasn't just a dancer tonight; she was a hunter seeking her prey.

Chapter Three

THE HEAVY METAL DOORS of the space station bar hissed as they slid open, revealing a dimly lit room filled with an eclectic mix of patrons. The air was thick with the mingled scents of various intoxicants and the hum of a dozen languages spoken by beings from countless different planets. Jack stood for a moment in the entryway, allowing his eyes to adjust to the low light. He scanned the room, wondering if Alexis was there and, if so, if he'd even recognize her.

After a cursory glance around the crowded room, he headed over to the bar where Kylix was bartending.

"Ah, Jack! Long time, no see," Kylix greeted him, his voice deep and resonant. "What can I get you?"

"Something strong." He settled onto a stool, then leaned against the cool surface of the counter.

Nodding, Kylix grabbed a glass and a couple of bottles from the back counter. Jack studied him as he poured equal parts from each bottle into the glass.

Kylix had been the bartender at The Abyss for as long as Jack could remember and, to Jack, the bartender was still a mystery. He was humanoid, but definitely not human. Like other alien beings, Kylix had pointy ears and could change his hair and eye color at will. He was also stronger and faster than the humans he resembled, and with much keener hearing and eyesight. Jack had run into other alien beings with such superhuman abilities. Lena, a half-Lyran, was just such a being. But Jack had never come across any other being who could do all that AND change their gender at will the way Kylix could.

Between the two forms, Jack preferred the female. For some reason, she seemed easier to talk to.

"Here you go," Kylix said a moment later, passing Jack the glass, now filled with a swirling deep blue liquid.

As he took a sip, the potent drink burned its way down his throat, setting fire to his insides. "Thanks," he managed between coughs.

"What brings you to the Outer Fringe this time?"

"I'm looking for a woman."

The bartender smiled. "I'm sure, given your reputation, you should have no trouble finding one."

"It's not like that," Jack clarified. "I'm looking for an old friend. Dark hair and blue eyes. Young. Attractive. Have you seen anyone matching that description?"

Kylix's features blurred and shifted. "Every time I look in the mirror," she cooed, now in her female form.

Jack gave a huff of laughter. "Funny. But seriously. Have you seen any new faces matching that description?"

Kylix narrowed her gaze at him. "Why are you looking for her?"

"Like I said. She's an old friend." When Kylix continued to stare at him, he continued. "Remember the holovault communique you gave me last time I was here?" She nodded. "It was from a close friend of mine who died under 'questionable' circumstances." He used his fingers to make air-quotes. "The woman I'm looking for is his sister. I'm afraid she might be here looking into the circumstances of his death, which puts her in danger."

He scanned the room again, his gaze stopping on the stage where a curvy female with short, spiky pink hair and very little clothing had just appeared. As the music started, she swayed in rhythm to the tune.

"Did the facial recognition software tell you she was here?"

"What?" He didn't have to fake being surprised but Kylix pinned him beneath her piercing gaze until he finally gave up. "Damn it. How'd you know about that?" Usually he was better at hiding his programs.

She smiled indulgently. "Nothing happens here that I don't know about. I considered removing your code from the program, but while some of your actions might be ethically questionable, you are, mostly, a decent man. And," she shrugged, offering a smile. "I was curious what you were up to." She leaned across the bar, putting her face closer to Jack's. "I believe your intentions are honorable."

"They are. Alexis is like a sister to me. I feel responsible for her." It was the truth, except the sister part. "And Michael's last wish was that I take care of her."

Kylix studied him a moment longer and then gestured towards the stage where the woman was dancing. "Talk to Eros—after she finishes her performance."

With newfound determination, Jack downed the last of his fiery drink and stood up. "Thanks, Kylix."

She merely nodded.

He wove his way through the tables, heading for the edge of the stage. All the while, his gaze never left the woman performing. Almost absently, he noted she was not a particularly talented dancer, but given her lush curves, he doubted anyone noticed—or cared. He let his gaze drink in the well-shaped legs, slender waist, and full, unbound breasts. There was so little material to her outfit, she was practically naked. With her green eyes, white lashes and aquamarine skin, he tried to guess what race she was. Thelarian, maybe? He hadn't met many Thelarians, the few he had all had the same colored skin and lashes.

The longer she danced, the more entranced he became. Her eyes sparkled like distant stars as she caught his gaze from up on stage; her seductive smile ignited a fire within him. He gestured with his hand that he wanted to talk to her and felt equal parts of relief and anticipation when she gave him a slight nod. He wondered if it might be possible to mix a little pleasure with business?

When her performance ended, Eros disappeared backstage accompanied by thunderous applause. She reappeared minutes later, wearing a cloak, but the clinging fabric did little to hide her lithe form as she strode toward him with long, confident steps.

"Can I buy you a drink?" he asked when she stopped in front of him.

"Sure, why not?" Her voice sounded melodious and inviting.

He led her to a quiet corner booth and waited for her to sit before sliding onto the seat opposite her. Then he raised his hand to summon a passing server. "What would you like to drink?"

"Veridian Tonic, please." She graced him with a dazzling smile that shocked him with its warmth.

He placed their order and waited for the server to disappear. "How long have you been working at The Abyss?"

"Not long." There was a throaty quality to her voice that sent his mind wandering to visions of nude bodies and tangled sheets.

"You planning to stick around long?"

She shrugged. "I don't know yet. Depends."

She didn't elaborate, and he didn't ask. People had a lot of different reasons for being at the space station and all of them were private.

Their drinks came, and after paying their server, Jack knew he couldn't stall any longer.

"I'm looking for someone," he told her. "A young human woman. Alexis Mattix. Kylix thought you might know her." Once again, he described Alexis.

Eros stared at him for so long, he wondered if he'd offended her with his question. Finally, she seemed to recover. "Why are you looking for her?"

"That's personal, but I'm worried she might be in danger." Her eyebrows furrowed. Then the music started up again, and another performer walked onto the stage. The crowd cheered, and he had to raise his voice to talk over the noise. "If you know anything about her whereabouts, I'd appreciate you telling me."

She leaned across the table to shout. "Not here. Let's go somewhere—quieter—to talk."

He nodded, not opposed to being alone with Eros. He slid out of the booth and held out his hand to help her up. She took it and he had only a moment to think that it fit nicely in his own before she withdrew it. "After you." He gestured for her to lead the way.

As he followed her toward the entrance, he caught Kylix's attention and waved his thanks for her help. Once outside the bar, he followed Eros down the hallway to the residential section of the space station.

They passed dozens of doors before she stopped at one and keyed in her access code. As Jack followed her inside, a heady mixture of incense and the faintest hint of something sweet—a scent that seemed to emanate from Eros herself—assaulted his senses.

The room was dimly lit, and exotic decorations cast mesmerizing shadows on the walls. A plush bed beckoned in one corner, its silky sheets practically inviting him into its embrace. In the opposite corner, a plush sofa and two chairs framed three sides of a clear smoke-colored glass coffee table. On the fourth side, mounted against the wall, was a large multi-functional screen.

"Drink?" She was already heading over to the microkitch built against the side wall.

"Sure."

He watched her take glasses down from a cabinet. Then she pulled a bottle of Galaxian Ale from the cooling unit. She filled both glasses and, leaving the bottle on the counter, carried them over, stopping just in front of him. She handed him one of the glasses and he raised it to his lips as she did the same. Their gazes briefly met over the rim. For a moment, he thought he saw uncertainty in her gaze just before she looked away.

Seeming to collect herself, she gestured to the sofa and chairs. "We can sit over here and talk."

"Okay." He followed her across the room and watched as she lowered herself into a chair. She seemed uncomfortable as she adjusted her cloak, pulling the front edges together to ensure that she was fully covered.

When she looked up to catch him watching her. "You said you were looking for Alexis?"

He had to remind himself that information was the only thing he wanted from this woman. "I am. I think she might be in danger."

She studied him for a long moment, as if trying to decide if he was telling her the truth. She must have decided he was. "Alexis left the station earlier today."

He blew out a frustrated breath. He'd been so close to finally finding her. "Do you know where she's headed?"

"Veridian Prime, though I don't know which city."

"That's okay." Alexis was obviously headed back home. When he and Lena left Outer Fringe, they would head that way and check on her.

Now able to enjoy the ale without worrying about Alexis, he finished the rest of his drink, then set the empty glass on the table and stood. "I should probably leave."

She set her glass down on the table and stood. He assumed she meant to walk him to her door. Instead, she closed the distance between them, stopping so close that he felt the heat of her body radiating like an invisible force field.

"Stay," she whispered, her lips curving into a siren's smile as she gazed up at him.

In the fraction of a second before her lips touched his, he ran the mental calculations. It would be a couple more hours before the Fleet Crystals in the *Black Jack* charged enough for them to leave. Lena was gambling on the lower levels and wouldn't want him disturbing her. Alexis was currently safe aboard a ship headed home. Bottom line—there was no need for him to leave Eros this minute.

As her lips found his, she unclasped the fastener holding her cloak together, and the material slid down her body like a caress, pooling on the floor around her feet.

Beneath the weight of his desire, Jack's resistance crumbled like ancient ruins. He kissed her back hungrily, the taste of her sweet and addictive, making him forget everything but the moment they were sharing. His hands found their way to her upper arms, pulling her closer, the heat between them threatening to consume them both.

She slid her hands under his jacket to push it off his shoulders, and he lowered his arms to let the coat fall to the floor. He didn't wait for her to pull at his shirt, but yanked it over his head and dropped it, already forgotten.

"Just as I imagined." Her words were as soft as the whispered touch of her fingers trailing across his chest.

"You are the most beautiful woman I've seen" he told her, a little surprised because he meant it.

"Do you really think so?" There was the sound of innocence in the way she asked, not like a woman fishing for a compliment.

By way of answer, he brushed a kiss against her neck, savoring the sweet smell of the perfume clinging to her body.

She raised her face to his, and he felt himself drowning in misty green eyes that stared at him as if he were something wonderful, something to be worshipped. He had to remind himself that it wasn't personal. She probably gazed at all her clients this way, but he could pretend.

He captured her lips in another kiss and her eager response ignited a fire inside him. He angled his head and urged her mouth open with his tongue, delving inside the instant she complied. As one hand pressed her to him, his other hand caressed a path up her waist until he cupped the fullness of her breast in his palm. When he stroked the side of it with his thumb, she moaned.

The fire she'd ignited turned into a blazing inferno and he knew he had to have this woman—now. He pressed himself against her, letting her feel his arousal, moving his hands up to hold her head in place while he plundered her mouth. Her short hair felt like silk between his fingers. He fisted his hands in it, unwilling to let her go.

Suddenly, she stiffened beneath his touch. Confused, Jack lifted his head and found her staring up at him with eyes open wide in—fear? Worry? There was something else not quite right and after a second, he realized that her shoulders appeared smudged and peach-colored flesh peeked out from beneath it. Plus, her hair was sitting sideways on her head and beneath it shown a skullcap.

She stepped away from him and he let her go, still a little confused. She reached up to pull the pink wig and skull cap off. Then she pulled out the pins holding up her hair. Long black hair spilled down about her shoulders. She tossed the wig and cap to the couch, bent her head as she reached up with her hands to her face. She lowered her hands and held them out so he could see the two green Winkskins sitting her palm. Still feeling perplexed, he looked up to meet her gaze and found himself staring into a set of familiar blue eyes.

With a growing sense of dread, he reached out and rubbed his thumb against her arm. When he pulled his hand away to look at the pad of this thumb, it was tinted an aquamarine color. "Oh, *krauk.*" He stepped back, alternately staring in horror at the wig, his thumb and the practically nude woman before him, an image that would be forever burned into his brain.

"Alexis?" he croaked, too shocked to say more.

"Hi, Jack." She smiled sheepishly. "Long time, no see."

Chapter Four

THERE WAS A PROLONGED moment of silence as Jack stared at her, his face a mask of horror and regret. Suddenly feeling mortified, Alexis crossed her arms to cover herself and offered Jack a weak smile. "I can explain."

"I doubt it." He seemed to have a hard time keeping his eyes on her face. Finally, he groaned and bent over, grabbing her cloak off the floor. Shaking it out, he took the two steps separating them and wrapped it about her shoulders, pulling it securely closed in front.

"Thank you." She wasn't sure whether she was warmed by his chivalry or irritated by his obvious rush to hide her from his sight. Minutes ago, he'd found her attractive enough. Silently, she cursed the ill fit of the wig.

She watched him back away from her, then, instead of looking at her, he dragged a hand across his face as if he could wipe the entire episode from his mind. His expression was tight, and she worried that her actions might have seriously damaged the friendship they had once shared.

"Jack?" She moved toward him, coming to an abrupt halt when he held up his hand to stop her. "You're mad, aren't you?"

"Mad doesn't even come close." He shook his head. "Alexis, what the hell were you thinking?"

That I love you. But she couldn't tell him that. "Don't you find me attractive?"

His laugh sounded choked. "You can't tell?" The front of his pants still strained to contain his arousal.

"Then why—"

"Don't finish that thought," he snapped. "You know why. You're too—"

"Don't you dare say I'm too young. I'm twenty-seven. Old enough to have been having sex for years." Anger warred with frustration.

"That's not what I was going to say." But she knew it was a lie. "You're Michael's sister."

"So? That doesn't mean you can't have sex with me." He gave a bark of laughter, which caused her to bristle with irritation. "You had your chance." She shrugged. "Your loss."

She grabbed her empty glass off the table, intending to pour herself another drink because the one she'd had was suddenly not enough.

When she turned to head into the microkitch, Jack was suddenly there, blocking her path. When she moved to step around him, he grabbed her by the upper arms to hold her in place. "I'm sorry, Alexis." His tone sounded calmer, tinged with regret. "You're right. What you do is none of my business. It's taking time for my brain to catch up to the fact you're no longer Michael's kid sister." She glanced at the hands gripping her arms and he immediately released her as his gaze searched her face. "Did I hurt you?"

"No," she lied, because heartache didn't count. She continued to the microkitch, refusing to look at him when he came up beside her and set his empty glass next to hers on the counter. She refilled both glasses.

"I'm not a child, Jack."

"I know." His tone sounded resigned as he picked up both glasses and handed her one. "Truce?"

They raised them at the same time and, in like fashion, threw back the contents in a single swallow. The icy cold liquid slid down her throat, sending a slow burn radiating throughout her body. She set the glass back firmly on the counter and then, feeling Jack's gaze on her, turned to face him.

"Truce."

"If we're through discussing your age and sex life," he said, "why don't you tell me what the hell you're doing out here?"

She winced at his tone and opened her mouth to reply, but he held up his hand to silence her.

"First, go change. Please. I don't know how you expect me to concentrate when all you're wearing is that cloak." His voice sounded unusually rough, and Alexis wondered if maybe his feelings weren't as brotherly as he pretended. A seed of hope took root deep inside.

"Okay." She pushed away from the counter and, going over to the dresser, pulled a black tubular piece of fabric from a drawer. Moving to the closet, she grabbed a pair of black heels.

When she turned around, Jack was watching her, his gaze smoldering hot. Still burning from his rejection, she wanted him to know what he'd given up, so in a move more daring than she thought possible, she released her grip on the cloak and let it slide once more to the floor.

Her reward was seeing Jack's mouth drop open in shock while his gaze heated with obvious desire.

"I'll be out in a couple of minutes." She was a little surprised when her voice sounded steady. Then she disappeared into the bathroom.

Once safely in the bathroom with the door closed, she felt her face heat as memories from moments before flooded back. Flesh and blood, Jack Marsden, holding her, touching her, surpassing every fantasy she'd ever had of him.

She thought back to when she realized he didn't recognize her. What had she been thinking? There was no way she could have carried off her deception. Yet she had tried—and almost succeeded. Even now, her lips burned from his kiss; her skin hungered for his touch.

Alexis sighed, knowing she'd do it all again if the opportunity presented itself. Not that such a possibility was likely. Jack wouldn't make the same mistake twice, and Alexis knew Jack would consider making love to her a major mistake. As the sister of one of his closest friends, she was off-limits. It didn't matter that her brother was dead, or that she was an adult. It probably wouldn't even matter if Jack knew how much she desired him, not that she'd ever reveal that bit of information. She'd die first.

Undressing, she stepped into the shower to wash away the skin tint. Once she was done, she stepped out and dried off. Before putting on the black dress, she picked up her Eros costume and, from the inside of the neckline, peeled away the tape holding the tiny vial of neon yellow liquid in place. *Starlight.* A rare and highly sought-after drug. Dominic had said Graxx was addicted to the stuff, so she'd set out to secure some. It had cost nearly one entire paycheck to purchase the quantity in this tiny vial. She couldn't afford to lose it or have it stolen, which was why she kept the vial on her. Plus, she wanted it readily available when she finally found Graxx. She had no illusions that Graxx would share information about the Luminite crystals willingly. She hoped the information he had was worth the expense of the drug.

She taped the tiny vial to the underside of one breast, where it would remain hidden from view, but easily accessible. Next, she stepped into the stretchy fabric tube and pulled the dress up over her body until she was covered from mid-chest to mid-thigh. She slipped on her heels and then peered into the mirror as she applied gloss to her lips and ran a brush through her hair. Then she checked the time and felt another surge of adrenaline. It was just past mid-evening—the time when the bar was busiest.

Stepping out of the bathroom, she headed across the room, stopping when she reached the front door. "It was nice seeing you again, Jack. We'll have to catch up, but some other time. I need to get back to The Abyss. You're welcome to stay as long as you want."

He stared at her, dumbfounded. "You can't leave. We need to talk."

"About what?"

"About Michael's death, for one. Do you know how long I've been looking for you?"

"Michael died nine months ago while committing a crime." She worked to keep her tone cool. "There's nothing left to discuss." She reached back and hit the wall panel, then listened for the hiss that told her the door had opened. "There's food in the cooling unit if you're hungry. Help yourself." She paused, unable to just walk away. "It was nice seeing you again."

Then she disappeared through the door and headed back to the bar.

Jack stared at the closing door, rubbing his forehead as he tried to make sense of what had transpired between them. He couldn't let her go. He still needed information from her.

Retrieving his comm device, he called Lena.

"I found her," he announced when Lena answered.

"So how'd it go?"

He felt his face heat at the memory of Alexis's nude body in his arms, the lust he'd felt for her. "Not great," he admitted out loud. "She wouldn't even talk to me."

"Well, you tried." He could imagine Lena shrugging.

"I'm not giving up yet. I'm going after her and this time, I'm not letting her walk away without talking to me."

"Yeah, good luck with that," she replied dubiously. "If you don't need me for a while, there's a game of Zypherian poker going on down in the bowels. I'd like to get in on the action."

"Sure. Try not to piss anyone off." Jack had learned a long time ago to never bet against Lena. She was a ruthless gambler and though she wasn't quick to anger, once that fuse was lit ... watch out! "I'll buzz you when I'm headed back to the ship."

"Roger that. And Jack?"

"Yeah?"

"Tread carefully. You lost a good friend. She lost the only blood family she had left. Remember how that felt?"

"Yeah. I do," he admitted. "Thanks."

Back at the bar, the room was alive with the hum of conversation, punctuated by bursts of raucous laughter and the clatter of glasses. Alexis moved almost absently through the sea of patrons, her thoughts still on Jack. She couldn't believe how foolish she'd been, allowing herself to become vulnerable with him. *Never again.*

Focus. Peering through the haze of smoke, she scanned face after face. Then, suddenly, in the farthest recesses of the establishment, she spotted a Raniform leaning against a grimy wall, nursing a glass filled with a noxious-looking drink. He had a scar bisecting his right eye.

That had to be Graxx.

Here goes nothing. She steeled herself as she began weaving her way through the crowd. Her heart pounded in her chest, adrenaline and the lingering sting of Jack's rejection coursing through her veins.

"Hey there," she purred, sidling up to him with a sultry smile that belied her inner turmoil. Leaning in close, she brushed her fingers against his arm. "You look like you could use some company."

Looking her up and down, there was something predatory in his gaze, like a wolf sizing up its prey. Alexis didn't flinch, didn't falter. Back when she was a cop, she'd gone undercover more than once. This wasn't her first up-close encounter with a potentially lethal criminal.

His scarred face broke into a wicked grin. "You've got that right, sweetheart. What brings a pretty little thing like you to the dark corners of the Outer Fringe?"

"Adventure." She tried to maintain her flirtatious demeanor, despite her disgust for this amphibian-like creature. "I'm always looking for something new and exciting. How about you?"

"Me?" Graxx laughed, taking a swig of his drink. "I'm just here for the work. And the money, of course."

Alexis leaned in closer, her voice low and conspiratorial. "I've heard whispers about a man named Graxx who frequents this establishment. They say he's the go-to guy for, shall we say, unconventional goods and information." She traced a finger along the rim of his glass. "You wouldn't know anything about that, would you?"

His eyes narrowed, his posture stiffening almost imperceptibly. "Now why would a sweet thing like you be asking about a dangerous character like Graxx?" His tone was laced with suspicion.

Alexis leaned back slightly, a coy smile playing at the corners of her mouth. "I'm in the market for information."

"Information, huh?" His eyes narrowed. "Why would I tell you anything?" he asked, his voice like gravel.

"Because I'm willing to pay for it."

Graxx's eyes widened slightly. He raised his webbed hand and stroked a finger-pad down her throat, leaving behind a slimy trail that made her skin crawl. His finger continued its path downward, stopping only when she grabbed his wrist to keep him from delving into her cleavage.

His gaze accusing, he glared at her. "I thought you said you'd pay for information."

She smiled, but didn't release her grip on his arm. "I will, but not with sex." Pushing his hand away, she released him and reached into her cleavage to retrieve the vial of *Starlight.* She held it out so he could see it, but then quickly palmed the vial before he could take it from her.

"Is that what I think it is?"

"*Starlight,*" she confirmed. "Some of the purist around, but it's not free."

"How do I know that's the real stuff?"

"How about a taste?" She offered with a sly smile, uncapping the vial and allowing a single drop to fall onto the tip of his outstretched finger. He popped the finger into his mouth and closed his eyes. She gave him a moment to savor the effect of the drug, then demanded, "Satisfied?"

"All right. What do you want to know?" His gaze stayed on the hand holding the vial.

"I want to know about stolen Luminite crystals."

His gaze flicked to hers and she saw a brief flash of alarm before he hid it. "Why?"

"That's my business."

At first, it seemed like he wouldn't answer. She watched as a bead of sweat formed at his temple, then trickled down his face. "Fine," he finally growled. "What do you want to know?"

Knowing she might only get one shot at this, she had to choose her questions carefully. "I know you're working on a ship that's currently transporting stolen Luminite crystal. I want to know who you're working for." She worked to keep her voice steady despite the unease stirring inside her.

"I don't know," he answered, a little too quickly.

"I don't believe you."

"It's true."

She studied him a moment and then slipped the vial back into her cleavage. "I guess I'll save this for someone who can be more helpful."

A flicker of uncertainty crossed Graxx's face before a mask of defiance quickly replaced it. Without warning, he pulled a knife from the back of his belt. The chaos of the bar seemed to fade into the background as Alexis focused her full attention on the glint of the blade and the dangerous gleam in Graxx's eyes.

"Give me the *Starlight* and walk away," he hissed, stepping closer with a menacing aura.

The smart play was to comply. "No. Not until I get some real answers."

Graxx looked ready to strike when a loud voice boomed out from behind them.

"What the hell's going on here?"

Alexis's breath caught in her throat as she recognized Jack's voice. For a fleeting moment, relief washed over her. Then Graxx spun her around and pressed the knife's blade against her throat. Years of training kept her calm, but the cold metal against her skin sent her pulse racing.

"Stay back, or she gets it." Graxx's voice sounded dark and dangerous as his grip on her tightened.

Chapter Five

"Bad move, friend," Jack growled, his heart pounding as every primal instinct urged him to protect Alexis.

"Stay out of this." The amphibious brute pressed the blade closer to Alexis's throat.

Jack gauged the distance between them, calculating every possible move, before sprinting forward with the reckless abandon that only came from fighting for something—someone—more important than oneself.

"Jack, no!" Alexis's cry echoed through the bar, but it was too late. The Raniform was already in motion, shoving Alexis into Jack with all the force of a freight train. They both stumbled, momentarily off-balance.

"Are you hurt?" he demanded, setting her back on her feet but not releasing her as he searched for signs of injury.

"No. No. Let me go." She shoved his hands away. "He's getting away."

She took off running and for a moment, Jack was thoroughly confused. Then he looked past her to see the Raniform racing for the exit.

"Alexis, wait!" Why did she have to be so damn impulsive? When she didn't slow down, he ran after her, pushing his way past the bar patrons, his long strides easily closing the gap.

They burst through the doors of the bar together and came to an abrupt stop.

"Where did he go?" Breathing hard, Alexis searched either side of the hallway.

"Over there!" Jack pointed to a shadowy figure disappearing around a corner. They charged after him, their footsteps echoing down the metal corridors as they navigated the crowded space station, dodging patrons and workers alike.

"Who are we chasing?" They'd reached the end of a hallway and stopped, not knowing which way their quarry went.

"Graxx," Alexis panted. "He's a mercenary."

He turned to face her. "Why in the hell are you chasing after a mercenary?"

She was leaning a hand against the wall as she tried to catch her breath. Her other hand was tugging up her dress.

"Because he has information I need."

"What—"

"Jack!" she interrupted. "Ask questions later. Right now, I have to catch him." She pushed away from the wall and stepped into the intersection of hallways. "You want answers? Then first, help me find him."

Jack studied her for a moment and then nodded. "He went that way." He pointed straight ahead.

"How do you know?"

He pointed to the floor where oily residue in the shape of a footprint was barely visible.

"Right." She took off down the hallway, Jack following close behind her.

They were entering the maintenance section and slowed their pace. The muffled sounds of the bustling space station gave way to the hum of machinery. A forest of maintenance shafts spread out before them, providing plenty of places to hide. Jack motioned for Alexis to stop so he could listen. A faint scurrying noise sounded off to the side.

"Left!" He turned sharply to dart down a narrow maintenance corridor. Graxx was several meters ahead of them, but when he turned to glance behind him, he stumbled over a stray pipe and slammed into a wall. With a last burst of speed, Jack tackled the Raniform to the ground.

Graxx refused to stay down. Using his immense strength, he lunged upward, flipping Jack off him. Jack hit the metal floor hard, but rolled back onto his feet almost instantly. As he lunged at the now-standing Graxx, the mercenary met him head-on with a fierce blow to the jaw, sending Jack staggering backward.

Before Graxx could capitalize on his advantage, Alexis stepped in with a swift roundhouse kick that was probably as much a surprise to Graxx as it was to Jack.

Despite Graxx's formidable strength, Jack and Alexis moved with a fluid grace, each step, each strike, seeming to flow naturally from the next, as if they had been fighting side-by-side for years. They circled Graxx with the precision of seasoned predators, working together to find and create openings, then striking with relentless determination.

It took longer than expected, but gradually, Graxx's movements slowed. Jack took advantage of the next opening to slam his fist into the mercenary's soft belly. As he bent over in pain, Alexis landed a devastating blow that sent Graxx crashing to the ground.

For a long moment, Jack and Alexis simply stood there, trying to catch their breath. Graxx glared up at them with a mixture of defiance and resignation, his once-threatening demeanor now replaced by defeat.

"What do you know about the stolen Luminite crystals?" Alexis demanded, her voice steady despite the adrenaline coursing through her veins.

Instead of answering, Graxx turned his head to spit blood on the floor by Alexis's foot. Then he glared defiantly at her until Jack grabbed his arm and twisted it.

"Alright, alright!" Graxx growled, as Jack applied more pressure to his arm. "It's true. There's a shipment of stolen Luminite crystals on board the *Nebula Marauder*."

"Where are you taking them?" she demanded.

"I don't know." Jack applied even more pressure. "Alright," Graxx gasped, pain etched into every line of his expression. "Veridian Prime, but that's all I know. We're supposed to get coordinates as soon as we make orbit."

"Who are they for?" Alexis asked.

"Don't know," Graxx wheezed, desperation seeping into his tone. "In my line of work, it's not healthy to ask too many questions."

Alexis stared at him, weighing his words. Her gut told her he had told them all he could and if there was a shipment of stolen crystals at the space station, then every second they spent here interrogating him for answers he couldn't provide was time wasted. She met

Jack's questioning gaze and nodded. They were done with Graxx. They could let him go.

Without warning, Jack delivered a swift punch to Graxx's jaw, knocking him unconscious.

"Was that really necessary?" Alexis's voice was tinged with disapproval.

He didn't care. "Can't have him alerting anyone else." He scanned the corridor for any sign of company, then dragged Graxx's limp body into a nearby supply closet.

"Let's go," he said, slamming the closet door shut. But when he turned around, Alexis was already halfway down the corridor, her long dark hair trailing behind her like a comet's tail.

"Alexis, wait!" he called out in frustration, sprinting after her.

He caught up to her and followed her to her quarters. She scowled at him when he followed her inside, but she didn't order him to leave.

"Care to tell me what's going on?" He watched her walk over to her closet and remove dark pants and a long-sleeved shirt.

"No time." She reached for the top of her dress and was about to push it down, then hesitated. "Turn around."

He reluctantly complied, but even then, he couldn't help sneaking glances at her reflection in the polished metal wall. She slowly peeled off her dress, revealing a perfect body that made his heart race and his breath hitch. He nearly groaned aloud.

He struggled to focus on their conversation. "Wh-why?"

"Why what?"

"Why don't you have time to talk?"

Alexis didn't hesitate. "Because I want to see this shipment of stolen crystals for myself."

"Are you out of your mind?" He knew all too well the danger that came with sneaking aboard a ship that transported illegal goods. The crew would rather kill an intruder than summon the authorities.

"Jack, this is my chance to find out more about Michael's death." Her voice cracked with emotion. "These stolen crystals are the key. I can't let this opportunity slip away."

"Then let me come with you." Desperation laced his words. "At least I can watch your back."

"No, thanks. I appreciate the offer, but I work alone." Her eyes met his, unwavering in their resolve. "It really was nice seeing you again." She headed for the door. "Lock up when you leave."

And with that, she disappeared into the bustling space station, leaving Jack standing in the middle of her quarters, his heart heavy knowing that the woman he cared for was about to embark on a dangerous journey from which she might not return.

Chapter Six

Reluctantly, Jack returned to the bar and took a seat at the counter. When Kylix looked his way, he raised a finger to request a drink. Acknowledging him with a nod, Kylix got to work, mixing a concoction that Jack hoped would help calm his frayed nerves.

"Here you go, Jack," he said, sliding the glass across the counter.

"Thanks." Jack took a sip. The biting bitterness of the alien liquor burned its way down his throat, leaving a warm trail in its wake.

"Did you find the woman you were looking for?" Kylix's knowing gaze told Jack he already knew the answer.

Jack answered him anyway. "Yeah, I did." *And then I lost her again.*

"Was she in trouble, as you feared?"

"Most likely," he said before he could stop himself. "But she made it clear that she doesn't need my help."

Remembering how she'd handled herself in the fight with Graxx, he had to admit that she seemed more than capable of taking care of herself. That didn't stop him from worrying about her.

Where and when had she learned to fight? he wondered, as he nursed his drink.

He was momentarily distracted when a woman slid onto the stool beside him. He glanced over and nodded in greeting. She was pretty—no, beautiful—with dark brown hair cascading down her back and violet-colored eyes that seemed to glow in the low light. Her air of mystery intrigued him, and under normal circumstances, he would have started a conversation.

Right now, though, another dark-haired beauty plagued his thoughts, filling them with worry and concern. So he glanced away from the woman and stared down into his drink, feeling a strange emptiness gnawing at him.

"Hey, Marlo," Kylix greeted the woman. "What brings you out this way?"

"Oh, you know. This and that," she replied evasively before ordering a drink.

As Kylix left to fix it, Jack swirled his drink, the ice cubes clinking in harmony with the rhythm of his thoughts. A moment or two later, Kylix returned with Marlo's drink and slid it to her.

"Thanks," she said before taking a sip. Then, before he could walk away, she asked, "Did you hear about the explosion on Helios Six?"

He nodded slowly. "I did."

"Know anything about it?"

"Like what?" Kylix asked.

"Like maybe who was behind it?"

"No. Sorry."

Jack hadn't been paying close attention, but the mention of the explosion brought back memories of another explosion. He caught Kylix's eye. "Any news of Nero?"

Kylix scratched his beard thoughtfully. "Not since the explosion." He glanced at Marlo, who was obviously listening. "Different explosion." Then he turned back to Jack. "What was that? About a year ago?"

Jack nodded. He and Nero had been friends, of sorts. They had flown together for a while, but Jack had lost track of the space pirate after they'd gone their separate ways. A year ago, he'd heard that Nero had been on board a ship when it exploded.

"Based on what I heard, I don't see how anyone could have survived that explosion." The thought was depressing.

"It seems unlikely." Kylix agreed. "Especially since no one's seen or heard from him since the explosion."

"Damn." He hated the thought that another of his friends might be dead. He needed to do a better job of staying in touch with people he cared about, he thought, his gaze wandering to the dwindling contents of his glass. He finished it and set several credits on the counter. "Thanks. See you around."

Giving Marlo a nod, he left the bar. Reaching the lift, he took it down to the docking level and stepped out. The heavy metallic clang of footsteps on the docking bay floor echoed through the vast expanse as he studied the sea of vessels stretched out before him, their gleaming hulls and alien designs a testament to the diversity of life that inhabited the Outer Fringe and surrounding galaxies.

Space station engineers scurried about, running diagnostics on the ships and fine-tuning their engines, while charging units whirred away, recharging the Kirellite crystals, better known as Fleet Crystals, that powered most ships. Jack's gaze scanned the room, searching for Alexis. Of course, he didn't expect her to be standing about, but that didn't keep him from being frustrated when he couldn't find her.

He started walking down the center of the bay, checking the names of the ships on either side of him, searching for the *Nebula Marauder*. When he found it, he stopped.

What now? Was Alexis already on board?

If so, he wondered how she'd slipped past the engineer who was working near the open hatch. He moved closer, analyzing the best way to sneak aboard when the engineer turned and he recognized Alexis; her lithe figure was clad in what was probably a stolen engineer's jumpsuit and her dark hair was tucked beneath a cap.

Her eyes widened in surprise at the sight of him. "Jack!" Her voice was barely audible above the cacophony of machinery and hurried conversations around them. "What are you doing here?"

He closed the distance between them in a few quick strides. "Looking for you." He glanced at the *Nebula Marauder* looming behind her, its sleek design hinting at speed and power. "You're really going through with this?"

She squared her shoulders, determination etched on her face. "I have to, Jack. You know I can't let this go."

"Alexis, please reconsider," he pleaded, his voice low and urgent. "We don't even know who owns this ship."

"That's one of the things I intend to find out—after I confirm there are stolen Luminite crystals aboard," she shot back, her tone resolute. "Michael didn't just wake up one day and say, hey, I think I'll steal me some Luminite crystals. He was working with someone and there aren't that many people crazy or resourceful enough to orchestrate these thefts. If I can find out who's responsible for the stolen crystals on board this ship, I'm that much closer to finding out how Michael was involved."

His thoughts raced, trying to find a way to talk her out of going on board, but like her, he, too, wanted to know more about Michael's death. "Okay, but I'm coming with you. You'll need backup."

Her expression momentarily softened, but then she shook her head. "I appreciate the offer, but it's too dangerous."

He smirked. "Stop. I already told you I was in. No need to tempt me with promises of danger."

"Jack ..." She hesitated, but deep down, she knew she'd be better off with his help than without it. "Fine."

"What's the status of the ship's crew?"

"I learned from one of the engineers that all ten members of the crew, which includes Graxx, are currently off the ship, but I don't know for how long."

"Then let's hurry. Ready?"

She nodded because, at that moment, she wasn't sure her voice would be steady enough to convince Jack she knew what she was doing.

As they mounted the steps and went through the hatch, she couldn't help but feel a sense of foreboding creeping over her, but she pushed the feeling aside, focusing instead on the task at hand: uncovering the truth about the stolen crystals.

No matter the cost.

Inside the *Nebula Marauder*, the narrow corridor was dimly lit and eerily silent. Their footsteps seemed to reverberate loudly in the oppressive silence, making each moment feel like an eternity as they ventured further into the ship. Jack, who seemed more familiar with the layout of the ship, led the way, with Alexis following closely behind.

They passed the galley and maintenance sections before Jack paused at a junction, considering which direction to take. Then he motioned for her to follow as he continued down the corridor towards the back of the ship.

Finally, they reached a massive door marked with the symbol for cargo storage. With a quick glance at Jack, Alexis swiped her hand over the access panel. A soft hum filled the air as the door slid open with a mechanical hiss. Before them lay a vast space filled with crates in various shapes and sizes. Some were neatly stacked, while others sat haphazardly around the room.

"Where do we even start?" She suddenly felt overwhelmed by the sheer number of crates.

Jack took another step into the room and looked around. Finally, he stopped and pointed. "Let's focus on the unmarked crates first. Those are likely our best bet."

Giving him a quick nod of agreement, they moved cautiously, stepping over cables and around machinery that littered the floor, heading for the unmarked boxes clustered near the far wall. The air was stale, making every breath feel heavy with anticipation.

When they tried to raise the lid on the first crate, they found it locked.

"How are we going to get this open without making too much noise?"

"Relax." Reaching into his pocket, he withdrew a small, high-tech tool and began working the lock. Within moments, the crate popped open with a nearly inaudible click.

She was impressed despite herself. "Nice."

"Not like I haven't done this before." The corners of his eyes crinkled with a hint of a smile, but the humor faded quickly, replaced by a steely resolve.

Lifting the lid of the box, they found only a pile of technical equipment, neatly arranged and secured.

"These are high-end communication devices. Not what we're looking for." His brows furrowed in concentration.

She nodded, masking her frustration. Moving on to the next unmarked crate, he used his tool again to unlock it. This time, they discovered a collection of sleek drones, their metallic surfaces glimmering in the dim light.

"No crystals here either." She was growing anxious.

Jack ran a hand through his scruffy hair, like he was thinking, then he bent down to examine the bottom sections of the other unmarked crate.

"Look there." He gestured to the bottom. "See how these four crates have a dusty residue along the bottom seam? That could be crystal dust settling to the bottom. Let's check these."

Alexis couldn't help but hold her breath in anticipation as Jack used his tool to unlock the lid of the first of the four crates. This time, nestled among layers of packing material, she spotted a shimmer of light reflecting off something within. Carefully removing the wrapping, Jack pulled out a crystal that seemed to glow with an inner yellow light.

"Is it Luminite?"

He turned the crystal over in his hand. "No. Kirellite." He set it back in the box and checked several more. They were all the same. He resealed the crate. "Either Graxx was mistaken or the stolen crystals are in one of these other crates."

They checked the next crate, but it, too, was filled with the more common Fleet crystals. Watching Jack move to the third crate, she couldn't help but worry that maybe this was a waste of time.

He examined the lid and pressed the button to activate the shipping manifest. "Drone parts." He gave a half shrug and set to work, using his tool to unlock the crate. Then he looked inside. "Well, what do we have here?" Reaching inside, he pulled out a crystal.

A sense of awe washed over Alexis. The crystal seemed to pulsate with an ethereal glow, casting a soft, violet light that danced across their faces. Its surface was smooth and flawless, each facet catching the light in a mesmerizing display of colors.

"It's beautiful," she whispered, her eyes fixed on the radiant gem.

"This is Luminite," he confirmed. "Hard to believe that just two of these beauties can power an entire spaceship."

"Do you see a lasered registration number on it?"

He held it up to the light, studying it from all sides. "I don't see one."

"Really?" She was perplexed. "All Luminite crystals are marked with a registration number before they leave the mine, so the government can trace them. Are you sure there's no number?"

"Here." He handed her the crystal. "See for yourself. No number."

She took it from him and turned the crystal slowly, carefully scrutinizing all sides. He was right. There was no number. Now, she had a hard time keeping her excitement in check. The crystals Michael was accused of stealing hadn't had numbers on them, either and she had a theory on why. "Someone is arranging to have crystals removed from the mines before they can be registered."

His gaze narrowed. "It would take someone pretty high on the food chain to pull off something like that."

"Exactly," she confirmed. "That's how whoever is doing this has avoided the government's attention. As far as the government is concerned, every registered crystal is accounted for."

"Crafty bastards." He took the crystal from her and put it back in the crate. Then he reached for another, smaller crystal before closing the box. "Here, take this small one, as evidence." He handed her the palm-sized unmarked crystal. Its surface was cool to the touch as she slipped it into her pocket. "Can we go now?"

She nodded, and they moved toward the door.

That's when they heard footsteps echoing through the ship.

"Quick, behind those crates!" Jack grabbed her arm and pulled her behind the stacked containers. She could feel her heart racing as they pressed themselves close together, straining to hear the approaching crew members.

Various scenarios of getting caught flashed through her head and none promised a happy outcome for her and Jack. Then, the footsteps got louder; they were punctuated by the heavy clang of equipment and the sound of mumbled voices.

"There," Jack whispered, nodding toward a small storage closet nestled between two towering stacks of crates.

Together, they hurried over to it and she tried the knob. "It's locked."

"No problem." Once again pulling out the small tool, he worked with practiced precision, his fingers moving deftly over the mechanism.

"Almost ... got it." He glanced nervously over his shoulder as if he expected a crew member to walk through the cargo hold doors at any moment.

Then she heard the soft click as the lock released, and Jack yanked the door open. He stepped inside, pulling her after him.

They had just closed the door behind them when they heard the metal hiss of the cargo hold door opening.

"Close call," he whispered as they stood with their bodies pressed awkwardly together in the tight space.

Alexis, acutely aware of his presence, felt the rapid pounding of his heart against her chest, matching the frenetic rhythm of her own.

"Try not to breathe too loud," he urged, his breath brushing across her cheek. "They'll hear us."

She nodded, feeling the heat rise in her cheeks. They listened as the footsteps drew nearer, the voices growing louder.

The closer they got, the more on-edge she felt. To stop her hands from trembling—and maybe to reassure herself she wasn't alone—she tightly gripped Jack's jacket. No doubt sensing her unease, he wrapped his arms around her and held her close, offering her the comfort she so badly needed.

Then she heard the distant hum of the ship's engines and felt the vibrations through the metal floor beneath them. As the vibrations intensified, her heart skipped a beat as she exchanged a glance with Jack, the reality of their situation beginning to set in. Jack's drawn expression and set jaw told her she had a right to worry.

The *Nebula Marauder*, a ship with unknown dangers and a merciless crew, was departing the space station—with them aboard.

Chapter Seven

JACK'S HEART POUNDED IN his chest as he heard an unknown number of *Nebula Marauder* crew members enter the cargo hold. Their voices were loud enough to be heard, but their words were unintelligible through the thick closet door. When their voices fell quiet, Jack mentally counted to one hundred. When still there was silence, he cautiously opened the closet door and peeked out.

"All clear." Stepping out into the room to give Alexis space to exit, he looked around. Everything looked the same, except for a new stack of crates in the center of the room.

"Now what?"

"I guess we get comfortable." He looked around dubiously.

"Or ... we could find an empty crew quarters." She hurried on when he gave her a questioning look. "Remember this ship is operating with only a skeleton crew. There should be a couple of unoccupied quarters. We find one to hide in until the ship reaches its destination."

He considered the suggestion. It was unlikely anyone would visit the cargo hold while the ship was in flight, so staying where they were held the least risk of detection. On the other hand, they had no idea where the ship was headed. Lack of food and water could quickly become an issue.

Giving Alexis a solemn nod, he went to the cargo hold door and listened. When he heard only silence, he pressed the access panel. The door shot open.

He stepped out into the currently empty corridor. After a moment's hesitation, she followed him. Together, they moved down the corridor, gazes darting around, alert to any danger of discovery.

They made their way down the narrow passage, each step measured and silent. Just as they reached an intersection, Alexis suddenly grabbed his arm and pressed herself against the wall. Jack froze, every sense on high alert as the sound of footsteps echoed around the corner.

The footsteps slowed and then faded away as an unseen crew member turned the other way. After a moment, Jack peered cautiously around the corner before whispering, "Clear!"

They dashed across the open intersection and continued along the corridor. Jack had been on ships similar to the *Nebula Marauder* and prayed that, like those other ships, the lift to the upper level was at the end of this corridor.

For a change, their luck held. They located the lift sitting empty, with doors open, and took it to the second level, where Jack thought the crew's living quarters were located. Their luck continued to hold when the lift doors slid open to reveal a quiet, deserted corridor. They stepped off and found the crew's quarters.

Now the tricky part. They assumed that all crew members were busy on the bridge or fast asleep behind locked doors. If they were wrong ...

Jack didn't want to think about that as he stepped up to the first door and pressed his hand against the cool surface of the access panel.

"Locked ..." he muttered, when the door didn't open.

Alexis moved to the door on the opposite side of the corridor and placed her hand against the access panel. "Locked ..."

They moved from door to door, frustration mounting with each one that didn't open. Finally, their luck changed, and a door hissed open. Relief washed over Jack as he shot Alexis a triumphant grin. Then, together, they slipped into a small, sparsely furnished chamber that offered them temporary sanctuary.

"Well, it's not much, but it's, um—"

"It's cozy." Her face brightened and she smiled.

"Yeah, okay. We'll stay here," he agreed. "Let me activate the lock so no one wanders in on us." He went to the door and input a key-code that would prevent anyone without the code from opening the door. When he finished, he turned around and spotted Alexis in the kitchen, looking through the cabinets. "What are you doing?"

She paused and looked over at him. "I'm hungry, so I thought I'd fix us something to eat."

The mere suggestion of food made his stomach growl. "I'll help."

It wasn't long before the two of them sat at the small table, about to share the flash-meal they'd prepared. Alexis filled two glasses with water as the scent of stew filled the space.

"Here." Jack scooped a portion of stew into a bowl and handed it to her. She took it with a nod and waited until he'd served himself before tasting the food.

She swallowed her first bite. "Not completely horrible."

He tried a bite, the taste of synthetic protein and rehydrated vegetables lingering on his tongue. "It's a bit of an acquired taste, but it beats rehydrated protein bars."

They ate in silence for a few minutes before Alexis raised her gaze from her bowl to him. "You never told me what you were doing in The Abyss. Just a routine stop?"

"Not exactly," he admitted. "I was looking for you."

Her eyes momentarily opened wider, registering her surprise. "Me? Why?" Her gaze narrowed then. "And why would you even think I was there?"

He sighed and set his spoon down so he could focus on the conversation. "I got a holovault communique from Michael telling me he was in trouble. The communique took six months to find me. By the time I got it and tried to call Michael back, he was dead. In his communique, he said he was in some sort of trouble, but he didn't go into specifics. He also thought you might be in danger, so I tried to get in touch with you, only you weren't answering my calls, and no one knew where you'd gone. So, I started hacking into various space station security systems, specifically their facial recognition programs, to add a program that would alert me if you were spotted. I got an alert that you were on the Outer Fringe space station." He paused, giving her time to consider everything he'd told her. "Your turn. What were you doing in the Outer Fringe?"

At first, he wasn't sure she was going to tell him, but then she heaved a sigh. "I'm looking for answers about Michael's death."

"Such as?"

"How Luminite crystals are involved, for starters. And why the Galathean PD shot him without even trying to take him alive."

"How do you know that?"

"Because I saw the body-cam footage."

Jack held up his hand to stop her. "What do you mean, you saw the body-cam footage? How'd you get a hold of that? Did you hack the GPD's computer system?"

"I didn't have to," she sighed. "I don't know why I thought you knew. After I completed my Tier-2 Education degree, I enlisted in the Galathean Police Academy. Michael wasn't exactly thrilled about it, but it was that or follow him into the military."

Jack chuckled. "I'm having a hard time picturing you as a Grid Cop."

She gave him a stern look. "Well, I was. Last year, I finally moved up the ranks to detective," she informed him. "Being a detective gave me access to Michael's body-cam footage and the evidence locker. That's how

I was able to examine the crystals Michael was allegedly stealing and discover they had no registration numbers on them"

That explains a lot. Especially why she's able to fight the way she can. "So you quit your job to start your own investigation into Michael's murder," he concluded. "What'd you learn?"

"That's just it. Nothing. I've learned nothing. In fact, I came away with more questions than answers." She huffed out a frustrated breath. "I even went to his office to question his co-workers."

A warning bell went off in his head. "You went to his office?"

She nodded. "You know what I discovered?"

This should be interesting. "What?"

"Nothing! Because his office is an abandoned building. I have no idea how Michael was earning the money off which he lived. Based on how he died, I'm left assuming he was a paid thief." She heaved a long sigh. "I don't want to believe that about him. So that's why I'm looking for answers."

Jack wondered how much of what he knew he should share. How much would Michael want her to know? In the end, it didn't matter because Michael wasn't here to offer his opinion and Jack hated seeing her upset. "Michael wasn't a thief," he finally said.

She nodded, but wouldn't really meet his gaze. "I know. I don't want to believe it either, but what other explanation is there?"

Michael, I know I promised to keep your secret, but the situation has changed. "Michael worked for the SDIA."

Her head snapped up as her gaze shot to his. "Michael worked for the Solaris Dominus Intelligence Agency?"

He nodded. "After our stint in the military, that's where he went."

"No. He'd have told me if he was an agent," she protested. "I'm his sister."

"That's precisely why he couldn't tell you."

"But he told you?" she accused.

"Not exactly. I figured it out on my own. After he admitted it, he swore me to secrecy. I have to think that if Michael was stealing those crystals, it was part of some undercover operation he was on."

"But why didn't the SDIA come out and clear his name?"

He shook his head. "I don't know."

"So, Michael dies with the world thinking he was just a low-life criminal." She shook her head. "Not nearly good enough."

He nodded. "I agree, but trying to find the answers could be dangerous. When he recorded the communique to me, I think he knew he might be killed. He also knew you'd try to find out more about his death and worried about your safety." He heaved a sigh as he studied her for a long moment. "I don't suppose you'd let it go if I asked?"

She shook her head. "Not a chance."

He gave a wan smile. "That's what I thought, so you leave me no choice."

"You're going to force me to stop?" she challenged.

He gave a soft bark of laughter. "Yeah, I've seen you fight. Don't get me wrong; I think I can take you, but probably not without serious damage to both of us. Thanks, but I think I'll pass. No, I've decided the only way I can honor Michael and his request to keep you safe is to help you."

"Really?" She rewarded him with a beatific smile.

"Don't thank me, yet. We might both still end up dead before this is over." He winked to show her he was kidding. Mostly. "I think I'll start by finding out more about this ship and its owner, since they're obviously involved in the crystal thefts."

"How will you do that?"

He raised his arm to show off his wrist device. "I'll hack into the ship's computer system. I don't know how long it will take to break through the ship's security and once I do, I'm likely to set off alarms. It won't take them long to find us when that happens, so we'll need an exit strategy and another place to hide."

"Okay, I'll study the ship's layout for alternate hiding places."

"Alright."

They put their plates into the recycler and then Jack sat back down at the table. He activated his wrist device's holographic screen and keyboard and set to work. For a moment, she simply watched him; she watched the way his fingers flew over the keyboard and his brow furrowed in concentration as he navigated through the ship's complex security systems. The soft glow of the screen illuminated his face, casting shadows that danced across his chiseled features. She sighed. Age had not robbed him of his looks; it had enhanced them.

Tearing her attention away from him, she moved to the small window in their cozy sanctuary and took a moment to gaze out at the seemingly endless expanse of stars, feeling both a sense of wonder and dread. The universe held so much beauty, yet it could also be cold and unforgiving.

"I sure hope we make it out of this alive." Her voice was barely audible over the hum of the ship's engines.

At her words, Jack pushed himself away from the table and walked over to join her, gazing out at the vast expanse of space.

"Hey." He gently nudged her shoulder with his. "We'll make it through this. I promise."

She turned to face him, her eyes searching his for reassurance. "I want to believe that, but the odds aren't exactly in our favor."

He couldn't argue with her, but something deep within him refused to give in to despair. He had to hold on to hope, for both their sakes.

"I know the risks." Gently grasping her shoulders, he dipped his head so he could look her in the eyes. "We're going to figure this out, okay? You and me, we're a team. We've got each other's backs."

As he spoke, memories of their brief but charged encounter in her apartment flooded her mind. The feel of his hands on her skin, the heat of his breath against her neck. Almost of their own accord, it seemed, his hands moved to cup her face, his thumbs gently brushing away the tears that had slipped down her face. At his touch, her breath hitched, her eyes widening when she saw a mixture of surprise and something else—something deeper, more primal—swirling in the depths of his gaze.

"Jack ..." she whispered.

And then he was kissing her. His lips firm and warm, molding perfectly to her own as if they were made for each other. For a moment, the universe fell away, and there was nothing but the two of them, lost in the sweetness of the moment.

Then reality came crashing back, and she pulled away, feeling flushed with embarrassment. Jack cleared his throat and looked down, seeming to find the floor incredibly interesting. "I, uh ... I should probably get back to work." He gestured vaguely towards the table.

She nodded, her own gaze fixed on the stars outside the window. "Right. And I should look for escape routes and new hiding places. Just in case."

They parted awkwardly, each retreating to their respective tasks. But even as she settled onto the couch in front of the small window, her mind kept drifting back to that kiss, to the feel of Jack's arms around her, the press of his body against hers.

Jack's efforts eventually bore fruit and he broke through the ship's computer security, gaining access to the owner's information.

"Simon Rourke." At the sound of Jack's voice, Alexis got up from her seat and walked over to stand behind him so she could see the screen. "That's who owns this ship."

"He's handsome," she noted aloud as images of a man in his early forties with short-cropped silver hair, lean and fit and exuding an air of authority, filled the screen. In one photo, he stood on the deck of a sleek spacecraft, his expression unreadable as he oversaw the loading of cargo. "In a cold, ruthless way," she quickly amended when Jack shot her a glare.

His fingers continued to dance across the keyboard, bypassing firewalls and security measures with practiced ease. The lines of code faded and were replaced with images and text .

"He owns Stellar Freight Solutions and Rourke Enterprises."

"I've heard of both," Alexis said. "Stellar Freight Solutions is a shipping company, and Rourke Enterprises specializes in technology solutions, but I thought both businesses were legitimate."

"What better way to move stolen goods than behind a legitimate front?" Jack muttered.

Delving deeper into the system, he came across a series of encrypted communications. Curious, he peeled away the layers of security until he gained access to a partition marked "Private Exchanges."

"*Krauk* ..." he breathed.

"What?" Alexis leaned closer.

Jack highlighted an audio message tagged with a familiar name.

Alexis squinted at the filename. *"Krauk!"*

Jack played the message.

Michael's voice filled the room—unmistakable, calm, and disturbingly transactional.

"Simon, I've uploaded the data from the SDIA's internal registry. Everything you need to keep your ships off their radar and your routes clean. In exchange, I want full partnership—no more middleman games. You give me access to your distribution network, and I'll make sure the SDIA stays blind.

"Payment terms remain as discussed. I'll be in touch when the next drop is ready."

The audio ended, and silence fell like a hammer.

Alexis stared at the screen, unblinking. "No. That ... that can't be what it sounds like."

Jack didn't answer immediately. His fingers had gone still on the keyboard.

"There's no trace of any SDIA tag in the metadata," he said quietly. "No tracer code. No false flags. If he was setting up a sting, he covered it way too well."

Alexis shook her head, but her voice was brittle. "Michael wouldn't do this."

Jack hesitated. "You said yourself—he was in deep. Maybe too deep. Maybe he lost the thread."

"No." Her voice cracked. "He was risking everything to stop Simon, not ... join him."

Jack looked away, jaw clenched. He didn't want to believe it either.

Suddenly, red warning banners flashed across the screen. Intrusion alerts.

"Damn it. We triggered an internal security protocol. We have to move."

"Right." Alexis wiped at her face and straightened, forcing herself into motion. "Let's go."

She moved to the door and palmed the access panel. It hissed open with a low breath of air, revealing an empty corridor.

She turned to signal Jack—but he wasn't beside her.

"Jack, come on! What are you doing?"

He was still at the console, frantically working.

"There's too much data to leave behind. I'm pulling everything I can. Maybe there's something in here that explains that message."

"You think there's a chance?" Her voice was trembling again.

"I have to believe there is." He tapped furiously at the controls. "Just a couple more seconds—"

"Jack!"

"Almost—" His voice caught as the download bar ticked past ninety percent. The tension in the air was a living thing.

"Got it!" he said, punching a button on his wrist device. The holographic screen vanished.

Alexis didn't wait. She grabbed his arm and hauled him into the corridor. Neither of them spoke as they moved, the weight of what they'd just heard pressing down like a storm cloud waiting to break.

Chapter Eight

THEY HAD BARELY STEPPED outside the room when the ship's alarms blared to life, a shrieking klaxon that sent a jolt of adrenaline through Alexis's veins. The red emergency lights flashed in rhythmic pulses, casting eerie shadows along the metallic corridor walls. The alert had gone out—every crew member now knew intruders were on board.

She and Jack had to move fast.

"Let's go." She motioned for him to follow as she bolted down the corridor, her pulse hammering in her ears.

They reached the end just as the pounding of boots echoed from the right. Without hesitation, she veered left, Jack matching her stride for stride.

Midway down, a side passage hissed open, and a crew member stepped into their path. His eyes went wide with shock when he saw them.

Alexis's heart leaped into her throat.

No time to fight. No time to react.

She dodged around him, catching a fleeting glimpse of his bewildered face as he spun toward them—too stunned to move for a split second. That second wasn't long enough.

By the time she risked a glance over her shoulder, the crewman had disappeared back into the passage. "He's gone to warn the others."

"Then we move faster."

She nodded, her mind spinning to recall the layout of the ship. The lift was no longer an option since that's the direction from which the crew members had been coming. "Next right, then down the maintenance shaft in the wall."

Reaching the maintenance shaft a short while later, Alexis yanked the lever. The access panel hissed open, revealing a narrow vertical tunnel vanishing into darkness. The air smelled of machine oil and faint ozone.

She was about to climb in when Jack's firm grip closed around her wrist.

"I'll go first," he said, voice low but commanding. "We don't know who's at the other end."

Before she could argue, he'd climbed through the opening, grabbed the ladder rungs and started down, disappearing into the shadows below.

Swallowing her frustration, she followed, feeling the chill of the metal bite into her fingers when she gripped the ladder rung. Every creak of the ladder, every breath, seemed deafening in the confined space. The deeper they went, the darker it became, the distant hum of the ship's engines vibrating through the walls.

Then Jack suddenly stopped.

"Wait," he whispered.

Alexis froze, pressing herself flat against the ladder. Her breath hitched.

Above them, voices.

A nervous sweat broke out along her spine. Had she closed the access panel? She thought she had, but doubt gnawed at her. Then she felt Jack's hand on her ankle, giving it a slight tug, letting her know to keep moving.

They descended deeper until, finally, he pushed open the lower access panel and peered out. "Clear."

She followed him into the corridor, forcing her breathing to steady. She looked around to orient herself, but the walls—all the same dull gray, lined with identical hatches and vents—blurred together in disorienting sameness.

"Well?"

She shot him a glare. "I'm thinking."

No time. No time. The walls seemed to close in around her.

Then she heard it—faint but growing louder.

Footsteps. Voices.

She tensed.

Coming from ahead. No, behind.

Krauk.

"Move!" She yanked Jack forward.

They raced past the maintenance shaft, heartbeats thundering in unison. They reached another intersection. Jack held up a hand to stop her. Then she heard it.

Boots. Close.

Too close.

They were boxed in.

Alexis's gaze darted to the doors on either side of them. Where did they lead? She couldn't remember. Panic clawed at the edges of her mind.

She grabbed a door handle. Locked.

Krauk.

She tried the next.

It opened.

They slipped inside nanoseconds before a voice rang out from the corridor: "They're around here somewhere! Find them, but don't kill them—Mr. Rourke wants them alive!"

Alexis barely had time to register the pulsating hum of machinery before Jack pressed his palm against the access panel, preventing anyone from opening the door from the outside.

She turned, scanning the room.

The engine room.

Great.

Throbbing with energy, the ship's power core pulsed in a hypnotic rhythm, throwing flickering light across walls lined with scattered tools and exposed wiring. A maze of metal catwalks crisscrossed overhead. There was no other door.

They were trapped.

"Damn it," Jack muttered. "I should have kept you safe."

Alexis rounded on him, eyes flashing. "Hey, we're not dead yet."

A hard pounding rattled the door.

"Not yet," he murmured grimly. "We will be if we don't lock this down."

Alexis's gaze landed on the tools magnetized to the wall. "What about those?"

Jack studied them, then nodded. "Might work."

She grabbed the largest wrench she could find, jamming it beneath the door. Too thin. She wedged another beside it, then kicked them both into place.

Another slam from the other side. The door jolted open a fraction.

"In there!" someone shouted.

Krauk.

Jack turned, eyes scanning. "We need a distraction."

Her gaze fell on the ship's power source—a crystalline structure thrumming with energy. "Can you do something about that?"

His smirk was tight. "Maybe."

He kneeled, prying open a panel. Alexis kept her eyes on the door, listening to the scrape of metal as the crew outside pried open the door, millimeter by millimeter.

The ship's lights flickered.

A shudder ran through the floor.

The engine sputtered.

Jack snapped the panel shut and stood.

"I loosened the connection." He slipped the tool back into his jacket. "Temporary fix."

She nodded. If he'd removed the power source entirely, life support would be lost, and they'd all die. Not the outcome she was hoping for.

Then she saw it.

The ventilation grate.

"Air shaft." She pointed to it. "It leads to the landing bay."

The pounding outside turned frantic.

Jack was already moving, unfastening the bolts. The grate hit the floor with a clang.

Alexis climbed in first. Jack followed, pulling the grate back into place as the engine room door burst open.

"Find them!" a voice barked.

Alexis ignored the ache in her limbs as she kept crawling through the narrow shaft. She used its twists and turns to track her progress against the image she'd memorized.

"Almost there," she whispered, mostly to herself.

Then she spotted a glow up ahead. The exit.

Reaching the grate, she peered through it into the landing bay. Empty.

She twisted around and kicked.

The grate clattered to the floor.

Praying no one heard, she dropped into the bay, scanning the row of shuttles.

Jack landed beside her, eyes glinting as he spotted what he hoped would be their salvation. "Emerson Space Runners. Nice."

"Can you fly one?"

He scoffed. "Please. I could fly one with my eyes closed."

She arched a brow. "Maybe leave them open."

He smirked. "Deal."

Then, with confident strides, he moved toward the nearest shuttle, and Alexis followed, hoping—praying—they would make it off this ship alive.

Climbing aboard the shuttle, Jack hurried up to the cockpit while Alexis hit the hatch control to close the shuttle door. Sliding into the pilot's seat, he studied the controls, his mind working faster than his pulse to memorize them. The interface wasn't what he was used to—sleek, streamlined, more modern than the interface on the *Black Jack*.

"Here goes nothing." He tapped in a quick sequence. The engines rumbled to life, their deep, resonant hum vibrating through the cockpit. Slowly, the shuttle lifted off the bay floor, but he didn't allow himself to relax.

Spinning the craft, he lined it up with the hangar doors. On the other side: space. Freedom.

"If the tech gods are listening, now would be a great time to bless me," he murmured, jabbing the button on the ship's console to signal the hangar door's control panel.

With a heavy *clunk*, the massive doors groaned and began retracting, revealing the infinite void beyond. Once the doors were fully open, Jack pressed the throttle, easing the shuttle forward.

And then—

The doors started closing again.

"Son of a—" Jack growled, fingers gripping the controls as the metal slabs began grinding shut. He hit the button to send another signal to the hangar door control panel, but the doors kept closing. Someone on the *Nebula Marauder* was controlling them now.

"Jack, stop!" Alexis's shout cut through the hum of the engines.

He didn't stop. Instead, he shoved the throttle all the way forward.

A roar filled the cockpit as the shuttle lunged toward the rapidly shrinking gap.

"Jack, NO!" Over the hum of the engines, Alexis's voice sounded raw with panic. He could practically feel the sheer terror radiating off her, but he couldn't afford to let it distract him. If his calculations were correct—

Focus!

As the shuttle's speed ramped up, the stars visible beyond the doors blurred. The gap between the doors seemed little more than a sliver now, an opening most sane pilots wouldn't attempt to fly through.

Jack wasn't most pilots.

His hands moved in precise, instinctive motions, adjusting the trajectory with razor-sharp focus.

"Alexis, trust me!" He tightened his grip on the controls as he spared her a quick glance.

Her knuckles were white as she clung to the edge of the co-pilot's seat, her entire body coiled with tension. "Jack, if we don't make it—"

"Stop." His voice cut through her fear like a blade. His gaze never left the closing doors. "We're going to make it. I promise."

She let out a strangled sob, but didn't argue. Maybe because, deep down, she knew he wouldn't make promises he couldn't keep. She hoped that was the case.

The last sliver of space between the doors was no wider than the shuttle's wingspan.

His heart pounded. The shuttle was moving fast and there was no room for error. If his timing was off even the slightest, they'd both die the instant the shuttle crashed into the doors.

"Almost there ..." His pulse was a drumbeat in his ears.

He heard Alexis suck in a sharp breath. "Jack, I—"

He didn't give her time to finish. He slammed his palm down on the button to activate warp speed while twisting the directional stick a fraction—just enough to tilt the shuttle as it shot forward.

Chapter Nine

FOR A FRACTION OF a second, the world became a blur of searing metal and flashing alarms. A gut-wrenching *screech* filled the cockpit as the outer edges of the shuttle grazed the doors—so close that sparks exploded in a shower of orange against the hull.

Then—silence.

They were through!

Jack let out the breath he hadn't realized he was holding, hands shaking slightly as he steadied the controls.

Behind them, the hangar doors slammed shut with finality.

Alexis sucked in a ragged gasp, her chest heaving. She turned wide, disbelieving eyes toward him. "You're—" She couldn't seem to find the words.

Jack exhaled sharply, lips curling into a smirk. "Amazing?"

She let out a breathless, half-crazed laugh, her eyes still wild. Then, without warning, she punched him—hard—right in the arm.

"Ow!" he yelped, rubbing the spot. "What the hell?"

"You're insane! We could have been killed!"

He grinned, ignoring the lingering sting. "Yeah, but we weren't. So, you know, maybe ease up on the punching next time."

She let out a shaky breath and sagged back against her seat. "Next time?" She closed her eyes. "I don't ever want to experience that kind of take-off again."

He chuckled, steering the shuttle away from the ship.

They were safe.

For now.

"Can you look at the navigation screen and tell us where the hell we are?"

"Give me a second to catch my breath." She shot him a sharp look as she activated the nav-screen and studied it for several long seconds. "We're still in the Outer Fringe, nearing the halo. And look—" She pointed out the front viewfinder. "There's the Solaris Dominus wormhole. The entrance can't be far—"

Her words were cut short as the shuttle unexpectedly lurched backward, throwing them both forward in their seats. Only their safety harnesses kept them from crashing into the front viewfinder.

"What the—" Jack's heart raced as he checked the readouts, trying to determine what had caused the abrupt change in course. "Damn it! It's the *Nebulae Marauder*. They have us locked in their tractor beam and they're pulling us back to their ship."

"Can't you do something?" Her voice held a hint of fear. "Feed the engine more power, maybe."

"Why didn't I think of that?" he growled facetiously. "The tractor beam is too strong." With the shuttle trembling under the relentless grip of the tractor beam, he knew they had little time.

"Take the controls," he ordered, his voice rough with urgency. "Don't let up on the thrusters. I'll see if I can reroute more power to the engines."

He sprinted toward the rear of the shuttle, passing by haphazardly stowed equipment. In the cramped space housing the ship's engine and power supply, aided by the soft glow from the emergency lights, he set to work, rerouting all available energy from the Kirellite crystals to the engines. He even tapped into the life support system because they'd only have one shot at breaking free; failure meant certain capture and, if their captors were not the law-abiding type—which seemed likely—possibly death.

"Come on, come on," he muttered to himself, feeling the weight of responsibility not just for his own life but for Alexis's as well. He couldn't bear the thought of failing.

"Jack!" She called from the front, anxiety lacing her voice. "Whatever you're doing back there, do it faster!"

"Almost there." He gritted his teeth as he made the final adjustments.

Then he rushed back to the front of the ship. Glimpsing Alexis's wide, frightened eyes, he felt a surge of protectiveness. "Make sure your straps are tight." He slid into the pilot's seat and slipped on his own harness. Then he hit the button that redirected all the ship's available energy to the engines.

The high-pitched whine of the engines filled the cabin as they strained against the tractor beam's hold. Jack's hands tightened on the controls, knuckles white, while Alexis muttered under her breath. It sounded like she was praying.

He followed her lead, but his prayer was less devout. "Come on, you *krauking* piece of junk. Move!" His fingers flexed on the throttle. The shuttle bucked and rattled under the strain.

Then, with a sudden lurch, the shuttle broke free of the tractor beam. Relief washed over them both, but there was no time to savor the victory. The momentum of breaking free sent the shuttle hurtling out of control at breakneck speed—directly toward the wormhole.

Jack fumbled with the controls, trying to slow their speed or alter their course, but there was no time. "Hang on!"

As soon as the shuttle pierced the outer wall of the wormhole, a strange sensation washed over them—an otherworldly blend of weightlessness and disorientation. For a suspended moment, it felt as if time itself had frozen, leaving them hanging in the void.

The wormhole's walls, translucent and pulsing like a living artery, glowed with eerie hues of violet and gold. Then reality snapped back with a jolt as the shuttle, rattling like it was being torn in half, passed through the inner wall, directly into the flow of traffic. Outside the viewport, light twisted into spirals—an endless kaleidoscope of motion, color, and distortion.

Then came the chaos.

Ships.

Dozens of them.

Passenger cruisers. Freight convoys. Courier darts. An entire interstellar migration of vessels rocketing through the transit lanes.

Jack's instincts took over as alarms blared from every panel. "We're in the core lane—this is high-traffic! I need to get us out before we become space paste!" He cast a quick glance at Alexis to see her tighten her harness straps, her eyes wide with well-deserved terror.

Suddenly, a StellarLux commuter liner screamed past them, its hull gleaming like a floating casino. The energy field from its engines buffeted their shuttle, threatening to send them into another spin. Jack gritted his teeth and yanked the controls, narrowly avoiding a spiraling tumble into the next lane.

Something blinked red on the screen.

"Drift bus incoming," Alexis read, squinting. "Five degrees and closing fast!"

A lumbering GovTran shuttle loomed like a monolith barreling toward them. Jack dove beneath it, the hull of their shuttle grazing the wormhole's inner boundary wall. A static charge exploded across the dash—blue sparks arcing.

"Crap!" Alexis tapped the nav screen rapidly. "Jack, the nav is glitching!"

"Nav's useless inside the wormhole," he shouted back. "This is all E-G-I, sweetheart!"

They corkscrewed between a modular cargo train and a glittering diplomatic yacht, missing both by a meter.

"E-G-I?" she asked, sounding breathless.

"Eyes and gut instinct."

Another ship—a dart-shaped Viper-class freighter—blasted through from a side entry tube, cutting them off.

"Who merges at that speed?!"

"Someone with bigger guns than ours." Jack braced himself as the shuttle clipped the Viper's wake. The little craft jolted sideways like a kicked can and his fingers danced over the manual controls as he tried to stabilize the shuttle's course using rapid-fire micro-thrusts. "I can't slow us down—not with the inertial dampeners failing."

Ahead, a sleek Starliner glided with indifferent grace, accompanied by two escort drones pulsing in tight formation.

"Gonna thread the gap," he muttered.

"Are you insane?!"

"Maybe." He yanked the control left, then right—barely squeezing through the two drones at light-speed.

Alexis made a strangled sound, somewhere between a gasp and a scream.

Jack glanced over at her and grinned. "Please—my grandmother could've flown that blindfolded."

She punched his shoulder, but before he could respond, another warning ping sounded—low and deadly.

A massive bulk hauler had dropped into their lane—a lumbering Titan-class freighter, slow, wide, and impossible to dodge.

Jack's eyes widened. "That's not a ship. That's a *moon with engines.*"

He yanked the control hard, trying to bank beneath it, but there was nowhere to go.

"No no no—," Alexis cried. "He's too close—"

The shuttle's nose cleared the hauler's front, but the massive side bulk scraped the port wing, slamming into them with the force of a meteor strike.

BOOM!

The shuttle spun, flung sideways like a toy kicked by a giant. Jack's shoulder slammed into the bulkhead, and his head cracked hard against the side panel. Stars burst across his vision, and a hot sting opened above his temple.

Lights died. Artificial gravity sputtered. Sparks rained from the ceiling as systems crashed.

Alexis shrieked as the world twisted.

The shuttle tumbled through the wormhole wall.

One second, they were spiraling in a vortex of light—

—and the next, silence.

Stillness outside.

Inside the shuttle, only the sound of Jack's ragged breathing and Alexis's shaky gasps filled the cabin.

She broke the silence first, voice trembling.

"Are we dead?"

Jack blinked, blood trickling down his temple.

He gave her a sideways glance. "Not yet."

And then, the console sparked one last time and died. The shattered console screen flickered once, then faded completely. Jack slumped back in his seat, breathing hard. He wiped the blood from his brow, grimacing at the sticky warmth.

Alexis finally unlatched her harness, the sound echoing loudly in the stunned quiet. She winced as she moved, her side aching from the impact.

"Well," she said hoarsely, "that was ... exciting."

He coughed a laugh, then winced.

They fell silent again, the enormity of what just happened creeping in. Beyond the cracked viewport, space stretched in every direction. No traffic lanes. No markers. No stars they recognized.

"Do you know where we are?" She leaned forward to peer out the front viewport, looking for a familiar constellation.

He shook his head. "No idea, but we can't stay here. Let me see if I can fix the engine."

He forced himself to his feet with a groan and staggered toward the back of the shuttle. The engine compartment was dim, lit only by the faint blue glow of residual power pulsing through exposed conduits. Jack dropped to one knee and opened a panel.

Most of the power he'd rerouted earlier was still bleeding through the main crystal feed, dangerously unbalanced. He worked quickly, re-stabilizing the core, bypassing a melted junction, and trickling just enough energy into the primary systems.

After several tense minutes, the engine gave a low, coughing whine—and then hummed to life.

He exhaled, half in relief, half in disbelief. Returning to the cockpit, he dropped into the pilot's seat and brought the navigation screen online. The image flickered, hazy and warped, but readable.

"We're back in Solaris Dominus." That was a relief. "Nearest inhabited planet's too far. This shuttle will never make it."

She frowned. "Then what do we do?"

Jack zoomed out. A faint beacon blinked six astral units away.

He pointed it out to her on the screen. "That's a Chronogeoscience space station orbiting a dead Wraith planet. Uncharted on most maps, but ... it's there."

Alexis's expression was wary. "Wraith planet?"

He met her gaze. "It's that or we wait to die out here. If they'll let us dock, we might be able to call for help."

She nodded slowly, but what else could she do? It's not like dying was the preferable option.

Jack keyed in the course. The engines groaned, but the stars shifted in the viewport as the ship turned.

"Heading out at zero-point-five astral units per hour. We should make our destination in twelve hours."

Alexis settled back in her seat. "Wake me when we're in ghost territory," she muttered.

He grinned faintly and adjusted their course. "You got it."

Outside, the shuttle limped into motion—scorched, battered, but moving—toward a planet long forgotten and a station they hoped would be their salvation.

The time it took for the shuttle to creep across open space toward the space station seemed interminable. By the time the space station finally came into view, the shuttle felt like it was barely moving. A twinge of hope ignited within Jack when he noticed the landing bay's metal outer doors already standing open.

"And ... here goes nothing." He directed the shuttle towards the gaping entrance, the engines groaning as they strained to maintain their sluggish speed.

As they neared the entrance, an unsettling vibration took over the ship.

"Jack ...?" Alexis began, her voice tinged with concern.

"I know. I feel it, too. Hold on."

They were mere meters away from the safety of the space station when the engines suddenly quit, leaving them in a sudden, eerie silence. Jack's heart leaped into his throat as he realized he had no way to steer the shuttle. They were now at the mercy of their own momentum, but as soon as the thrusters burned off their residual store of energy, even that would be gone.

"Brace yourself, Alexis!"

The shuttle glided through the bay opening. Then the artificial gravity kicked in and the bottom of the shuttle hit the bay floor. Its momentum carried it several meters into the bay, accompanied by the screeching of metal raking against metal.

A meter from the innermost shuttle bay wall, the shuttle ground to a stop and, with the engines dead and the control panel fried, the resounding silence was disconcerting.

"You okay?" His voice was hoarse from the strain of the last few moments.

"Think so." She rubbed her shoulder where the harness strap must have dug in. "That was one hell of a landing."

"Better than the alternative." He tried to mask his own relief with humor, knowing they had cheated death once again.

Outside the shuttle, they heard the grinding sound of the bay doors as they automatically closed. Looking out the shuttle's viewport, he waited for the safety light to turn green, which would let them know that the internal atmosphere had normalized and it was safe to leave the ship without first putting on their space suits and oxygen tanks.

It took longer than expected, but the safety light finally blinked to green.

"Ready to get off this shuttle?" He was already moving to the shuttle's door. "Let's go introduce ourselves to the residents."

Chapter Ten

Opening the shuttle's door, Jack exchanged a wary glance with Alexis before stepping out into the deserted landing bay. Their footsteps echoed through the cavernous space, magnifying their sense of isolation.

"Strange." He scanned the area. "You'd think someone would've shown up to greet us by now, especially since we breeched their force field."

"Maybe they're not that happy to see us." She kept her voice soft while she looked all around. Everything was eerily quiet and still. The only sound other than their footsteps was the hum of the life support systems.

As they ventured further from the safety of their shuttle, the automatic lighting in the shuttle bay flickered sluggishly, casting eerie shadows on the walls.

Jack looked back at her. "I have a bad feeling about this. You stay here while I go look around."

She followed him across the room, halting when he turned to face her. "There is no way you're wandering around this place and leaving me behind."

"It's perfectly safe."

At that moment, the station emitted a long, low groan that echoed off the walls, much like an ancient building settling.

Alexis jutted out her chin, daring Jack to say anything more.

He only sighed. "Come on. Let's go find somebody."

They left the landing bay and headed down an empty corridor. The dim lighting gave the space station the feeling of being trapped in a perpetual twilight, while the sound of their footfalls reverberated off the walls like ghostly echoes.

"Maybe everyone is sleeping," Alexis suggested.

"You ever heard of a station where everyone slept at the same time?" Jack tried to suppress the unease creeping up his spine.

They explored hallway after hallway, finding nothing but abandoned rooms and more evidence of the station's emptiness. In the cargo bay, auto-pilot supply pods sat unused, their metal surfaces gleaming dully under the weak light. Further down the corridor were labs filled with dormant equipment.

Jack noted the old-fashioned computers sitting on tables like relics of a forgotten past. "I don't think anyone's been here for a while." Then he gestured to the door. "Let's keep looking and see if we can find the command center."

They followed the signs directing them to the command center, encountering no other beings along the way. On the bright side, they found no corpses meaning the residents had left the station, as opposed to dying there.

When they finally entered the control hub, an eerie silence hung heavy in the air, broken only by the faint hum of machinery.

Jack looked around, searching for the main computer. "We know life support is still working, or we wouldn't be standing here. Let's see what else is working." He went over to the main computer and tapped the screen to wake it.

"While I find out what systems are still operational, why don't you look at the data log? Maybe we can find out how long ago this station was abandoned, and why."

"All right." Alexis set to work accessing the old-fashioned data-recorder.

Jack started the diagnostic scan of the space station. As he waited for it to run, he heard Alexis sigh and looked over.

She looked up from her reading to meet his gaze. "Well, I know why the station is empty. It was evacuated when the funding ran out. Thirty years ago!"

He shrugged. "It could be worse." At that moment, a *ping* indicated the diagnostic scan was complete. He studied the results. *Damn it. We can't catch a break.* "Well, the good news is we won't suffocate. The bad news is, we'll have plenty of time to enjoy the isolation. The comms are fried."

Alexis sighed. "Now we know what worse looks like."

She tried to sound calm, but Jack knew she was worried. Hell, he was worried, but he didn't want her to sense it. "Hey." He reached out to gently touch her arm. "It'll be okay. The Comm-Net is the fastest means of communicating, but it's not the only means. We'll figure it out. Right now, though, we're both exhausted, so let's start by searching for food and water, okay? We'll find a place to rest, maybe catch a couple hours of sleep, and then we'll worry about communications."

"Okay." She nodded bravely. "Maybe, if we're really lucky, we might even find a bottle of brandy."

"Yeah, one can hope."

When they reached the residential wing, they entered the first room.

Jack walked around, surveying the space. "Not bad. It might even be nicer than our previous lodgings."

"I wonder if the food synthesizer still works," Alexis speculated aloud, spotting the industrial-sized machine mounted in the kitchen. She pressed the "on" button and, amazingly, the panel lit up. Taking a chance, she made a selection. Jack came to stand beside her as they waited for the machine to stop humming. When the access door opened, they both stared at the tray of food within.

"What do you think?"

He reached over and pulled out the tray.

She stared at the gray meat surrounded by dark-blue round discs.

Jack lifted the tray higher and inhaled, his nostrils flaring. "Smells funny. What's it supposed to be?"

"Chicken and potatoes."

He glanced at her and then looked back down at the tray of food. He walked over to the recycler and threw the whole thing away. "I don't think we can risk it. What else is here?"

He began opening pantry doors and located a handful of Food Stasis Pods. "This looks promising." He carried them over to the table and set them down. Then he went over to the sink and turned on the faucet. Brown liquid drizzled out.

"I'm not drinking that."

He couldn't blame her. "I didn't see any water bottles. Let's split up and search the rest of the rooms. Bring anything useable back here."

After searching all the rooms, they stood together surveying the results of their search piled on the table.

"Twelve bottles of water and twenty-one Food Stasis Pods," Jack summarized. "It's better than nothing."

Alexis wasn't sure she agreed. Six bottles of water each wasn't much. Even if they rationed themselves to one bottle a day, they'd be lucky to still be alive at the end of the second week.

As if sensing her mood, Jack stepped close and, placing his arm around her, pulled her in tight for a hug.

"We're not dead yet." His voice held quiet determination. "And I'm pretty sure I saw a tachyon generator in the main control room. If it's still functional, I can try to power up the station's communication array. There's a chance I can tap into the old wormhole-relay laser system and send a tight-beam signal straight to the Outer Fringe. If the relay on the other side is still active, someone will get the message almost instantly."

Alexis pulled back enough to meet his eyes. "And if the relay isn't active?"

Jack smirked. "Then I get creative. Worst case, I rig up a supply pod to carry the message manually."

Feeling slightly more optimistic, Alexis gave him a small smile. "Thanks, Jack. I'm sorry I got you into this, but I'm glad you're with me. Now, let's see if the food in these FSPs is edible."

Once again, Jack found himself sitting at a table, having just finished a meal with Alexis. With the scent of beef stew still wafting through the air, he allowed himself to enjoy the comforting domesticity of the moment.

"That's the best meal I've had in ages." Its comforting warmth seemed to melt away the space station's lingering chill, and he eased back into his chair with a contented sigh. "You know what would make this whole being-stranded-alone-on-an-abandoned-space-station experience better? Is if you had your Eros dance outfit on beneath those clothes." He waggled his eyebrow at her to let her know he was teasing.

She smiled in return, but her heart raced at his words, and she couldn't help but remember the way his gaze had lingered on her when she'd been up on stage at The Abyss, or the way he'd kissed her before realizing who she was.

She fought back a blush, struggling to find the perfect flirty comeback, when an ominous groaning sound reverberated through the station.

"What was that?" Her voice sounded as shaky as she felt.

"It's probably nothing," he said when the sound didn't come again. "Old stations like this make all kinds of weird noises."

Alexis studied his expression, searching for reassurance. When he offered a crooked smile, she nodded slowly. "Okay, if you say so."

They finished their meal in silence and then Jack cleared the table, tossing the used Stasis Pods into the recycler.

"I'm going to check on the generator," he told her. "Want to come?"

She nodded and followed him out of the quarters.

Arriving at the control room, Jack found the generator humming steadily. He scanned the console—several lights flickered weakly, but one stood out: COMMUNICATION ARRAY CHARGING. He let out a slow breath and began tapping commands into the dusty interface.

"Come on, baby," he muttered under his breath. "Talk to me."

As readouts flashed across the screen, his heart raced with hopeful anticipation. If he could get a signal through to Lena—

"How does it look?"

He met her gaze, unwilling to sugarcoat the truth. "Looks like we still need to wait before I can send anything out, but everything else seems solid. A little patience and we'll have our rescue party en route." He didn't point out that their message getting through to the Outer Fringe depended on there being a relay hub between them and the space station to catch the message and forward it on.

"I hate waiting." She moved closer to him so she could watch the console's progress. The seconds ticked by with agonizing slowness until finally—

"Ready!" he announced. With a quick keystroke, he sent the message racing into the darkness of space.

He stared at the screen for a moment longer before turning to her with a smile. "Okay. Message has been sent. While we wait for a reply, let's check out those supply pods."

They left the control room and made their way back down the dim hallways. The eerie silence closed in around them once more, punctuated only by the sound of their footsteps.

They reached the cargo bay, and Alexis couldn't suppress a feeling of triumph when she saw the supply pods lined up, their sleek forms like small rockets. Jack went to the first one and checked it.

"No good. Dead crystal."

She watched as he checked and passed on two more, feeling her frustration mount. Then—

"Finally." He grinned, his eyes lighting up as he checked the fourth pod. "Looks like this one's operational."

He opened a panel on the side and pulled out a glowing power crystal, inspecting it with an expert eye. "It's still in pretty good shape."

She studied it. "You think it could power our shuttle?"

He shook his head, sparing her a glance. "Too small. Not even if we combine it with the crystal you picked up back on the *Nebula Marauder*."

She fished into her pocket and pulled out the small crystal she'd nearly forgotten about. It glimmered faintly in her palm before she tucked it away again with a sigh.

"The pod is programmed to return to its planet of origin," Jack explained. "I'll program it to play a distress signal, providing our coordinates." Replacing the crystal, he gave the pod an affectionate pat. "We might as well head back to the room and get some rest while we wait to see if Lena replies."

"Lena?"

He gave her a quizzical look. "Yeah. My chief engineer. She's back at the Outer Fringe space station with my ship, probably wondering what the hell happened to me."

She was doing her best not to get upset that there were things about Jack she didn't know. "You have your own ship?"

Now his brows furrowed. "Yeah, of course. The *Black Jack*. She's not much, but she gets around. How else did you think I got to the Outer Fringe space station?"

She'd assumed he'd booked a ticket on a passenger vessel, like she had, but she kept this to herself. She nodded slowly while processing the information. "How big is your crew?"

He shrugged. "Not big. Lena and I make up the entire crew."

Unbidden, the green-eyed monster reared its head, making her want to know more about his relationship with Lena. She stopped herself just short of asking. "Yeah, some sleep would be good."

They left the cargo bay behind and retraced their steps through the winding halls of the station.

Entering the quarters, they paused, eyes drawn to the one bed. Alexis glanced from the bed to Jack and back again. "I can—"

"I can take the chair," he interrupted her, scratching at his neck with a sheepish grin.

"Don't be silly." She crossed her arms, feigning indifference. "The bed's more comfortable. We're both adults; we can share it. All we're going to do is sleep."

He hesitated, then gave a shrug of agreement. They moved to opposite sides of the bed and stretched out. For a moment, they lay stiffly, each acutely aware of the other's presence. Then Jack pulled the cover over them both with a resigned chuckle. Alexis let out the breath she hadn't realized she'd been holding and relaxed.

"See? Not so bad."

She turned her head to look at him in the dim light. "Don't get any ideas," she warned with a smirk.

"Too late." His voice was low and sultry.

Despite everything—the danger, the uncertainty, the weight of all they'd been through—Alexis found herself smiling softly. She shook her head and settled deeper into the pillow, the tension in her shoulders easing for the first time in days. The gentle rhythm of Jack's breathing filled the quiet, steady and reassuring, like an anchor in the storm her life had become. For the moment, they were safe. Wrapped in that fragile calm,

Alexis let her eyes fall closed ... and finally surrendered to sleep.

A deafening, metallic rending tore through the station, like steel being ripped in half.

Alexis jolted awake, heart hammering, the sound still echoing in her ears. Jack shot upright beside her, already swinging his legs over the edge of the bed.

"What the hell was that?" he snapped, grabbing for his boots.

"I don't know, but it wasn't nothing," Alexis said, fumbling into her own shoes as adrenaline surged through her.

They bolted into the corridor, the sharp scent of heated metal and ozone trailing through the air like a warning. The station seemed to shudder around them as they sprinted toward the control room, every footstep echoing their rising fear.

Jack dove for the main console, fingers flying across the keys. Alexis moved to the adjacent screen, eyes scanning readouts for any sign of damage or breach.

"There!" She pointed at a section of the console where an alert flashed angrily: ORBITAL STABILIZERS MALFUNCTIONING.

Jack cursed under his breath. "The space station's orbit is decaying."

She stared at the console, trying to process his words while reining in her dread. "But we should be okay. Total failure could take months," she argued.

He glanced at her. "I think it's already been months." He moved further along the console, keyed in a command and then pointed. "Look at this."

"What is it?" She moved closer to get a better look at the corkscrew pattern on the screen.

"It's the space station's orbital coordinates for the past ninety rotations around the planet. It's been slowly descending toward the planet. See this line?" He pointed to a line that stretched across the screen, mere millimeters below the lowest point of the corkscrew pattern. "We're here and that line right below it? That represents the planet's atmosphere. Once the space station's orbit reaches that line, it's game over."

"How much time do we have?" She tried to ignore the sudden ringing in her ears. When he turned to her, she didn't like how serious he looked.

"Not long."

"Days?" He shook his head, and her heart fluttered in her chest. "Hours?"

He spared her a quick look, his expression clearly reluctant. "More like minutes. Maybe."

Oh, krauk!

Chapter Eleven

"FOLLOW ME." JACK LED her out of the control room, and they sprinted for their quarters, ducking inside to grab the water bottles. Jack led her back out, urgency in each step as they headed toward the cargo bay.

Reaching the supply pod, he punched commands into the console. The panel lit up in response, and he quickly opened the pod's hatch. He leaned inside, inspecting the interior. It was empty, other than storage netting tacked to the side. More important, the width, depth and length of the compartment were barely large enough to accommodate the both of them. The fit would be tight.

Like a coffin.

He quickly dismissed the thought as he retrieved an oxygen tank from a nearby shelf and shoved it into the empty pod.

"Time to go." He climbed into the pod and laid down. Then he held out his hand to Alexis. "Your turn."

Suddenly, a disembodied voice echoed from the pod: "Ten. Nine."

She froze, staring at him in horror. "You want us to use this as an escape pod?"

"Eight. Seven."

"Alexis! This is our only chance to survive." He shook his outstretched hand with gentle insistence.

"Six. Five."

Her eyes were wide with fear, but when he thought she'd balk again, she took his hand and let him help her into the pod.

"Three."

He gave her just enough time to settle on top of him before he opened the oxygen tank, allowing a small stream of air to hiss out. Then he pressed the button that closed the pod's upper panel.

"Two."

"Brace yourself." He placed a hand at the back of her head, cradling it to his chest as he wrapped his other arm around her, feeling the way her body shook. If they were going to die, he would allow himself these last moments of being close to her.

Then everything happened at once. The station heaved and as Jack looked out the pod's small window, he saw the ceiling tear away from the walls and disappear. A high-pitched tone sounded, and then they were shooting through the launch tube at an incredible rate.

Images rushed past in a blur and then, suddenly, they were outside the station, traveling through the blackness of space. Jack held his breath, praying they got far enough away that the pod wasn't sucked in along with the station when it crashed and burned through the atmosphere.

He didn't have long to wait until he caught sight of the station's fiery entrance into the planet's atmosphere. Then, as the supply pod shot further away from the planet, he lost sight of even that, and there was only darkness and the gentle hissing of oxygen.

"How are you doing?" His voice sounded muted in the chamber.

"Honestly? I've never been more scared in my life."

He tightened his arms about her. "I'm sorry, Alexis. I should have taken better care of you." He felt her return his hug.

"I'm the one who's sorry, Jack. It's all my fault. I should never have dragged you into this." He felt her lift her head and peer up at him, though it was too dark to see. "Would you hate me if I told you how glad I am that you're with me now?"

Her soft words tore at him as he fought to ignore the feel of her body pressing against his. "Hate is the polar opposite of what I'm feeling." He groaned as his body betrayed him, hardening until the stiff length of him pushed against her lower abdomen.

"Kiss me, Jack." The whispered words fell across his face in a gentle caress, so faint he wondered if he'd heard them at all. Still, he hesitated and felt her body shift as she brought her lips closer to his. "Please, Jack. Don't make me beg."

All the reasons he shouldn't kiss her flashed through his mind; none of them mattered if they were about to die. No longer able to resist, he damned the consequences and captured her lips with his, devouring their sweetness with a longing born from years of denial. Her response was no less timid.

Lost in mind-numbing sensations, limited by the small confines of the pod, Jack made love to her the only way he could—through his kisses. His mouth caressed hers and when her lips parted on a sigh, his tongue delved into the moist recesses beyond, stroking her tongue in a primitive mating rhythm.

At that moment, it didn't matter that they were shooting across the heavens, with death waiting to greet them at the end of the journey. Life was perfect.

Slowly, the reality of their situation returned, and Jack reluctantly pulled away from her enticing lips. "We need to stop." His breath was coming in gasps. "We're using up too much oxygen."

She pulled away and lowered her head to his chest once more, nodding to show she understood the gravity of their predicament. They lay in silence, the only sound the gentle hiss of the dwindling oxygen supply. Jack's mind raced, trying to calculate how much time they had left, but the variables were too many. The size of the tank, the rate of consumption, the distance to the nearest habitable planet or space station—all unknowns in the vast expanse of space.

Time felt elastic within the confines of the pod, stretching and contracting unpredictably. Minutes bled into hours, or perhaps it was mere seconds slipping by, impossible to discern. The sensation was disorienting, like floating in a liminal space where the usual rules of time no longer applied. The silence that enveloped them grew heavy and profound, as if the very air held its breath in anticipation.

Jack's senses were heightened, attuned to every subtle shift in Alexis's breathing, every twitch of her muscles against his. He marveled at the softness of her hair brushing his chin, the way her body molded perfectly to him, as if they were two halves of a whole finally reunited.

As the pod continued to shoot across space, Jack's thoughts wandered to the events that had brought them to this moment. The dangerous mission, the narrow escapes—all leading to this final, desperate gamble. He knew the odds were stacked against them, but with Alexis in his arms, he found a strange sense of peace. If this was to be their end, at least they would face it together.

The hiss of the oxygen tank grew fainter with each passing moment, a grim reminder of their dwindling supply. His chest tightened as he purposely drew in shallower breaths, the air thin and stale. Their time was running out.

Alexis hadn't moved in some time and he realized she'd passed out, her body growing heavy and still against his own. Part of him was grateful she wasn't awake to face the looming specter of death.

The lack of oxygen turned his thoughts into a kaleidoscope of memories and regrets. He thought of the countless missions he'd undertaken, the close calls and narrow escapes that had led him to this moment. He thought of his friends, some of whom he hadn't seen in a while; all of whom he'd never see again. Friends like Lena, Adrian, Nero, Lazureth ...

There were others, too many to recall. And then, with clarity as if it had happened yesterday, he remembered the first time he laid eyes on Alexis. It had been a bright, warm afternoon during a rare leave from his and Michael's military duty. Since he'd had no home of his own, Jack had accepted Michael's invitation to go home with him.

Walking in the door, the modest family home was filled with laughter and the scent of freshly baked bread wafting from the kitchen. They'd followed the sounds and smells to the kitchen where Jack first laid eyes on Alexis.

She was only fourteen then, yet she possessed an almost ethereal beauty that seemed to glow against the backdrop of ordinary life. Jack recalled watching her from the doorway, her dark hair tumbling in soft waves around her shoulders as she chatted animatedly with her mother. There was a quiet confidence in the way she moved—a graceful blend of youth and an old soul that belied her tender age. She'd gazed up at him when Michael introduced them and he'd felt an unexpected stir—a mix of admiration and a deep, protective instinct. Over the course of a week, her fierce determination and quick wit drew him in like a moth to a flame.

After all this time, he was still drawn to her. The only thing that had changed was that she was no longer a child, no longer off limits. With that thought came his last regret, that he wouldn't have more time with her.

But if this was to be their end, he could think of no one else he would rather have by his side. The thought was chased by a deep sorrow because Alexis was too young to die.

The hissing sound faded to a whisper, then ceased altogether, plunging the pod into an eerie silence. Jack's lungs burned, screaming for air that would not come, and his vision blurred at the edges. He tightened his arms around Alexis, holding her close as if his embrace could shield her from the icy grip of death.

Then death came for him, in the form of a searing white light, brighter than any star he had ever seen. The gateway to the afterlife. A wry smile tugged at the corner of his lips as he dismissed the notion; with the life he'd led, the sins that stained his soul, he knew damn well that Heaven's gates would remain firmly shut to the likes of him. Perhaps the light had come for Alexis. Yes, that made more sense.

The light pulsed and throbbed, growing brighter with each passing second until it consumed his entire field of vision. His eyes watered and his head pounded, the pressure building behind his temples until he thought his skull might shatter. There was no use in fighting it any longer, so he surrendered himself to the darkness.

Chapter Twelve

ALEXIS STIRRED FROM HER unconscious state, the sound of Jack's voice gradually pulling her from the depths of darkness.

"Alexis ... Alexis, wake up. We made it."

As she slowly opened her eyes, the first thing she saw was Jack's face, mere inches from her own, his eyes filled with a mixture of relief and joy. His smile, though weary, was genuine and comforting.

"Jack?" she croaked, her throat dry and her voice hoarse. "What ... what happened?"

"We were rescued," he explained. "A passing ship picked up our distress signal and pulled our pod into their docking bay."

She frowned, fighting through the fog in her brain to make sense of his words. Rescued? A ship? She blinked, realizing the pod's hatch was open, and the air felt different—fresher. Gradually, the events of their harrowing escape came flooding back: the desperate flight from the *Nebula Marauder*, the daring plunge into the wormhole, taking refuge in the space station only to discover it wasn't the haven they'd hoped for. And finally, climbing into the supply pod and the agonizing uncertainty of whether they would survive the journey as the pod shot across space to the nearest planet.

As her senses slowly returned, she became acutely aware of her body's position—draped across Jack's muscular frame, their limbs intertwined in the cramped confines of the supply pod. A flush of embarrassment, mixed with a tingle of excitement, crept through her as she realized the intimacy of their situation.

With a determined effort, she attempted to push herself up, her hands pressing against the firm planes of his chest. Her movements were sluggish, her muscles stiff from the prolonged inactivity. As if sensing her struggle, Jack gently grasped her waist, his strong hands providing support as she maneuvered herself into a kneeling position, straddling his hips.

For a moment, their eyes locked, a silent acknowledgment of the unspoken tension that always seemed to simmer between them. Jack's gaze held a tenderness that made her heart flutter, but there was also a glimmer of something else—a hunger, a longing that he quickly masked.

As soon as she found her balance, Jack smoothly shifted beneath her and, in one fluid motion, used his powerful arms to lift himself out from under her, to a standing position, before stepping out of the pod. The sudden absence of his warmth left her feeling strangely bereft, but she had little time to dwell on the sensation as Jack extended his hand down and gently but firmly helped her out of the pod.

As she stood on shaky legs, her gaze flicked over their surroundings, taking in the sleek lines of the unfamiliar ship. The walls were pristine white, adorned with intricate geometric patterns that seemed to glow with a soft, pulsing light. The air carried a faint scent of ozone, mixed with something sweet and exotic, like the nectar of a rare flower.

"Don't worry, you're safe here."

At the sound of the strange voice, Alexis whirled around to face the man with vibrant red hair and kind eyes standing behind her. Seeming to notice Alexis's wariness, he offered them both a reassuring smile. "Welcome aboard the *Windswept.*"

At that moment, the bay doors slid open with a soft hiss and two men strode in. Jack's gasp coming from beside her caused her to turn back to him. Seeing his stunned expression sent a jolt of apprehension through her. She stepped closer to him, her eyes fixed on the two men. The one with the piercing blue eyes and short silver hair strode forward, his gait confident and purposeful. His companion, equally tall and imposing, followed a step behind. His dreadlocks, a deep ebony hue, were adorned with silver and gold beads woven meticulously throughout, catching the light with each turn of his head as his midnight-blue eyes scanned the room with a keen intensity.

"Never took you for a void-drifter," the silver-haired man said to Jack, his voice filled with amusement. "Personally, I would have chosen a luxury ship to entertain a beautiful woman, but I guess a supply pod is one way of keeping her close."

Instead of taking offense, Jack laughed and extended his hand. "Nero Blackwell. Man, I thought you were dead, killed in that explosion."

The man chuckled, a deep sound that seemed to fill the space between them. "I won't say it wasn't a close call, but reports of my death have been exaggerated." His voice was smooth and confident. "You should know better than to believe everything you hear, Marsden."

"Well, I'm glad you're alive, but where the hell have you been this last year?"

"Lying low while I get used to this." He raised his right arm and for the first time, Alexis realized it was mechanical. "I escaped the explosion with my life, but sadly, not with my arm."

"I'm sorry about that," Jack said, sincerity lacing his words, "but it's damn good to see you."

It was only then that Jack seemed to remember Alexis was there. He turned to her, apologetic. "Alexis, this is Nero Blackwell, an old buddy of mine, from way back." Then Jack turned to the other man. "Dracke, it's good to see you again," he said, shaking the man's hand. "Alexis, this is Dracke. Nero's next-in-command."

With the pleasantries out of the way, Alexis felt her guard drop ever so slightly. If Jack trusted these people, then perhaps she could, too.

"Let's go someplace else to talk," Nero suggested, leading them out of the docking bay. "Do either of you need medical attention? I've got a pretty good medical officer."

"No, we're fine," Jack assured him. "Fortunately, you found us as our air ran out. We wouldn't say no to some food and drink, if you can spare it. Our last meal was resynthesized mystery stew."

"Of course." Nero glanced back at them. "On our way to the galley, I'll show you where you can stay and freshen up. Follow me."

As he led them through his ship, Alexis noticed the sleek metallic corridors stretching out before them like a labyrinth, every turn revealing yet another passage-way. She couldn't help but wonder how large a ship this was.

Finally, they arrived at the crew's quarters. The doors slid open with a soft hiss, revealing a series of private rooms. "These are both empty." Nero gestured to two adjacent doors. "They're not the most luxurious accommodations, but they're clean and comfortable. Each room has its own refresher unit for your clothes and shower-misters for bathing." He turned and pointed down the hall. "The galley is that way, third door on the right. You can't miss it—the aroma of our chef's famous Solarian Stew will guide you there." He chuckled, a glint of pride in his eyes. "If you're not partial to stew, we have other options. Join me there when you're ready. I want to hear how you both ended up in that supply pod."

With that, Nero turned on his heel and strode away, his mechanical arm catching the light as he disappeared around the corner.

Alexis stepped into the first room, marveling at the sleek yet functional space. The silver-framed bed looked inviting after their harrowing ordeal, and the viewport offered a stunning view of the star-speckled void beyond. She was about to settle in and catch her breath when she heard footsteps behind her. Turning, she saw Jack enter the room. The door slid shut with a soft hiss behind him.

Confusion flickered across her face. "I thought you'd be taking the other room." She gestured towards the door. "But if you prefer this one ..." She took a step towards the door, ready to leave and give Jack his privacy, but he reached out, gently catching her arm.

"Wait." His voice was low and earnest. "I think it's best if we stick together for now." She raised an eyebrow, a silent question hanging in the air between them. He sighed, running a hand through his tousled hair as he searched for the right words.

"Look, it's been a long time since I last saw Nero, and while I trust the guy, and he did just save our lives, he's still a space pirate. We can't afford to let our guard down completely." His gaze softened, a flicker of concern dancing within their depths. "I'd feel better knowing you're close by."

She couldn't deny the genuine concern etched in his features or the logic of his words. Despite Nero's timely rescue, they were still in unfamiliar territory, surrounded by a crew of space pirates whose true loyalties remained with their captain.

"Alright."

His shoulders visibly relaxed, relief washing over his face. "Thank you." He stepped back to give her some space. Despite the obvious weariness that clung to him, there was an undeniable strength in his presence, a quiet resilience that seemed to radiate from within. She found herself drawn to that strength and resilience.

A flicker of something unspoken passed between them before he looked away.

It was as if the confines of the pod had stripped away the barriers between them, leaving them raw and exposed in each other's presence. Feeling suddenly awkward, Alexis moved about the room, pretending to check it out, all the while very much aware of Jack. Their paths met in front of the refresher unit, and both reached for it at the same time. The brush of Jack's hand against hers sent a jolt of electricity through her.

Instead of pulling his hand away, he gently took her hand, his touch sending a wave of warmth through her body. She turned to face him, her breath catching in her throat as she saw the raw hunger in his eyes. The intensity of his gaze made her knees feel weak, and she leaned closer, drawn to him like a moth to a flame.

"Alexis ..." Her name sounded like a whispered prayer on his lips. He leaned in, his face mere inches from hers. She could feel the heat radiating from his skin, could see the flecks of gold in his hazel eyes. For a moment, the universe seemed to shrink down to just the two of them, standing on the precipice of something profound and life-altering.

But as Jack's lips hovered a hair's breadth from hers, she felt a sudden rush of uncertainty wash over her. Sure, she had kissed him in the pod when she thought they were both about to die. They hadn't died, though, and the weight of unresolved tensions and unspoken feelings came crashing down upon her like a tidal wave. She realized with startling clarity that if she kissed him now, in this moment of vulnerability and heightened emotions, there would be no going back. Their re-lationship, already precariously balanced on a knife's edge, would be irrevocably changed.

With a shaky breath, she forced herself to step back, breaking the spell that had fallen over them and putting some much-needed distance between their bodies, but not yet pulling her hand from his.

"Jack, I ..." Her voice trailed off as she struggled to find the right words. She took a deep breath, trying to calm the racing of her heart. "I don't think this is a good idea."

His brow furrowed, confusion and a hint of hurt flickering across his handsome features. "What do you mean?"

Of course, he was hurt. She sighed inwardly, her gaze dropping to their intertwined fingers. The warmth of his touch sent a shiver down her spine, but she couldn't allow herself to be swept away by the intensity of the moment.

"We've been through a lot together." She took a breath, trying to work up the nerve to continue. "I can't deny that there's something between us, but given all we've been through recently—" She looked up at him, her eyes searching his. "I don't want to complicate things further by rushing into something we might regret later."

His expression hardened ever so slightly, but he nodded slowly, his thumb gently caressing the back of her hand once more before he released it. "You're right." His voice was low and gruff. "I got caught up in the moment, the relief of being alive and safe." He cleared his throat. "We shouldn't keep Nero waiting. You can shower first. After you undress, hand me your clothes through the door and I'll put them in the refresher to clean."

She didn't know what she'd expected. Maybe she hoped he'd argue with her, tell her that his feelings for her were stronger than any situation in which they found themselves. It didn't help that she knew her feelings were totally irrational.

She stepped into the bathroom and closed the door. After she undressed, she gave her clothes to Jack and stepped beneath the fine chemical spray of the mister, wishing it was a soothing shower with real hot water.

All too soon, her shower was over, and she was dressing in freshly cleaned clothes. When Jack took his turn in the bathroom, she put his clothes into the refresher.

After both had showered and dressed, they made their way down the corridor towards the galley, the tantalizing aroma of Solarian Stew growing stronger with each step. The scent was a complex blend of savory spices and tender meat, hinting at the hearty meal that awaited them. Jack could practically feel his mouth beginning to water in anticipation.

"Welcome to the galley," Nero announced, looking up as they entered, a broad grin spreading across his face. The spacious room was alive with the clamor of pots and pans, the sizzle of searing meats, and the chatter of crewmembers gathered around the long, communal tables. The walls were adorned with an eclectic mix of trinkets and trophies from distant worlds, each one telling a story of the ship's many adventures.

At the center of it all stood Nero, his imposing figure commanding attention as he oversaw the preparation of the meal. His mechanical arm moved with a fluid grace, deftly stirring a large pot of stew that simmered over a glowing heating element. The savory aroma that wafted from the pot was enough to make Alexis's mouth water, reminding her of how long it had been since she'd had a proper meal.

Nero handed the ladle to one of the crew members and moved to the large table near the center of the room where Dracke was already seated, gesturing for Jack and Alexis to join him there. As soon as they sat, steaming bowls of stew and glasses of a pink beverage were placed before each of them.

As they ate, Nero launched into an account of his harrowing experience from a year ago. The words flowed easily from him, painting a vivid picture of the day he boarded a Turin freighter to save a kidnapped child. As the story unfolded, Alexis leaned in closer, hanging on every word.

"Room after room was empty," he said, his voice tightening. "Too empty. That's when I knew—something was wrong. It felt like a trap." He leaned forward, voice dropping to a rasp. "I deployed a spider-bot to scout ahead. It pinged back an image I'll never forget." A pause. Then, grimly: "A Traxian bomb. Armed and counting down." The silence crackled with tension. "The *Windswept's* transporter was worthless thanks to the freighter's shielding. My only chance was the Quantum Leap Device strapped to my belt. I bolted for the shuttle bay, hit the trigger, and vanished a heartbeat before the blast tore apart the rest of the freighter."

He lifted his mechanical arm, the metal catching the light. "But not fast enough." His gaze went hard. "The explosion ripped through the hull like paper—and with it, my arm. If Dracke and the crew hadn't been nearby, I'd be another smear of frozen blood drifting through space." He flexed his metal fingers, the faint whirr cutting through the stillness. "Been a year now. Still trying to get used to this damn thing."

"Damn, Nero." Jack shook his head. "You could have let someone know you were alive."

"Believe me, I wanted to." His gaze hardened. "But I had reason to believe that the bomb was set there specifically to take me out. I needed whoever was behind it to think they'd succeeded—at least until I could figure out who they were and confront them."

Alexis felt a shiver run down her spine. He'd recounted the tale so matter-of-factly, with the same this-shit-happens-all-the-time attitude Jack had. When she was a police officer on Veridian Prime, she'd thought her job was dangerous, and it was, but obviously, her job was not nearly as dangerous as that of a space pirate's.

Jack raised his glass in a toast, pulling her from her thoughts.

"To the stars that guide us, the friends beside us, and the luck that finds us—here's to journeys well-traveled and stories yet to be told!" Their glasses clinked together, the sound echoing through the galley.

"Alright, I've told you my tale." Nero leaned back in his seat after taking a swallow of his drink, curiosity evident in his dark gaze. "Now, I want to know how you two came to be shooting across space in a supply pod."

"Where do I start?" Jack mused, taking a sip of his drink. "I suppose it started with Michael's death."

"Your military buddy?" Dracke asked.

Jack nodded. "I'm surprised you remembered. That was a long time ago."

"As I recall," Dracke said with a smirk, "that first year you flew with us, all you talked about was the trouble the two of you got into together." His expression grew serious. "I'm sorry to hear he's passed."

Jack nodded to acknowledge the condolence. "Alexis is Michael's sister. We both found the circumstances of his death suspicious. He was killed while stealing Luminite crystals."

"Michael wasn't a thief," Alexis felt compelled to point out.

"I caught up to Alexis in the Outer Fringe. She'd gotten a lead on a shipment of stolen crystal. We thought if we could find out who's behind these thefts, it might help us understand Michael's involvement, so we sneaked onto the ship to see what we could find out. Unfortunately, we were still in the cargo hold when the ship took off."

He explained how they'd hidden in an empty crewmember's quarters, how breaking into the computer system had alerted the crew to their presence and how they'd stolen a shuttle to escape, only to be caught a short time later in the ship's tractor beam.

"Breaking free of the beam sent us spiraling into a wormhole. Then a freighter clipped us, sending us flying back out of the wormhole. By then, we'd lost the *Nebula Marauder*, but our engines were fried. We limped to the nearest space station, thinking we were saved, only to discover the station was abandoned, and its orbit was in the final stages of decay. The only thing working at that point was the auto-piloted supply pod, so in we went."

"Holy *krauk*!" Dracke exclaimed.

"You certainly know how to keep things interesting." Nero raised his glass to take a drink but, at that moment, his mechanical hand spasmed and the glass shattered in his grip, splattering liquid across the table. "Damn it!" he swore, shaking his clenched fist free of the liquid.

Alexis and Dracke were already using napkins to clean up the spill.

"Sorry about that," he apologized through gritted teeth. "I'm still having trouble with this damn mechanical limb. Dracke's designed a more sophisticated model, but we don't have a good way to power it. Most of the standard batteries and energy cells burn out too fast. And of course, Luminite crystals are regulated and expensive."

At the mention of the crystal, Alexis remembered the crystal in her jacket pocket. She'd intended to keep it as proof that crystals were being stolen, but Nero had literally saved hers and Jack's lives. They owed him. Now it seemed like the crystal could serve a higher purpose. Retrieving it from her pocket, she held it out to them.

"Would this unregistered crystal help?" She watched Nero's eyes widen in surprise.

Dracke reached over and took the crystal from her so he could study it more closely. After a moment, he gave Nero a subtle nod.

But Nero shook his head, refusing the offer. "We can't accept that. It's much too expensive."

Alexis met his gaze with unwavering determination. "You saved our lives. We can't put a price on that. Please take this as a small measure of our thanks."

Nero hesitated, seemingly torn between gratitude and concern. He glanced at Jack, who nodded in agreement with Alexis.

"It didn't cost us a thing. It was part of the stolen shipment we found on the *Nebula Marauder.* At first, we thought we were only dealing with a crystal theft ring, but after looking through the *Nebula Marauder's* computer, I think the stolen crystals are a small part of a bigger problem. That's where we need to focus our attention. So, please, take the crystal with our thanks."

Somewhat reluctantly, Nero accepted the crystal. "Thank you." His voice was rough with emotion. "You don't know how much this means to me."

Jack sat back in his chair. "That meal was excellent. My compliments to the chef. Mind if I use your comm-unit? I left Lena and the *Black Jack* at the Outer Fringe space station. I'll call her to come pick us up and we'll get out of your hair."

Nero grinned. "You're welcome to use the unit, but there's no need for Lena to come all the way out here. We're actually headed to Outer Fringe ourselves. We should be there in about five hours."

Chapter Thirteen

"ANY LUCK REACHING YOUR chief engineer?" Alexis asked when Jack walked into their room a half-hour later.

"Yes, and it's a good thing we still have a couple of hours before we reach the Outer Fringe because it's going to take every minute of that for her to calm down. She's mad as hell that I didn't tell her what I was up to."

"She was worried about you." Alexis had to fight to suppress a bout of jealousy. She needed to know if it was warranted, so she asked the question uppermost in her mind. "Are you two ...?"

"Are we what?"

"Involved?"

He shook his head. "No. We tried it once, when we first started flying together, but it didn't take."

Alexis was surprised. She found it hard to believe any female could resist Jack.

"We should probably take advantage of the travel time to Outer Fringe to grab some sleep," he said, breaking into her thoughts. "I can't remember the last time I slept. That brief period of unconsciousness in the pod doesn't count."

Alexis's gaze scanned the room. Why were they always finding themselves in rooms with only one bed?

"I can sleep on the couch," he offered, as if reading her thoughts. "You can have the bed."

He walked over to it, but she stopped him. "That couch is too small for either of us to be comfortable on. Besides, we shared a bed at the space station before we realized the orbit was decaying. There's no reason we can't share this bed." Plus, after everything they'd been through recently, she felt safer with Jack close by. Of course, she didn't share that with him. She was supposed to be a hardened police officer, able to face dangers as nonchalantly as he appeared to.

"All right." He looked at her like he wanted to say something more but kept silent and merely strolled to the near side of the bed. The side closest to the door, she noted. Where, if someone were to break in, he could easily insert himself between her and the source of danger. Ever protective.

Smiling to herself, she walked around to the other side of the bed. Jack pulled the top cover back. Then, removing only their shoes and weapons, they lay down.

"Lights off," Jack said aloud as he pulled the cover over them, and the room was plunged into darkness.

For what seemed forever, Alexis lay there, staring blindly at the ceiling, acutely aware of every sound and movement Jack made.

"I have a confession to make."

The sound of his voice surprised her because she'd thought he had fallen asleep. "What's that?"

He shifted slightly, turning his head to face her in the darkness. "When we were in that supply pod, and I thought we might not make it out alive ... it made me realize some things. Things I've been trying to ignore or push down, but I can't anymore."

She held her breath, her heart pounding in her chest as she waited for him to continue.

"Alexis, I ... I care about you. A lot. More than I probably should, given our situation and everything that's at stake. But nearly losing you, it put things in perspective." He paused, as if searching for the right words. "I'm not saying I'm in love with you. I don't know if I'm ready for that—yet. But I know you mean a great deal to me. And I'd like to see where this thing between us might go. If you're open to exploring it."

Alexis was silent for a long moment, processing his confession. A warmth blossomed in her chest and spread through her entire being. This was what she wanted, wasn't it? She swallowed hard against the lump forming in her throat.

"I realized some things too." She took a deep breath, bracing herself for what she had to say next. As much as her heart yearned to embrace the possibility of a relationship with Jack, she knew she couldn't. At least for now.

She turned to face him, even though she could barely make out his features in the darkness. "Jack, I ... I'm so grateful for your honesty. And believe me, there's a part of me that wants nothing more than to explore these feelings between us. But we have to think about the bigger picture here."

She could sense his confusion, could almost hear the gears turning in his head as he tried to understand where she was going with this.

"Uncovering the truth about my brother. It has to come first. Getting involved romantically would only complicate things. Distract us—distract me from what I need to do." Each word felt like a knife twisting in her gut, but she pressed on. "I care about you, Jack. So much that it scares me sometimes. Which is why, when we get back to the Outer Fringe space station, we need to go our separate ways. You've almost died three or four times since you started helping me. It's hard enough that I lost my brother. I can't lose you, too."

The silence that followed was deafening. Alexis could hear her own heart pounding, could feel the weight of Jack's gaze on her even in the pitch black.

Finally, he spoke, his voice rough with emotion. "I can't say I'm not disappointed, but I understand. And you're probably right." He rolled away from her then. "Good night, Alexis. Try to get some sleep."

"Good night, Jack." She could barely get the words out over the lump in her throat, but she managed. She rolled over, facing away from him so he wouldn't notice the tears coursing down her cheeks. Cutting ties with Jack might be the right thing to do, but it had also been one of the hardest. Instead of feeling good about her decision, she felt very much bereft and alone in the dark, and it took a long time before she fell asleep.

Alexis's eyes fluttered open, and she froze. It took her a moment to register where she was—and that Jack's arm was draped across her waist. They lay closely intertwined, his breath warm against her neck.

Her heart skipped, and she tensed involuntarily. The movement startled Jack awake. He pulled back quickly, blinking in confusion.

"Uh ... sorry," she mumbled, disentangling herself so she could sit on the edge of the bed. She ran a hand through her hair, willing her pulse to slow. "I guess we were more tired than we thought."

Jack sat up too, his expression unreadable. "Yeah." His tone was polite but distant, and it stung more than Alexis wanted to admit. "We should get moving. We'll be arriving at the space station soon," he added after glancing at his chrono.

"Right." She forced a nod, rose from the bed and headed into the bathroom, needing a moment away from him to collect herself. This new distance between them was what she'd asked for, after all.

As they left their room several minutes later and made their way to the bridge, Alexis kept her eyes focused ahead, determined not to look at Jack. The air between them felt heavy, laden with all the things left unsaid.

When they entered the bustling command deck, they found Nero and Dracke huddled over a holo-display, while a few crew members monitored various stations. A massive viewport revealed the sprawling cylindrical silhouette of the Outer Fringe space station looming closer by the second.

Nero glanced up at them. "There you two are. Sleep well?"

Jack mumbled something unintelligible as he joined the group.

"Good," Nero replied with a knowing smirk. "We'll be docking soon." His gaze flickered between Jack and Alexis. "Once you locate Lena, meet us back in The Abyss for a drink. I didn't press you earlier because I figured you were exhausted, but I'm keen to hear more about these stolen crystals and how they might relate to Michael's death. Maybe I can help. Just because no one's seen me in a year doesn't mean I haven't been around."

Jack glanced at Alexis, silently seeking her input.

She was grateful. While she'd told Jack they'd part ways as soon as they reached the space station, the truth was she had no damn clue what move to make next in her investigation. A drink with Nero might provide her with more information—something she couldn't afford to pass up. She gave Jack a subtle nod of agreement.

"We'll be there," he promised.

Nero turned back to his display, dismissing them with an absent wave. "Good. See you soon."

Alexis lingered a moment longer than necessary before heading for the exit, with Jack at her side. Her mind raced through possibilities as they navigated the corridors leading to the docking bay. She vowed to stick around long enough to learn whatever she could; after that, she'd part ways with Jack like she'd promised herself.

Waiting for the ship to dock seemed like it took forever, Alexis thought, especially since she and Jack spent the time waiting in silence. Finally, though, she felt the ship shudder slightly as it connected with one of the station's docking arms. Jack shot her a sideways glance, but she kept her focus on the red atmosphere light mounted on the inner docking bay wall, visible out the side viewport.

As soon as the light turned green, she reached for the hatch lock, jerking her hand away when her fingers brushed against his hand, already gripping the lock. He gave no outward sign that her touch affected him and disengaged the lock.

"Do you know where to find Lena?" she asked as they left the ship.

"Sure. She'll be where the action is. You're welcome to go with me or you can go with Nero and Dracke to The Abyss." He didn't wait for her to decide, but started walking off.

For reasons she didn't want to examine too closely, she hurried after him. Reaching the main lift, they took it up to the next level, into the bowels of the space station.

Walking through the labyrinth of shadowy corridors that seemed to stretch on forever, Alexis couldn't help but feel wary. This was where most of the black-market trading and gambling occurred.

Alexis studied the busy chaos around her. Traders hawked their wares from stalls crammed into every available space while gamblers huddled in dark corners, playing their games.

"How are you possibly going to find her in this crowd?"

Suddenly, she heard a vibrant voice rise louder than the others, shouting obscenities.

"Found her." A hint of a smile broke through his brooding exterior as he pointed towards a flash of purple hair visible among a group of brutish gamblers.

Alexis wasn't sure what she expected Lena to look like, but it wasn't a petite, pale woman with enormous black eyes and spikey purple hair. One moment she was visible and then the next, she was swallowed by the crowd of riffraff surrounding her. Alexis thought she might feel intimidated if she were in Lena's shoes, but Lena looked perfectly at ease.

She gave a throaty laugh as she won her game. When she glanced around and spotted them, she tapped out and cashed in her gaming credits.

With a nod to the rest of the gamblers, she walked away, heading toward Jack and Alexis.

"Jack!" She cuffed him on the back of his head when she got close enough. "That's for ditching me. Don't do it again." Then she hugged him tightly. "This is for not getting yourself killed." After a long moment, she released him and stepped back, eyeing Alexis curiously. "You must be Alexis."

As the two women sized each other up, Alexis felt another unexpected pang of jealousy. She pushed the feeling down, reminding herself that she had given away the right to feel that way.

"It's nice to meet you." She tried to keep all inflection out of her tone.

"Hmmm, we'll see," Lena said. "Someone mind telling me what kind of shit you two have gotten yourselves into?"

"Not here." Jack cast a look over at the gamblers, though no one appeared to be listening to them. "I'll explain later. Nero and Dracke are waiting for us at the bar."

At that, Lena looked shocked. "Blackwell's alive?" Jack smiled and nodded. "Well, ain't that something?"

They headed back through the corridors that would take them to the lift. As they walked, Jack told Lena briefly about getting trapped on the *Nebula Marauder,* their quick trip through the wormhole, their desperate escape in the supply pod and their rescue by Nero.

"You must be star-kissed," she exclaimed, "to have survived. What I don't get is why you were on the *Nebula Marauder* in the first place."

"It has to do with Michael's death," he started. "Alexi—"

"Where do you think you're going?" A voice boomed, interrupting him. Three imposing figures suddenly materialized from the shadows, effectively blocking their path.

"Pit Jackals," Lena spit out quietly beside him, referring to the lower-level gang responsible for overseeing the gambling.

"Look, we don't want any trouble," Jack said, attempting to de-escalate the situation. "Let us by so we can access the lift and we'll be out of your way."

"We'll let you by as soon as you pay the access fee." The center man's gaze lingered on Lena, clearly expecting her to hand over her recent winnings.

"Over my dead body," she snarled before Jack could silence her.

His thoughts raced, weighing their options. They could offer the men a couple of credits, but he doubted that would buy them safe passage. These thugs were spoiling for a fight.

As if to prove him right, the thug holding a meter-long lead pipe in his hand suddenly lunged at him, swinging the pipe toward his head. With practiced ease, Jack ducked beneath the attack, grabbing the thug's arm and twisting it before using his momentum to throw the thug against a wall.

Alexis, suddenly confronted by one of the other thugs trying to grab her, stepped aside and executed a precise judo throw that sent her assailant crashing to the ground.

From a few steps back, Alexis spotted the third thug attempting to flank Lena. "Behind you!" she shouted, her voice urgent but steady.

Lena whirled around as the third thug lunged at her from behind, his arms outstretched to grab her. With an almost preternatural speed and agility, she twisted her lithe body to the side, causing the man to stumble past her. In a flash, she was behind him.

Alexis watched in awe as Lena leaped onto the thug's back like a violet-maned wildcat, her movements fluid and precise. She wrapped her slender arms around his thick neck in a vise-like chokehold, locking her hands together and squeezing with a strength that belied her petite frame.

The man sputtered and gasped, his eyes bulging as he clawed frantically at Lena's arms. But her grip was unrelenting, her face a mask of calm determination as she maintained the pressure. He staggered forward a few steps, trying to slam her against the wall to break her hold, but Lena held fast.

Her luminescent skin seemed to glow in the dim light of the corridor as she tightened her chokehold even further, cutting off the thug's air supply completely. His struggles grew weaker and more uncoordinated until finally, with a shudder, his eyes rolled back in his head, and he crumpled to the ground, unconscious.

Lena landed gracefully on her feet as the man collapsed beneath her. She straightened up, not even breathing hard. "Thanks for the heads-up."

With all three assailants down, Jack gestured for Alexis and Lena to follow him. "Let's get out of here before they come to."

They continued on until they reached the lift, and Alexis didn't breathe a sigh of relief until the doors were closed.

"Nice moves back there," Lena commented, standing beside her. "You really know how to handle yourself."

"Thanks," Alexis replied, her tone measured but appreciative. "You had some pretty good moves yourself. I don't think I've ever seen anyone move that fast."

"She's half-Lyran," Jack explained.

Lena winked at her. "True, but it doesn't change the fact that men are always underestimating women."

Chapter Fourteen

WALKING INTO THE ABYSS, Jack noted the usual eclectic mix of patrons gathered, their murmured conversations and laughter blending with the low thrum of bass from the sound system. He scanned the crowd and spotted Nero and Dracke over by the bar, leaning casually against the counter and talking to Kylix who, in his usual striking style, was mixing a drink with one hand while gesturing animatedly with the other, his bright eyes flicking between the two men. Whatever was being said earned a low chuckle from Dracke and a wry smirk from Nero.

As soon as Nero noticed Jack, Alexis, and Lena approaching, he clapped Kylix on the shoulder. "We'll catch up later."

Dracke gave the bartender a nod before the two of them stepped away from the bar and crossed the room to meet the newcomers.

"Hey, look who's still alive!" Lena greeted them warmly, her smile broad as she closed the distance. "Long time no see, boys."

Nero grinned, pulling her into a quick but firm hug, while Dracke offered a rare, approving smile. "Been too long," Nero agreed. "Let's grab a table."

He gestured toward an empty booth tucked into the far corner. As the group followed him, Jack and Alexis both gave Kylix a wave in greeting. The bartender returned it with a two-finger salute before going back to serving drinks.

They slid into their seats, exchanged a few lines of small talk, and placed their drink orders. When the server returned and set their drinks down, Nero leaned in, his voice dropping.

"Alright. Tell us what's going on."

Jack did, speaking in hushed tones as he recounted everything they'd uncovered about the stolen crystals and Michael's suspicious involvement. He finished with how he'd hacked into the Nebula Marauder's computer and discovered the ship was owned by Simon Rourke.

"Simon Rourke?" Lena mused, her brow furrowed. "I've heard that name before. Can't quite remember where, though."

"He's a wealthy business executive on Veridian Prime." Jack pulled up an image of Simon Rourke on his wrist-mounted computer and then showed it to each of them. "This is him. Does he look familiar to any of you?"

Nero leaned in closer, his brow furrowing as he studied the image intently. "Lucas Myers." The name came out little more than a whisper. "I thought he disappeared years ago."

"Who?" Alexis asked.

"Simon Rourke," Nero replied. "That's not his real name. He's actually Lucas Myers, a well-known IT criminal who vanished about a decade ago."

"Any idea what this guy might be up to with all those stolen crystals?" Jack asked. "It's not like a guy that rich needs to risk prison by selling stolen crystal."

Dracke shook his head slowly, clearly as confused as the rest of them.

"I don't know but there's someone who might," Nero suggested slowly, drawing everyone's gaze. "His name is Coda Varek. He worked with Lucas back in the day. They were partners but had a huge falling out when Coda almost went to prison. Coda said that Lucas framed him, but could never prove it. He disappeared before he could be sent to jail. I ran into him years later on Purgo-Max and you should know that he won't talk to just anyone."

As he spoke, Nero reached into his pocket and pulled out a small pouch. He opened it and dumped a dozen metallic discs onto the table. Each disc was engraved with intricate symbols. He sorted through them until he found the one he wanted and then handed it to Jack. "This is Coda's favor token. He gave it to me years ago. Use it, and he should talk to you."

Jack took the token, feeling its weight in his hand as he studied the intricate symbols etched into the metallic surface that seemed to dance in the dim light of the bar. Then he met Nero's gaze with a determined nod. "Thank you."

The significance of Nero's gesture settled upon him. In the shadowy underworld they navigated, trust was a rare commodity, and the exchange of favor tokens held a significance that transcended mere words. He knew he couldn't let this gesture go unanswered. It wasn't because Nero had given him access to Coda Varek. It was because Nero had entrusted the token to him instead of to Alexis, which meant that if Alexis wanted to talk to Coda, she'd have to go with him. Which suited

Jack fine because he had no intention of letting her go off by herself to finish this investigation.

"Mind if I borrow that?" He gestured to Nero's pouch. After Nero handed it to him, he reached inside and withdrew a small, unassuming device. It was a Mnemoglyph, a tool used to imprint one's unique emblem onto a favor token. The device fit comfortably in his palm, its sleek surface cool against his skin. Reaching into the pouch again, he carefully extracted a single, pristine blank disc. It gleamed in his palm, the polished Stellurium alloy catching the light and reflecting it back in a mesmerizing display.

He fit the disc into the Mnemoglyph and then pressed an icon on his wrist device before pressing it against the Mnemoglyph. The small device started to glow, a soft, pulsing light that grew in intensity.

Slowly, an intricate pattern appeared;—a symbol that bore testament to Jack's identity, his history, and his unbreakable word.

As the last line of light faded, Jack opened the Mnemoglyph and withdrew the token.

"Here." He handed the token to Nero. "In exchange for your help."

Nero raised an eyebrow, taking Jack's token with a nod. "Fair enough, Marsden. I appreciate it."

Jack inwardly smiled, his eyes flicking briefly toward Alexis as he returned the Mnemoglyph to its pouch and handed it back to Nero, who tucked it back into his pocket.

Lena raised her glass. "Time to finish our drinks and get going." The others followed her lead, each taking a last sip of their beverages before placing the empty glasses on the table. Then, as a group, they stood and walked toward the entrance.

"Good luck out there," Kylix called out to them as they left The Abyss, her ice-blue eyes sparkling with sincerity as she shifted seamlessly from female form to male form. As many times as Jack had watched the transformation, he wasn't sure he'd ever get used to it.

Outside the bar, the group stopped.

"Thanks again for everything." Jack reached out to shake hands with his old friend. He hoped he'd see him again.

"I'd tell you to stay out of trouble," Nero said, "but something tells me I'd be wasting my breath. So instead, I'll tell you to be careful."

"Be safe," Dracke added gruffly, not one for lengthy goodbyes.

"Will do," Jack replied, his voice low and determined. He waited until they walked off before turning back to Alexis and Lena.

"Back to the *Black Jack*?" Lena asked.

Jack nodded. He was looking forward to getting back to his ship. The *Black Jack* was more than a means of transportation; it was a symbol of survival, a sanctuary amid the chaos of the galaxy.

"Coming?" he asked Alexis. She didn't look happy.

"I don't suppose there's any chance you'll give that favor token to me?"

He smiled. "Not on your life."

She nodded slowly. "Then I guess I'm coming with you."

They turned to follow Lena down the corridor.

"Hey." He reached out to briefly touch Alexis's arm. "You going off on your own won't stop me from pursuing the truth behind Michael's death, but we both might discover the truth faster if we work together. What do you say?"

She looked at him, her eyes holding a storm of conflicting emotions. When she finally nodded her agreement, he felt something inside him shift; it felt like a heavy weight lifting and, for the first time since they'd lain on that bed together, he breathed a little easier. As long as she was by his side, as long as they were both alive, there was still a chance for a future together.

The purr of the *Black Jack's* engines reverberated through the ship as it touched down on one of the Purgo-Max landing pads hours later. Jack cut the engine and waited for a disembodied voice to talk over the comm. He didn't have to wait long.

"Name, number and purpose." The voice sounded bored.

"Jack Marsden. Three. We're here to see Coda Varek. We have business to discuss."

"Coda Varek, huh?" The voice sounded less bored now. "What kind of business?"

Jack frowned, but kept his voice even. "The private kind."

"That'll be five thousand credits for a one hour stay."

Behind him, Alexis gasped, but Jack held up his hand to silence her. He was familiar with the Starlashed faction. It controlled access to the underground city with a mix of brute force and extortion.

"You're fume-fried if you think I'm going to pay that. Two thousand credits for three hours," he countered. "Plus one thousand credits for you."

He waited while the guard thought about it, and then a moment later, the landing pad began descending below the planet's surface.

Jack flipped off the comm and leaned back in his chair. Beside him, Lena snorted.

"Never underestimate the power of greed," she muttered, turning to head back into the ship. "I'll pull a thousand credits out of petty cash," she hollered back at him.

As soon as the pad was fully descended, Jack spied the grizzled Starlashed guard out the front viewport. He was leaning against a nearby post, arms crossed, and a skeptical glare in his eyes.

"Alright." Jack glanced at Alexis and Lena. "Let's do this."

They disembarked from their ship with Alexis and Lena following a pace or two behind Jack. As they approached, the guard's stance shifted almost imperceptibly, his hand drifting closer to the pulse blaster holstered at his side. Up close, Jack noted the guard's weathered face bore the scars of countless battles, a testament to the harsh realities of life on Purgo-Max. With his free hand, the man held out a transfer unit and Jack tapped his wrist-device against it, transferring the two thousand credits to the faction's account. Then the guard held out his hand and Jack placed the small pouch holding one thousand credits into it.

"It's a pleasure doing business with you." Smiling, the guard slipped the pouch into his pants pocket. "Enjoy your stay."

Then he walked over to the *Black Jack* and slapped an external Ship Anchor Mechanism to the hull. Jack watched as the guard entered a code and then leaned forward, pressing his face against the e-SAM while the device scanned his retina. When he stepped back, the light on the outside of the device turned green, showing it was in standby mode. At the end of three hours, the e-SAM would activate, anchoring the *Black Jack* in place, and it would cost a lot more than two thousand credits to set it free.

Jack turned to the women. "We need to hurry." He gestured for them to follow him as he started down the corridor that led to the heart of Purgo-Max.

The hum of ceiling lights sounded above them as Jack, Alexis, and Lena made their way along the gently declining corridor. Ahead, the steel-plated access doors to Purgo-Max's underground tunnel system stood like the mouth of some long-dead beast, flanked by a steel guard's booth and flickering floodlights. The Gritwalker faction controlled security and two of their guards stood outside the booth—one tall and broad with a jagged scar down his jaw, the other wiry and twitchy, his eyes flicking between them with too much interest. Above them, a small, spherical security drone wobbled erratically near the ceiling, its anti-grav propulsion sputtering.

As they approached, the larger Gritwalker stepped forward, arms crossed over a plated chest. His cybernetic eye whirred faintly.

"State your business," he barked.

"Our business is with Coda Varek," Jack replied.

The guard raised his arm to read his wrist-device and tapped the screen. "Varek know you're coming?"

"No," Jack admitted with a sigh.

"Then it's going to cost you." The guard grinned.

Trips to Purgo-Max were always costly, and Jack did his best to mask his disgust. "How much?"

"Hmmm. First, we have to open the gate. Then one of us will need to guide you to your destination. And you'll need protection along the way." He pretended to think about it. "Five thousand credits."

"What?! I just gave all my cash to that Starlashed motherf—"

Alexis placed her hand on his arm and he fell quiet.

"No cash? That's okay. We accept alternate forms of payment." His gaze drifted slowly over to Alexis and Lena, his implication clear.

Jack's jaw clenched, anger flaring in his eyes. His impulse was to wipe the smirk off the guard's face with his fist, but before he could decide how to respond, Lena spoke up. "What's wrong with your security drone?" She pointed to the unstable spherical drone.

The Gritwalker glanced up, then back at Lena. "What's it to you?"

She shrugged. "I'm pretty good with tech, and I know how much the Ferric Network is going to charge you to fix it. Let me look at it. If I can fix it, you escort us to Coda Varek's residence for free."

The guard hesitated, then shrugged. "Knock yourself out, but try anything funny, and you'll be surface-side before you know it."

Lena approached the malfunctioning drone. It was out of her reach, but just as Jack started to walk over to help, she jumped into the air and grabbed it. Pulling it down, she held it with one arm while using the other to open the access panel. For several seconds, she poked around at the various chips and wires. Then, withdrawing a multi-tool from her belt, she set to work, her fingers a blur as she manipulated the delicate circuitry.

The Gritwalkers watched her closely, their postures tense. After a few seconds, she slipped the tool back into her belt and snapped the access panel closed.

"There." She stepped back as she released the drone. With its anti-grav stabilized, it floated smoothly once more. "Good as new."

The lead Gritwalker studied the drone, then nodded. "Not bad." Then he turned to his companion. "Let her through and take her to Varek's."

Lena's dark eyes sparked in anger. "That wasn't our deal."

The guard scoffed. "No, that's my deal. You fixed one lousy drone so you get free passage. Your friends stay here—unless they pay."

Jack was already mentally bracing himself for the fight to come. Last time he'd visited Purgo-Max, negotiations had taken a turn for the worse and he and Lena had been forced to kill several guards who'd gotten too greedy. Fortunately, the head of the Gritwalkers had determined the deaths were justified—by Purgo-Max laws—and they'd walked away from the incident, but not before making a few enemies. Another fight would likely lead to another death, and Jack wasn't sure this time they'd be allowed to leave.

He glanced at Lena and noted the way she was pursing her lips. Her thoughts were likely flying the same orbit his were, so yeah, things were about to go supernova. Easing his hand across his chest, he prepared to pull his small blaster from its hiding place beneath his jacket. On the other side of him, Alexis must have picked up on the change in mood because she stepped away from him, giving herself room to fight.

Chapter Fifteen

AT THAT MOMENT, A third Gritwalker appeared, walking up to the gate from the other side. He studied them as he stepped through the booth and, a second later, surprise registered on his face. He stepped out and approached the Gritwalker guard, leaning close to whisper in his ear. The guard's expression grew serious. Then he stormed off, walking through the booth to the other side and disappearing around a corner.

The third guard addressed the one who'd moved back into the booth. "Open the gate. Now."

It looked like the other guard wanted to argue, but he did as instructed and slowly, the large metal gate opened.

"Follow me," the newcomer told them, stepping through the gate to the other side. Jack wasn't sure what had just happened, but he stepped through the gate with Alexis and Lena following him.

"Where are you going?" the third guard asked as soon as they were safely through to the other side.

"We came to talk to Coda Varek," Jack told him.

"I'll take you."

Jack exchanged confused glances with Alexis and Lena, but when the guard started walking, they hurried to catch up to him.

"I don't understand what happened back there," Jack finally said to the man.

"Not here," he muttered, not bothering to look at Jack.

The guard led them down a series of tunnels, glancing over his shoulder from time to time to ensure they were still behind him. After several turns, he stopped in an empty side passage and finally spoke. "Name's Sebastian."

Jack nodded, waiting for more.

"You two," he pointed at Jack and Lena. "I remember you. Last time you were here, you took out some Gritwalkers."

Lena looked disgusted. "They didn't give us much of a choice."

Sebastian held up his hand to stop her. "You'll get no argument from me. Those two had been stirring up trouble for a long time. There were plenty of us who wanted them gone, but taking out faction members is risky business. You saved us the trouble. So, consider this escort a favor."

"We appreciate that," Jack said.

"Unfortunately, not everyone down here is your fan, so let's get moving before we run into those who'd like some payback for what you did to their friends." He turned and led them further into the maze of tunnels.

Eventually, the tunnel opened into a vast underground chamber, and the group stepped into the marketplace. It was abuzz with activity as people bartered for black-market items, shouting their wares and haggling over prices. Above them, tangled webs of cables and pipes crisscrossed the ceiling, casting eerie shadows on the rough-hewn walls.

"Stay close and keep your eyes open," Jack murmured to Alexis and Lena, his gaze darting around as they navigated the bustling underground city.

"I've never seen anything quite like this place." Alexis looked around with equal parts of amazement and apprehension.

"It's your usual gathering of criminals and reprobates," Lena muttered, her gaze darting around.

The trio followed the guard through the marketplace until they reached the other side. Then he led them down another passageway, the noise from the marketplace growing fainter the further away they walked.

Eventually, they reached another massive chamber sitting at the juncture of half a dozen tunnels. Smaller cables branched off from the large ceiling cables like tentacles reaching into the side tunnels. The surrounding air practically crackled with electronic energy.

The openings to the side tunnels all looked identical to Jack except for the graffiti sprayed on the walls beside each opening.

They finally reached a reinforced door marked with the Ferric Network's emblem—a jagged gear surrounded by circuit patterns. Sebastian motioned them forward and tapped on the entry panel.

"Thanks ... I think." Jack turned toward the door.

Sebastian gave a nod. "Varek lives at the end of this tunnel." Then he turned and left them there, disappearing back into the tunnel from which they'd come.

The three watched him until he disappeared from view.

Then the door to the tunnel opened and a Ferric Network faction member stood, blocking the entrance.

"We're here to see Coda Varek," Jack told him. This time, he pulled the favor token from his pocket and held it up, letting the guard take a closer look. After a moment, the guard stood aside so they could enter.

"His door is at the end," the guard told them. "Make sure you don't stray."

Jack nodded and, sparing a quick backward glance to make sure Alexis and Lena were still with him, started down the tunnel. There were metal doors spaced far apart on either side, but Jack continued past them until he reached the very end.

Here goes nothing. He knocked on the intimidating metal door, noting the security camera mounted atop.

"State your business," a disembodied voice demanded.

"Jack Marsden, requesting an audience with Coda Varek." He held the favor token up to the security camera so its round surface caught the dim light.

Above him, he heard the whir of the camera as the lens zoomed in for a closer look at the token. A few moments later, the metal door ground open. Jack exchanged wary glances with Alexis and Lena before stepping through the opening.

Coda Varek's residence was a study in contradictions—a posh, meticulously arranged room carved into the rough, subterranean walls of Purgo-Max. Plush chairs and gleaming holo-screens contrasted with the dark industrial corridors outside.

Coda, a lean man whose handsome features belied a lifetime of hardship, greeted them with a cool nod. He held out his hand for the token, and Jack handed it over.

"How did you acquire this?" His tone wasn't accusatory—but it was sharp.

"Nero Blackwell gave it to me."

"When, exactly?"

"Approximately twenty hours ago," Jack replied.

The brows above Coda's luminescent eyes rose slightly. "So, he's alive."

It was more of a statement than a question, but Jack answered anyway, since Nero hadn't asked him to keep it secret. "Yeah. He survived the explosion."

A slow smile tugged at Coda's mouth. "That's good to know." He flipped the token into the air, letting it somersault a few times before catching it and sliding it into his pocket. Then he turned his unreadable smile on the group. "I'm Coda Varek. What do you want?"

"We want to know about Simon Rourke," Jack said.

"The entrepreneur?" Coda asked dryly. "I only know what I've read in the newsfeeds."

"That's not entirely true." Jack ignored the man's faint smirk. "Nero said you and Simon have history—that you knew him pretty well back when he went by Lucas Myers."

Coda's smirk faded. "If 'knew him pretty well' means we were partners until he framed me for hacking into government systems, dumped the evidence in my lap, and then vanished with millions in stolen data—then yes. I knew him *very* well." His voice held the bite of a wound long scabbed over but never healed.

Jack exchanged a glance with Alexis. At her small nod, he went on. "Her brother—my friend—Michael—was killed during a Luminite crystal heist. Only Michael wasn't a thief, and the crystals weren't registered. We started digging and found a shipment of unregistered crystals on one of Simon's vessels. Now we're wondering how that ties to Simon ... and to Michael's death."

"Is he transporting them here to Purgo-Max?" Lena asked.

Coda's expression shifted, eyes narrowing. "No. I would've heard if someone was offloading unregistered Luminite here."

The four of them shared a look.

"Then what's he doing with them?" Alexis wondered aloud.

"You knew him best," Jack said. "Any ideas?"

"I don't guess," Coda said curtly. He gestured to the sitting area. "Sit."

They obeyed. Coda remained standing, arms folded as he spoke.

"Back then, Lucas and I were developing a distributed computing system—something we believed could one day link every system in real-time across the galaxy. I wanted secure, decentralized access. Lucas wanted control. Pure and simple. He was obsessed with systemic dominance—controlling traffic, communications, even energy flow. The tech wasn't there yet, so his ambitions stalled."

His voice dropped an octave, disgusted.

"I walked away from the project. He walked away with my reputation—and a future I'd spent my life building."

He paused, then strode across the room to a console and tapped at the keys. News snippets bloomed in the air.

"Let's see what the galaxy's favorite liar is up to."

He scrolled until a headline stopped him.

Rourke's Galactic Connectivity Enhancement Project Hailed as Software Breakthrough of the Century

Rourke's Latest Tech Poised to Revolutionize Wormhole Travel

Coda's jaw tightened. He said nothing for a long beat, just stared.

"You think this is why he needs the crystals?" Jack asked.

Coda's eyes flicked to him. "I do. This is his dream, all grown up and government-funded. If he's using unregistered Luminite, it's because he doesn't want official eyes on what he's building. That means he's hiding something. And the only thing he'd ever want to hide—"

"—is control," Jack finished grimly. "The wormhole network."

Coda nodded. "If he's built a machine that can integrate with Intergalactic Wormhole Transit Authority's systems—and I suspect he has—he could manipulate travel across entire sectors."

Alexis went still. "We have to stop him."

"Agreed," Jack said.

"I hate to be the voice of reason," Lena interjected, "but shouldn't we get proof first?"

"Good point," Jack said. "We can't move on Simon without hard evidence."

"But how do we get it?" Alexis asked.

They all turned to Coda.

Coda scoffed. "Don't look at me. This isn't my fight."

Alexis's expression hardened. "You don't care? He framed you. Destroyed your life."

Coda leaned back, folding his arms. "And the galaxy watched it happen. No one came knocking to help. I learned a long time ago not to get involved in other people's crusades."

"It's not just our crusade," Jack said quietly. "If he takes control of the wormhole network, he can control everything—supply lines, communications, off-world medicine, escape routes. Billions of lives. Still not your fight?"

Coda was silent. Then, softly, "Billions of lives didn't lose *everything* because of Simon. I did."

Alexis took a step forward, her tone sharper now. "Then help us make him pay for that."

Coda didn't move.

Jack spoke, calm and deliberate. "When we bring him down—and we *will* bring him down—he'll know your name was on the knife. That *you* were the one who helped unravel everything."

Coda's jaw clenched. He stared at the console. For a long moment, no one spoke.

Then he exhaled slowly and turned toward them.

"You want proof?" he said. "I might have a way."

He walked back to the console and pulled up a system diagram. "If Simon has compromised the IWTA's systems—which seems likely—then he's built himself a back door into the wormhole network. Something subtle. Something only someone who knows his code could spot."

"You know what to look for," Jack said.

"I do. But we can't find it remotely."

"Why not?" Alexis asked.

"These systems are shielded. Government-grade encryption, redundant firewalls. Nothing short of local access will do."

Lena frowned. "So what does that mean?"

Coda pointed to a glowing hub on the star map. "You'll have to go to the Hydro Terra Nova wormhole station. It's the central control hub. If there's a back door, it'll be there."

"Let me guess," Lena said. "We break in."

Coda's grin was faint, humorless. "Now you're catching on."

Chapter Sixteen

ALEXIS SCOFFED. "THOSE STATIONS aren't exactly open to the public. How do you propose we get close to their computer? The security on any station is tight."

"You can't go to any station," Coda told her. "You'll have to go to the IWTA's central hub station."

She could only stare at him in disbelief. "Are you crazy? The security on that station is tighter than a Xargonian's grip."

Coda chuckled dryly. "Well, you're mostly right. It's tight, but getting past it isn't impossible."

"I trust you'll explain what you mean?" Jack requested.

"Sure. Security at that station is multi-level. First, only official IWTA shuttles are authorized to dock at the station, so you'll need to secure a ride on one. There are two such shuttle stations on Hydro Terra Nova, which is, as you know, the closest habitable planet to the wormhole's central hub. It doesn't matter which shuttle you catch, but you'll need a shuttle pass. And don't go in armed. You will be screened, and the authorities have a zero-tolerance policy regarding individuals bearing weapons and explosives." He held up a second finger. "Second, once you arrive at the station, you'll need to show security your employee ID to get into the station. Then," he held up a third finger, "once inside the station, personnel are allowed only into the areas for which they are authorized and there is a separate access card for each area. The security codes on these cards change every shift based on a randomized program, so it's impossible to anticipate what code will be used for any specific shift."

"How do you know so much about the security at the wormhole stations?" Alexis asked, curious.

Coda smiled, his eyes glinting with a hint of mischief. "Because I helped design it, which is how I know the system isn't impossible to get past."

Alexis exchanged surprised looks with Jack and Lena.

"Are you telling us we can get by using access and employee ID cards purchased from a black market syn-pass dealer?" Lena asked.

Coda shook his head. "No. The security measures I designed are too intelligent to be fooled by fake IDs.

You'll have to use real access and ID cards to get past security."

"And how do you suggest we do that?" Lena asked.

"Steal them, of course," Coda said simply. "And then you have to make sure the people whose cards you've stolen cannot report the theft."

"No," Alexis shook her head, feeling ill. "I'm not killing someone to steal their credentials."

Coda shrugged. "While killing them is an obvious solution, it doesn't have to be the only solution. I'm sure you'll think of something else."

She looked first at Jack and then Lena, but their expressions remained carefully blank, leaving her to wonder if she was the only one objecting to killing innocent people. Before she could question them, Coda continued.

"Once you clear security, you still need an authorized card to the server room, preferably from someone just starting their shift. Otherwise, if their card expires while you're inside the server room, you could find yourself locked inside with no way out."

"I don't like it," Lena said. "We can't lurk around the server room waiting for someone to use their card and then jump them. That'll draw all sorts of attention."

"We also can't go around stealing random cards until we get lucky," Alexis added. Images of the three of them racing around the wormhole station, stealing card after card, flashed through her head. There had to be a better way. Then she remembered a ploy she'd used on an old undercover case. "What about maintenance workers?"

All three turned to look at her.

"I once worked undercover as a maintenance worker. No one noticed me and my access cards opened the door to every office because I was expected to clean them all. Maybe it's the same at the wormhole station?" She turned to Coda. "Do you think the maintenance crew has access to the server room? I mean, someone has to clean it, right?"

"No," he said, dashing her hopes. "They have special bots to clean the server room because the temperature has to stay at a constant level. Those computers run hot. Add a couple of warm bodies to the room and suddenly you have alarms pinging everywhere as the temperature rises. Which is something else you need to be aware of." He paused, stroking his chin as if deep in thought. "But I wonder ..."

He turned back to his computer and typed rapidly. A minute later, he pulled a schematic up on his holo-screen. "This might work." He pointed to a room on the schematic. "See that? That's the server room." He tapped a few more keys on the computer and another image with red lines appeared, overlaying the first.

"Each of these red lines represents a ventilation shaft. See this one? It feeds cold air into the server room. Now follow it back the other way." He ran his hand along the image and stopped a short distance away. "It runs right past this maintenance closet." He smiled and looked up at Alexis. "That's how you can get into the server room."

She nodded, liking that plan.

"Jack and I know our way around computers, but it could take a while for us to find the back door in Simon's code," Lena said.

"Not a problem," Coda told her. "I know exactly what to look for. I'll write a search program and save it to a data chip. You insert the data chip into the computer, and it'll scan all the coding. Once it finds the back door, it'll copy that code and any other relevant code to the chip."

Lena nodded. "That works."

"Will finding the back door be enough proof?" Alexis asked.

This time, it was Jack who answered her. "No. We have to identify the computer using that back door. Once we locate that computer, we need to examine its code—and we need to know who it belongs to."

"Exactly," Coda agreed. "We're assuming that when you ping the computer on the other end of that back door, you'll find Simon's supercomputer." He glanced from Jack to Lena. "Shall I include that in the program I give you?"

Jack nodded. "Thanks. That would help. What do we owe you for this?"

Coda shook his head. "Watching Simon's plans fail will be payment enough. Now, please have a seat while I work on this program." Then he turned away from them and began typing at his computer.

Alexis went with Jack to the seating area and sat on the couch. Lena, she noted, walked over to Coda's workbench, obviously curious about what he was working on.

After a surprisingly short amount of time, Coda pulled a data chip from the computer port.

"I've transferred the files you'll need to this chip." He handed it to Jack. "The schematics, the search program, and the reverse ping to locate the base computer—everything." His luminescent eyes bore into Jack's. "Be careful. If Simon catches wind of what you're doing ..."

"He won't," Jack assured him, pocketing the chip. "We'll be in and out before he even knows we were there."

Coda gave a curt nod and turned toward the door, ready to see them out.

But Lena hadn't moved. She was still at the workbench, her face bathed in the cool glow of a microscope's interface. "These are incredible," she said, almost reverently.

She looked up, her black eyes gleaming. "Nanobots, right? I've used them before, but these look next-gen."

"They're my latest project," Coda replied, a hint of pride sneaking into his voice. "Been refining the programming for months."

He joined her at the bench and picked up one of the sleek, iridescent nanobots with a pair of fine-tipped tweezers. "Each one has a quantum processor that lets it adapt in real time. They work as individuals or as a coordinated swarm."

Lena leaned in, her mind racing with possibilities. "Medical infiltration, high-efficiency repairs ... surveillance. Even sabotage."

"Exactly," Coda said. "But they're not toys. Balance is everything—give them too much autonomy, and they start making decisions you didn't authorize."

"How do you stop that from happening?" she asked.

That was all the invitation he needed. Coda launched into a rapid-fire explanation of his redundancy loops, cascading shutdown protocols, and self-limiting code branches. Lena soaked in every word, her thoughts buzzing faster than the nanobots.

When he paused for breath, Lena glanced at him and said softly, "Would you sell them?"

The question caught Coda off-guard. "They're not for sale," he said immediately. "They're not ready."

"I'm not asking for a full swarm," she said, tone careful. "Just a sample. A hundred, maybe less."

Coda eyed her, clearly torn. "Even if I were willing—which I'm not sure I am—do you have any idea what they cost to build? The quantum filaments alone—"

"Name your price," Lena said.

He did.

The number hit her like a gut punch. Her smile faltered, and she stepped back from the bench.

"Right," she murmured. "That's ... a little more than I have."

"Then we're done," Coda said, cool again, motioning toward the door. "No hard feelings."

Lena hesitated. For a heartbeat, she looked like she might argue—but instead, she gave a stiff nod and turned away.

Jack and Alexis were already halfway to the exit when they heard Lena's boots stop short.

She stood frozen at the doorway, staring at the floor.

"I want them," she said, more to herself than anyone else. "*Krauk*, I want them."

Slowly, she reached into her jacket and pulled out a small, round disc—metallic, etched with a pattern that shimmered in shifting light.

Jack saw it first. "Lena—no."

Alexis gasped. "Is that—? You're not seriously—"

Lena turned back to Coda and held the token up between her fingers.

"I'll give you a favor token," she said, steadying her voice. "For the nanobots."

Coda's eyes narrowed. "That's no small offer."

"I know."

He stepped closer, arms crossed. "Are you sure that's what you want to do? A favor token is binding. Irrevocable."

"I know that too."

Jack looked like he might intervene—but one glance at her face stopped him. Her mind was already made up.

Coda studied her for a long moment, then exhaled slowly. "All right. One token." He grabbed a Mnemoglyph off the bench and held it out to her.

She hesitated for a moment, the weight of her decision pressing down on her like a physical force. Then, with a deep breath, she placed the token into the Mnemoglyph to etch her promise into the disc. Then, replacing the device on the workbench, she handed the glowing token to Coda.

As it left her fingers, a sense of finality settled over the room. The die was cast, the deal struck. There was no turning back now. Coda's fingers closed around the token, its soft glow extinguished as he pocketed it with a satisfied smile.

"A pleasure doing business with you." His voice was as smooth as silk. "Now, let me package these for you."

Coda turned and began rummaging through a series of drawers, his movements precise and purposeful. He pulled out a small vial and a transfer pipette. Working carefully, he transferred nanobots from their container into the vial.

Lena leaned in closer, her breath catching in her throat as Coda worked. She forced herself to pay attention when he launched into an explanation of the care and maintenance of the nanobots, his words washing over Lena in a steady stream. He spoke of charging cycles and diagnostic routines, software updates and troubleshooting procedures. She drank it all in, committing every detail to memory, determined to master these incredible machines.

Minutes ticked by as Coda meticulously filled the vial, each nanobot selected and placed with the utmost care. Lena watched, transfixed, marveling at the precision and skill on display. In the background, she could hear Jack and Alexis shifting restlessly, their impatience growing with each passing moment.

Finally, with a soft snap, Coda closed the lid on the vial and held it out to Lena, his luminescent eyes glinting with a mix of pride and something else, something harder to define. "They're yours now. Use them wisely."

She took the vial and held it like the precious cargo it was. When she met Coda's gaze, a silent understanding passed between them. This was more than a transaction, more than a simple exchange of goods. It was a pact, a promise, a bond forged between two technophiles.

As Lena slipped the case into her pack, Jack cleared his throat pointedly. "We should get going." He glanced at his chrono. "Our time's almost up."

Lena blinked, startled out of her reverie. She checked her own chrono and realized with a start that he was right. They had mere minutes before their ship would be locked down, stranding them on Purgo-Max.

With hurried farewells, Jack, Alexis, and Lena left Coda's workshop, the metal door clanging shut behind them with an ominous finality. They stood for a moment in the dimly lit tunnel, the hum of distant machinery filling the air like a pulsing heartbeat.

A creeping sense of unease settled over Alexis as they raced through the tunnels, back the way they'd come, their footsteps echoing in the eerie stillness. The twists and turns of the route back to the main corridor seemed to blur together, each passage looking much like the last. Had they taken a left at that junction, or a right? Was this the same set of flickering, half-broken lights they'd passed on the way in, or a new set entirely?

Doubt gnawed at the edges of her mind as they pressed on, the minutes slipping away like sand through an hourglass. Jack took the lead, Alexis and Lena followed closely behind him, their eyes darting from side to side, searching for any landmark or sign that might guide their way.

As they rounded a corner, Lena suddenly stopped short, her brow furrowed in concentration. "Wait!" Her voice echoed off the damp walls. "I remember this spot. We turned right here, not left."

Jack paused, glancing back at her with a mix of surprise and skepticism. "Are you sure?"

She nodded, her gaze distant as she seemed to dredge up the memory. "I'm positive. There was a symbol spray-painted on the wall, something that looked like a coiled serpent. It caught my eye as we passed."

Alexis chimed in. "She's right. And a little further down, there was a junction with a broken light panel. We took the left fork."

"Okay," he said, nodding sharply. "I trust you. Let's go."

They set off again, their pace quickening as they followed Lena's and Alexis's directions. The tunnels looked more familiar now, the twists and turns falling into place like pieces of a puzzle. They passed the broken light panel, the exposed wires sparking and hissing in the damp air. Exiting the left fork, she spotted the coiled serpent, its paint faded and chipped.

Finally, they reached the Gritwalker's gate. No one appeared to stop them as they passed through it. Then they were racing up the corridor where the docking shafts rose like great, yawning mouths. The *Black Jack's* designated shaft was easily identifiable, the green light of the e-SAM device blinking steadily on its hull.

As one, they broke into a run, their footsteps ringing out in a staccato rhythm. Alexis's heart pounded in her chest, adrenaline coursing through her veins as she pushed herself to keep pace with Jack and Lena.

As they neared the docking shaft, Alexis risked a glance at her chrono. Less than five minutes remained until their time was up, until the e-SAM would lock onto the *Black Jack* and trap them on Purgo-Max. She gritted her teeth, willing her legs to pump faster, harder.

Lena, thanks to her half-Lyran genetics, reached the ship first, her lithe form a blur as she raced up the ramp and disappeared inside. Alexis and Jack followed close behind, their boots clanging against the metal as they stumbled into the cargo bay.

"Go, go, go!" Jack shouted, slamming his hand against the hatch control. The hydraulics whined and hissed as the hatch rose to seal them inside.

He didn't wait for the ramp to close fully. He sprinted towards the cockpit just as the engines roared to life. Lena was already in the pilot's seat, her hands flying over the controls with practiced ease.

"Strap in!" she yelled over the rising whine of the engines. "This is going to be close!"

Alexis flung herself into the nearest seat, fumbling with the harness as the ship lifted off. In the co-pilot's seat, Jack did the same.

The ship rose swiftly, the docking platform falling away beneath them as they ascended the long, vertical shaft. Alexis gripped the armrests tightly, her knuckles white with tension and her gaze fixed out the side portal, watching the e-SAM's blinking light reflecting off the shaft walls.

Green, green, green ... the light pulsed in time with her racing heartbeat. They were so close, the mouth of the shaft yawning wide above them. Just a few more seconds ...

And then e-SAM disengaged, and they were free, shooting into the planet's dismal atmosphere. Only once they finally reached the star-studded expanse of open space did Alexis relax in her seat, a laugh of pure relief bubbling up from her chest. They'd made it with not a moment to spare.

Jack turned around in his chair, his grin wide and infectious. "What a rush!"

Chapter Seventeen

Hours later, back at the Outer Fringe space station, the neon-lit entrance of The Abyss loomed before Alexis, casting an eerie glow on the faces of the patrons milling about. After their long flight back, Alexis, Jack and Lena were eager for a proper meal and stiff drink. The Abyss was the perfect place for both.

Alexis stepped through the doorway, Jack and Lena close behind her, and was immediately assaulted by a cacophony of music, laughter, and the clinking of glasses. The air was thick with the mingled scents of alcohol, smoke, and the tangy spice of alien cuisine.

She scanned the interior, noting the diverse crowd—humans and various alien species gathered around tables or hunched over the bar. She spotted an empty booth in a secluded corner and tilted her head toward it, signaling for the others to follow. As they moved through the bar, people glanced at them, but then quickly looked away. One of the many unspoken rules at The Abyss was to mind one's own business.

As she reached the booth and slid onto the worn leather seat, Alexis couldn't help but feel a flicker of unease as she thought about what they were planning to do. The wormhole network was massive and highly regulated. Security would be tighter than any they'd encountered thus far, and while she wasn't sure what side of the law Jack and Lena typically found themselves, she'd devoted her entire career to upholding the law. To break it now, even for a justifiable reason, made her anxious. And then, of course, there was Simon. If he learned what they were up to, he would take measures to eliminate the threat, which meant there was the very real possibility that one or more of them could die before this adventure was over.

"You okay?" Jack gently touched her elbow as he slid into the booth beside her.

Startled out of her reverie, she gave him what she hoped was a reassuring smile and nodded.

He gave her a quizzical look, and she thought he might press her for an answer, but then the server appeared at their table to take their orders.

"Alright," Jack said as soon as the server left. "We need to discuss how we're going to do this." Alexis looked around, worried. "It's okay," he assured her. "There's too much noise for anyone to overhear us." He pulled out his computer tablet. "The first thing we need to know is the station's shuttle schedule." He spent the next couple of minutes typing before he stopped and smiled. "The first shuttle for the day shift leaves at oh-four-hundred."

"That's good," Lena said. "It'll still be dark. We can get there early and wait in the parking lot for lone maintenance workers to arrive."

"You're not planning on killing them, are you?" Alexis was still concerned.

Lena shook her head. "No. I don't believe in senseless killing. We'll drug them and leave them someplace to nap."

"We need uniforms," Jack said. "We—"

He fell silent as the server materialized beside their booth with a tray of food and drinks. He waited until the server handed them their drinks, each one a swirling galaxy of color, set the plates of food on the table, and left.

"About the uniforms," Lena said, a smile touching her lips. "I know a guy who knows a guy who can supply those, but he's not cheap." She turned to Jack. "How many credits can you give me?"

He tapped the unit around his wrist and studied the screen. "A hundred?"

She rolled her eyes. "Come on, Jack. Be serious."

He sighed and held out his wrist. "Fine. Take what you need." He didn't sound happy as he held his wrist over hers. When the transfer was made, he glanced at his device. "A thousand credits!"

"Relax," she admonished him. "You'll get it back. I promise."

Alexis was confused by the exchange. "You can buy three wormhole station uniforms for a thousand credits?" In her experience as a cop, such things cost ten times that amount.

Lena snorted. "No way. But with a thousand credits, I can buy my way into a game on the lower level. Then I'll play until I've won enough money to buy what we need."

"Seriously?" Alexis thought maybe Lena was joking, but when she looked at Jack, his expression was confident.

"She's that good," he told her.

"Damn right I am." Lena set about cutting her food.

The uncertainty of what lay ahead settled over Alexis as she ate, turning her food to rubber in her stomach. She tried to lessen her unease by talking through their plans out loud.

"We'll have to get into the server room fast," she said. "We have to give Coda's program as much time to run as possible and hope we don't get caught waiting for it to finish."

Jack nodded as he swallowed a bite of his food. "And if we get caught, we'll be lucky if going to prison is the worst thing that happens to us."

Her mouth set in a determined line, Alexis pushed aside her plate and looked from Jack to Lena, gauging their reactions. "I'm sorry I got you both into this. I'm doing this to prove my brother's innocence, but you two don't have to take the risk. If you want to walk away, I'll understand."

Jack's gaze met hers, unwavering and resolute. "You really think I'd let you do this alone? It's personal for me, too."

His words warmed her more than she cared to admit, but he turned his attention to Lena before she could respond.

"But Lena," his tone grew serious. "There's no reason for you to—"

Lena cut him off with a dismissive wave of her fork. "Oh please," she scoffed, popping another bite of food into her mouth. "The wormholes effect all of us. Besides, you think I'm going to let you two have all the fun? I'm in."

Alexis smiled despite herself, the weight on her shoulders easing slightly. Their loyalty was both inspiring and humbling.

Lena finished the last of her food. "I'd better get to the lower level and win those extra credits. Meet you back at the ship?"

"How about we meet at my apartment?" Alexis suggested. "The rent's paid up for a few more days. It might be more comfortable than the ship."

"Sounds good." Lena wiped her mouth with a napkin and pushed back from the table. Alexis gave her the room number and a passcode to get in, then Lena slid out of the booth. "Don't wait up for me," she told them, giving them a wink before turning toward the exit.

"Stay safe," Jack called after her.

"You know it!" Her voice echoed back as she walked away.

Alexis watched her leave, a mix of admiration and concern swirling in her chest as Lena's petite frame disappeared into the sea of patrons.

"Don't worry. She knows how to take care of herself." Jack's voice pulled her from her thoughts.

She gave him a grateful smile and then leaned against his shoulder for a moment, allowing herself a precious second of comfort.

They finished their meal and drinks, left enough credits on the table to cover their tab, and left the bar.

Outside in the corridor, Jack fell into step beside her, his presence a familiar comfort. They walked in silence, navigating the passages that led to Alexis's apartment.

When they reached it, she paused and turned to Jack, a flicker of vulnerability in her eyes. "Thank you, Jack. For everything. I don't know if I could do this without you."

His gaze softened, a rare moment of unguarded emotion. "I'm here, no matter what. We're in this together."

With a deep breath, Alexis punched in the code, then pressed her palm against the access panel until the door slid open with a soft hiss.

The apartment was a welcome respite, a small haven amidst the storm of their recent adventures. Alexis moved through the space with practiced ease, shedding her jacket and boots as she went.

"Make yourself at home," she called over her shoulder, heading towards the microkitch. "I think I have a bottle of wine stashed somewhere."

Jack settled onto the worn couch, his gaze roaming across the walls, taking in the eclectic mix of holos and artifacts. "Are these yours?"

She glanced over from the microkitch to see him gesturing to her artwork. "No, they were here when I rented the apartment. I liked the way they looked, so I left them there."

He went back to studying them until the clink of glasses drew his attention. He looked over to see Alexis approaching, a bottle of deep red wine in one hand and two glasses in the other.

She set the glasses down on the low table and poured a generous amount into each glass before handing one to Jack.

"To old friends and new beginnings." She raised her glass in a toast.

He touched his glass against hers, a wry smile tugging at his lips. "And to the trouble we always seem to find ourselves in."

They sipped the wine in comfortable silence, the weight of the mission momentarily lifting. Alexis curled up on the opposite end of the couch, her eyes distant as she swirled the crimson liquid in her glass.

After a few moments, she gave a soft snort. "Do you remember that night?" she asked, a hint of nostalgia in her voice.

He chuckled softly, his eyes sparkling. "How could I forget? You were what, sixteen? And determined to prove yourself."

"Yeah, I don't even know why I thought of it." She tried to hide her face behind her hand. "I was so naïve back then. I thought I could handle anything."

"It was my second visit to your house with Michael. You snuck out in the middle of the night, stole your brother's hover bike, and ended up in the seediest part of the city, trying to make a deal with that tech smuggler ... what was his name again?"

"Raxon Flux," Alexis supplied, shaking her head at the memory. "I'd crashed my computer and needed to replace it before my folks found out. Raxon said he'd sell me one I could afford. I had no clue what I was getting myself into or that the computers he was selling were stolen."

Jack took a sip of his wine, his expression turning serious. "I heard you sneak out and decided I should follow you. I'm glad I did. When I found you in that alley, surrounded by Raxon's goons, I thought my heart was going to stop. I'd never been so scared in my life, and that's after serving two years of active military duty."

Alexis shuddered at the memory. Had she actually thought she could broker a deal with the notorious gang? She'd wanted to prove herself, to show that she was as capable as her older brother, but she'd quickly found herself in over her head.

"I thought for sure I was done for," she admitted softly. "But then you showed up, all bravado and quick wit. I don't know how you talked us out of there."

Jack's eyes sparkled with mischief. "It's a gift. I have a way with words."

Alexis snorted again. "More like you scared them. All that time you spent lifting weights in the military, I think each of your biceps was bigger than their thighs. And you had that scar across your cheek. You looked badass."

He pretended to be insulted. "Are you saying I don't look badass now?"

She smiled. "You still look badass, even though you've had the scar removed. But back then, you had this crazed look in your eye."

"That crazed look was because I couldn't stop thinking about what they would have done to you if I hadn't been there."

Alexis grew serious, setting her wine glass down on the table. She turned to face him fully, reaching out to place her hand over his, her eyes searching his. "I'm not sure I ever thanked you for saving me that night."

"You did. As I recall, you kissed me."

"You remembered." Her voice was so soft, he barely heard it.

"I never forgot," he told her truthfully. "It's probably good that Michael and I shipped out the next day. That night, I was finding it hard to remember you were my best friend's sixteen-year-old sister." He brushed his thumb over her knuckles, a gentle, reassuring touch. "I've always felt protective of you, Alexis. From the first moment Michael introduced us, I knew you were special. I knew I'd do anything to keep you safe."

The air grew thick with unspoken emotion.

"Jack, I'm not sixteen anymore." Her voice was barely above a whisper as she leaned toward him.

"Don't I know it," she thought she heard him mumble, but then he was leaning closer.

Closer.

Their lips met in a tender kiss, and she melted into his embrace. His fingers tangled in her hair as he pressed her to him.

Finally. Her mind felt hazy with desire and emotion. *Finally, we're crossing that line—*

Jack's kiss was gentle yet passionate, his lips moving against hers with a tenderness that belied the intensity of his desire. The world around her faded away, the gentle hum of the environmental systems replaced by the pounding of her heart and the soft sighs of her breaths.

Time seemed to stretch and bend, seconds turning into minutes as they lost themselves in the kiss. Jack's hands roamed over her back, tracing the curve of her spine through the thin fabric of her shirt. Alexis shivered at his touch, a delicious warmth spreading through her body. She nipped playfully at his lower lip, eliciting a low groan from deep in his throat.

They explored each other with a languid passion, savoring every touch, every taste. Jack's lips trailed along her jaw, his teeth grazing the sensitive skin of her neck. Alexis tilted her head back, a breathy moan escaping her as his tongue soothed the slight sting. Her hands slid under his shirt, fingers splaying across the hard planes of his chest, feeling the rapid beat of his heart beneath her palm.

The galaxy could have been ending outside the walls of her apartment, but in that moment, nothing else existed but the two of them. Years of unspoken longing, of stolen glances and lingering touches, poured into every kiss, every caress. It was a dance they had been performing for as long as Alexis could remember, a push and pull of attraction and restraint, and now, finally, they were letting go.

But as the heat between them grew, a flicker of uncertainty passed through her mind. She pulled back slightly, her breath coming in short gasps as she searched his eyes. In their depths, she saw the same mix of desire and hesitation that she felt. Now was not the time to start a meaningful relationship. There was too much at stake to risk the distraction.

As if by mutual agreement, they slowly disentangled themselves, the urgency of the moment fading into a comfortable intimacy. Jack settled back against the couch, his arm draped across her shoulders, holding her close. She leaned into him, her head resting in the crook of his neck, breathing in his familiar scent—a mix of leather, blaster oil, and something uniquely Jack.

They sat in comfortable silence. The worries of the mission and the dangers that lay ahead seemed distant, almost unreal. For this one perfect moment, suspended in time, there were only the two of them, the warmth of their bodies pressed together, the steady beat of their hearts in sync.

Alexis couldn't remember the last time she'd felt so content, so utterly at peace. The past seemed far away, a distant echo she was content to ignore. She shifted slightly, sinking deeper into the warmth of his embrace. His arm was strong and reassuring across her shoulders, pulling her closer.

As his hand began to gently stroke her hair, a soothing rhythm that matched the steady beating of her heart, she sank deeper into tranquility until sleep claimed her.

Chapter Eighteen

THE DOOR TO THE apartment burst open, startling Jack awake. Beside him, Alexis jerked upright. He hadn't realized they'd fallen asleep on the couch. Instinctively, he reached for his weapon, only to realize it was Lena standing in front of them, a triumphant grin on her face.

"I got them!" She practically danced where she stood. "The maintenance uniforms, the fake IDs, the access cards—everything we need to infiltrate the wormhole station!"

"That's great," he mumbled, running a hand through his tousled hair. He looked over at Alexis, who looked a little disoriented, her eyes heavy with fatigue.

"Lena, what time is it?" Her voice sounded froggy.

Lena's grin faltered slightly as she took in their disheveled appearance. "Oh, um, I don't know, exactly. I didn't mean to wake you, but I was just so excited about the uniforms ..."

Jack rubbed a hand over his face, trying to clear the cobwebs from his mind. "No, no, it's fine."

He stood up, stretching his muscles and wincing slightly at the stiffness in his joints. Alexis followed suit, though he noticed she wouldn't meet his gaze.

So much for our moment of peace, he thought wryly, a twinge of disappointment in his chest. "Alright." He was glad his voice sounded stronger. "Let's see what you've got, Lena."

She nodded, her enthusiasm returning as she laid the maintenance uniforms on the table, along with two black bags. The dark blue jumpsuits were nondescript except for the IWTA emblem on the front. Alexis picked up one suit to inspect the emblem.

"Wow! These look legit." She laid the suit back on the table. "I'm impressed."

Lena grinned. "That's because they are legit. My source intercepted a shipment of uniforms that included several IWTA maintenance uniforms. Of course, until now, he's not been able to sell any. No one's been willing to risk the security measures. He was happy to get rid of them, so I got a good deal on them."

"Nice." Alexis gestured to the nearest black bag. "What's in there?"

Lena opened the bag and withdrew the contents, laying the items on the table. Alexis stared at a woman's locket, several hypodermic injectors and a small vial of blue liquid. She looked questioningly at Lena, who was still grinning.

"The locket is actually a digital thermometer, with an alarm. It won't set off any security alarms because it's so common. This one, of course, has been modified to be extremely sensitive." She gestured to the blue liquid in the vial. "That's Somnalex-9. It's a black market somnolent and very strong. We fill the hypodermic with it, inject our victims and they'll sleep for hours."

"Good thinking." Then Jack gestured to the other bag. "What's in there?"

Her black eyes sparkling with mischief, Lena opened the bag and dumped its contents onto the table. Three sets of ChromaMorph wigs and face masks fell out. "I thought these might come in handy."

ChromaMorph Polymer wigs and face masks were the latest in hyper-realistic disguises. Jack reached out and picked up one of the masks. The synthetic mesh of the nanofibers felt like actual flesh to the touch. "These must have been pricey."

Lena shrugged. "What can I say? I was on a lucky streak." She held her wrist out to Jack. "Here's your thousand credits back." She touched her wrist device to his, completing the transfer.

The ease with which she transferred that amount of money told Jack she'd been very lucky indeed. There was no telling how much money she had pocketed, even after buying all this stuff.

Returning his attention back to the masks, he carried one into the bathroom and stood before the mirror. He synced the mask to his wrist device, searched the web for an image at random. Then, pressing the mask against his face, he pressed the micro-button along the jawline. The nanofibers seemed to come to life and attach themselves to his face like a second layer of skin. As he watched, the color of the mask changed until it matched his skin tone perfectly. Beneath the subtle contouring of the mask, his nose appeared longer, his cheekbones flatter and his jawline rounder. Soon, he looked exactly like the person whose image he'd selected and nothing like himself. When he moved his mouth and raised his eyebrows, the mask moved with him.

He pressed the button along the jawline, peeled off the mask, and carried it back to the table. "Nice job. Now we don't have to worry about whether we'll look like the people whose ID badges we steal."

A heavy silence settled over the apartment. The weight of the impending mission hung in the air, a palpable presence that couldn't be ignored.

Jack stretched, his muscles rippling beneath his worn shirt. "We should get some rest. Tomorrow's going to be a hell of a day."

Lena yawned, her purple hair falling into her face. "I call dibs on the shower." She turned to Alexis. "Can I borrow a nightshirt?"

Alexis went to the closet and found two nightshirts. She gave the smaller of the two to Lena, who took it and headed towards the bathroom.

As the sound of running water filled the apartment, Alexis busied herself with straightening up the tiny living room. She tried to ignore the way her heart raced every time she caught Jack's eye, the way his presence seemed to fill the space around her.

"You okay?" he asked softly, his gaze searching her face.

She nodded, forcing a smile. "Just nervous, I guess. It's a lot, you know?"

He moved closer, his hand brushing against her arm. "I know. But we've got this. I mean, it can't be any worse than shooting across open space in a supply pod, right?"

Alexis thought back to their time in the pod, the way they'd clung to each other as the universe twisted and swirled around them. At least they'd been together.

"Yeah, we've got this." She hoped she sounded more certain than she felt.

For a moment, they stood there, the air between them charged with unspoken words and unresolved tensions. Alexis felt herself leaning in, drawn to him like a moth to a flame.

Then Lena emerged from the bathroom, a cloud of steam billowing behind her, and the moment was broken. Alexis stepped back, her cheeks flushed. "Bathroom's free."

Alexis met Jack's gaze. "You go ahead. I'll make up the couch for you while you shower. Lena and I can share the bed."

He nodded and disappeared into the bathroom. As Alexis busied herself with making up the couch, she tried not to think about how much she wished he were sharing the bed with her.

Get it together, she scolded herself. Right now, there isn't time for distractions.

When she finished, she noticed Lena was already in bed, sound asleep. Deciding she would shower later, Alexis changed into the other nightshirt and crawled into bed beside Lena. When Jack finished his shower and came out of the bathroom, she closed her eyes and pretended to be asleep. She listened as, beside her, Lena's soft snores filled the room. The sound of Jack's footsteps was barely audible as he crossed the room to the couch.

"Good night, Alexis," she heard him whisper, the sound warming her from within.

Maybe, she thought, as sleep finally claimed her, maybe when this is all over, we'll see where this thing between us could go.

Hours later, they sat around the table in Alexis's apartment, printouts of the wormhole station's schematics spread out before them. The only sound was the soft hum of the atmospheric-integrity force field outside the window, keeping the vacuum of space at bay.

Jack looked up from the plans, his gaze turning first to Alexis and then to Lena. "Let's go over the plan one more time."

Both women nodded, their expressions somber. The weight of what they were about to attempt hung heavy in the air, the risk of failure all too real.

"First, we fly to Hydro Terra Nova," Lena began. "We'll find a remote place to land the ship and then take a rental car to the IWTA Shuttle Station. That way, we don't draw too much attention to ourselves."

"Then we wait in the parking lot for maintenance workers to arrive and we inject them with Somnalex-9," Alexis said.

"We'll scan their faces and feed the data into the ChromoMorph masks and wigs," Jack continued. "With the disguises and ID cards, we should have no trouble getting past security. Once inside, we'll need to find another maintenance worker and take their access card to get into the maintenance closet."

"Once inside," Alexis said, "we'll use the air shaft to gain access to the server room. I'll stand watch while the two of you run Coda's program."

"After we've downloaded the data, we leave the same way we got in, through the air shaft," Lena finished.

"Then we catch a shuttle back to the planet, ditch the uniforms and masks and catch a ride to where we parked the *Black Jack*," Jack finished and Alexis and Lena both nodded. "Now, let's talk about everything that could go wrong and come up with our contingency plans."

For the next two hours, they discussed the different ways their plans could go wrong—everything from maintenance workers resistant to the effects of the somnolent to getting caught in the server room.

"Piece of cake," Lena said when they'd finished.

"Yeah." Alexis wasn't feeling nearly as confident as Lena sounded.

Jack, seeming to sense her unease, reached out to cover her hand on the table with his. "We got this."

She met his gaze, drawing strength from the confidence and determination she saw there. He was right. They had to try. She nodded, letting him know she was on board with the plan.

He gave her hand a squeeze and then checked his chrono. "It's time," he told them. "Let's do this."

With the rally still lingering in the air, the three left Alexis's apartment and set off for the *Black Jack*.

A grayish dawn hung low over the horizon, the twin moons of Hydra Terra Nova fading behind rising mist as the planet-side shuttle station flickered to life. Steel towers blinked with red lights and service drones buzzed between landing pads, prepping for the early-morning transit runs. The trio—Jack, Alexis, and Lena—stood in the shadowed corner of a half-abandoned hovercraft lot, each dressed in a blue uniform and wearing their wigs and masks.

They'd landed the *Black Jack* earlier at a public pad several kilometers away and then rented a hover car to take to the station. They'd parked nose-first between two rusted cargo haulers where the car was less likely to be noticed.

"First shift's due in ten." Jack's voice sounded slightly muffled beneath the mask. "We stick to the plan. Quick, quiet, no blood."

"Easy peasy," Lena muttered.

They'd decided she should be the one to approach and subdue their targets, given her superhuman speed and strength. Following a quick injection of Somnalex-9, their victim should lose consciousness almost immediately.

The first few people to arrive at the shuttle station were office workers, based on the way they were dressed. Soon after, a carload of maintenance workers arrived.

Alexis was beginning to wonder if they'd have to rethink their plans when a dusty bronze hover cycle pulled into the lot with a lone rider. He parked on the far side, in the designated hover cycle parking area. After securing his cycle, he started walking to the front platform. When he passed beneath one of the parking lot lights, Alexis saw his blue uniform.

About to alert Lena, she turned in time to see Lena slip away, into the shadows. Jack touched Alexis's arm and they hurried after her.

Lena moved with the stealth and grace of a Solarix shadow leopard, creeping up behind the man—silent and efficient. In one smooth motion, she jabbed the hypodermic into the worker's neck. His body tensed and hung, momentarily suspended upright. Jack and Alexis quickly moved forward, taking a place on either side of the worker as his legs gave out. Supporting his weight, they walked the now unconscious man back to their hover car.

Lena moved ahead of them to open the back door. It took some doing, but Alexis and Jack maneuvered him into the back seat. Then, Lena scanned the man's face using her hand-held holo-scanner.

"Facial structure: 94% match to Jack," she announced. "We probably won't find a closer match. She tapped the device to send the scanned image to Jack. Before closing the hover car door, she plucked the man's ID card from where it was clipped to the front of his uniform and handed it to Jack. He clipped it to the front of his uniform.

"Image received," he confirmed a second later. "Uploading to ChromaMorph now."

A soft ripple moved across Jack's mask and wig as the nanotech engaged. His cheekbones sharpened, nose narrowed, and short dark hair lengthened into the man's shaggy auburn mop.

"Well?" He turned to the women. "How do I look?"

Alexis peered closely at his face before turning to take another look at the unconscious man.

"The resemblance is uncanny," she admitted, for the first time feeling like their plan might actually work.

A quarter of an hour later, a public transit shuttle arrived. A tall woman in her fifties with silver-streaked hair and wearing a blue uniform stepped out of it. Lena moved fast, timing her approach perfectly with the woman's turned back. One soft pfft of the injector and the woman collapsed into her arms.

With Jack's and Alexis's help, they carried the woman back to their hover car, where Lena scanned her face. "Match with Alexis: 89%. Close enough with the wig. Sending the image to you now."

Alexis waited for the soft beep that let her know the image had been received and then uploaded it to the ChromaMorph app. A moment later, she felt the nanotech fibers moving across her face. She winced as her facial structure reconfigured, cheeks hollowing slightly, lines forming at the edges of her eyes. The hair of her wig elongated and turned silver-black. She gathered it into a bun, much like the one in which the woman's hair was styled. She adjusted the locket thermometer around her neck. Then, finding the woman's

ID badge, she clipped it to her uniform. "How do I look?"

Jack studied her closely before turning to look at the unconscious woman. "You're thinner than she is, but the face and hair are a close match." He turned to Lena. "Now we need to find someone for you."

They moved back into the shadows to continue waiting. Soon, another lone maintenance worker arrived, but Alexis, who was standing a little in front of the others, shook her head.

"Too tall," she whispered to them.

They allowed the worker to walk past them and continue to the platform where other shuttle riders waited. It was important they find someone similar in size and build to Lena. Finally, a slender, short man in a blue uniform and a mop of curls appeared. He strolled past where the trio waited, a music chip dangling from his ear.

Lena grinned. "He'll do."

He never saw her coming. A minute later, the man was safely ensconced in the car and Lena's luminescent complexion had faded into an earthier tan, her purple hair darkened and coiled into curls. Her pointed ears subtly rounded.

"Ow." She rubbed her jaw as the morph settled. Then she turned to face the others. "Well?"

"Looks good," Alexis assured her.

With all three sleeping workers safely tucked into the hover car with the sedative running through their systems, the team took a few minutes to memorize the names and positions of the workers they were impersonating. Then Alexis headed for the shuttle terminal and entered the loading zone. Lena waited for a count of twenty and followed after her, making sure not to stand too close as she waited for the shuttle. A few minutes later, Jack entered the loading zone.

They didn't have to wait long before the shuttle landed and they were able to board. Jack took a seat near the rear by the emergency hatch, eyes forward. Alexis sat by the window near the front, arms folded with just the right amount of supervisory disdain. Lena dropped into a middle seat, legs stretched out, bobbing her head in rhythm with the music still playing from the borrowed music chip.

No one spoke. The shuttle lifted with a hiss of compressed air and set off. A long time later, the IWTA's central hub station grew visible on the horizon—tall, gleaming, and bristling with antennae and scanning towers.

The docking tunnel smelled faintly of ozone and bleach. Bright overhead lights turned every shadow into a spotlight. Security drones floated above the entry checkpoint, projecting red scanning beams, while two guards manned the entry gate.

The shuttle riders disembarked, queuing up before the gate. Alexis and Lena held back, assuming places further back in line, letting Jack go first. If there was a chance the masks wouldn't pass through the facial scanner, he wanted to be the one to assume the risk.

One-by-one, each person in line stepped forward and turned to look into the facial scanner as they presented their ID to the guard. One-by-one, the guard raised the gate to let them pass.

Then it was Jack's turn.

"Next," the guard said.

Jack stepped forward, projecting calm, mentally reciting his title and name. Technician Roen Tavar. Technician Roen Tavar. He presented the stolen ID badge and let the facial scanner sweep across his features.

It felt like forever as he waited. Then the scanner flashed a green light, but the bar remained down.

"What's in the bag?" The guard gestured to the bag Jack was holding.

"Supplies." Jack opened the bag to let the guard peer inside. When they'd packed the bag, they'd made sure to not include anything that would set off alarms inside a space station.

The guard barely glanced into the bag before waving Jack forward as he raised the bar.

Jack exhaled slowly and walked through the gate. Behind him, the bar descended back into place.

"Next."

Jack moved a short distance away before stopping to stoop down like he was adjusting the fastener on his boot. Several more workers entered the station before it was Alexis's turn.

Surreptitiously, Jack watched as she stepped up to the gate, posing as Supervisor Malen Korr.

The guard actually smiled. "Back so soon, Malen?"

Alexis forced a curt nod. "You know how it is. Place can't run without me," Jack heard her mumble as she turned toward the facial scanner. Once again, it felt like time stood still as he waited, but then the scanner blinked green and the bar went up.

"Next," the guard barked after Alexis stepped through. Without glancing toward Jack, Alexis moved past him, up the corridor and around the corner. Per their agreed upon plan, she would wait there. Jack and Lena would join her as soon as Lena cleared security.

Jack tore his gaze from the intersection and looked back to the gate as Lena stepped forward and looked into the scanner.

Jack held his breath. They were so close.

The scanner's light blinked red, reflecting off Lena's altered features for what felt like an inordinate amount of time. He watched her rub her forehead and wondered if something had gone wrong with her mask.

By the gate, the guard's eyes narrow as he studied Lena.

"You okay there, Karlo? You don't look so good."

Instead of answering him, Lena turned and met Jack's gaze. Seeing her crazed look, he braced for danger.

Oh, shit!

Chapter Nineteen

Jack started back for the gate, hoping he reached it before all hell broke loose. He was only a couple of meters away when Lena turned to the guard and gave him a sleepy grin.

"I'm good. Too much to drink and not enough sleep, if you know what I mean."

The guard snorted and thumped the scanner. It blinked green and he raised the bar. "Don't let 'em catch you sleeping on the job."

Lena winked and walked through the gate, not stopping until she reached the intersection around which Alexis had disappeared.

Jack hurried after them. Phase one of their plan was complete. They were in.

Most workers, upon gaining access to the central hub station, reported to security to get their access cards. However, since getting a card meant first passing a biometric scan, Jack, Alexis and Lena by-passed the security station and regrouped in a side corridor beneath flickering maintenance lights.

While they were alone, Jack tapped his wrist device to pull up the station schematics, which he studied for several long seconds. Then he tapped his wrist device again, and the schematics disappeared.

"This way." He motioned for them to follow as he moved further into the wormhole station, heading in the general direction of where, according to the schematics, the central computer core was located.

They had nearly reached the restricted lower-level junction when he raised a hand, freezing them in place.

Footsteps echoed from around the corner. Then a lone maintenance engineer appeared, early 30s, walking briskly—his belt jangling with tools and his access card visible on his hip.

Jack gestured to him. "He's got what we need. Do you have any more Somnalex-9?"

"We're out," Lena told them.

"Then we'll have to do this the old-fashioned way," Alexis said. "I'll intercept. Get ready."

The trio slipped into an alcove beside a rusted coolant control panel. As the worker passed, Alexis stepped out casually.

"Hey," she said, pretending to adjust her comm unit, "you got a sec? My calibrator's acting up."

The man blinked. "Do I—?"

Too late. Jack came from behind, clapped a hand over his mouth while wrapping his other arm securely around the man's chest. He dragged him, kicking and squirming, back into the alcove.

Alexis hurried after him and shoved her thumb into the side of the man's neck. In the next instant, the suddenly unconscious man slumped and would have fallen to the floor if Jack hadn't still been holding him.

"What did you do?" He was both surprised and impressed.

"It's a trick I learned on the force for dealing with difficult suspects. He won't be out long, so we should probably stash him someplace before anyone sees us.

"We can use this," Lena announced, pushing a gray wheeled utility cart. "I found it over there." She waved toward the back of the alcove.

They dumped the man into the cart and then looked around for a way to hide him from view, coming up empty.

"The maintenance closet we want isn't far," Jack told them. "Let's take him there—fast."

"Take this" Lena snatched the man's access card off his belt and handed it to Alexis, who led the way.

They rolled the cart through the auxiliary corridors, passing three maintenance droids and a janitorial

AI who gave them a friendly beep before continuing on its way. Eventually, they reached Utility Closet K-22—-adjacent to the server room's north wall—and used the access card to open the door.

Inside, the cramped closet smelled of ozone and grease. They shut and locked the door behind them, stacking two crates against it for extra security.

"We need to make sure he doesn't come to and escape while we're busy," Jack said.

"Maybe this will work." Alexis was on the other side of the closet where she'd been examining the supply shelf. When Jack looked over at her, she tossed him a roll of adhesive stripping.

"Perfect." He set to work and with Alexis's help, soon had the man's wrists and ankles bound. Then he tore off an extra strip of adhesive to cover the man's mouth. "That should hold him for a while."

Meanwhile, Lena had been emptying the contents of Jack's bag on the floor. Handheld plasma torch, mag-seal patch panels, thermal shears, noise-dampening foam, and safety visors lay before them.

Jack grabbed a visor and put it on. "Time to make a door."

Lena knelt beside the wall's wiring conduit and opened a panel. A dull hum greeted her—proof that the main shaft ran behind it. "This is it."

Jack fired up the thermal shears, sparks hissing as he sliced a square panel out of the wall. The metal gave way slowly, layer by layer, until the last piece dropped with a muffled clank.

Behind it, a narrow air shaft stretched into darkness—barely wide enough to crawl through.

"Ladies first," Lena said, grabbing a glow rod and sliding into the shaft head first. "If I get stuck, tell my mother I died doing something illegal and totally badass."

She wriggled forward and Alexis followed next, clutching her pack. Jack followed last.

The shaft ended behind a wall vent in the server room—a gleaming, sterile space filled with tower-like computer columns, each rimmed with pulsing blue light.

Lena used a silent cutter to unhook the grate. Pushing it aside, she dropped lightly to the floor and crouched low. One by one, Alexis and Jack followed.

They moved quickly.

Jack and Lena reached the central terminal. Jack pulled out Coda's sleek black data chip and inserted it into the port beneath the main console. The system lights flickered.

In another part of the room, Lena used her wrist device's micro-cable to connect it to the terminal. "Initiating trace-sweep now."

Meanwhile, Alexis positioned herself near the ventilation intake. She opened the thermometer locket and held it in front of her. "Temperature's good."

She focused all her attention on watching the temperature gauge. If the room's temperature spiked, it would trigger both an alarm and the room's carbon-dioxide suppressant gas. Both could prove dangerous to their future health.

Jack and Lena worked in silence, the sound of the air processors blending with the soft clatter of keystrokes.

"These subroutines are nested deep," Jack muttered a few minutes later. "Simon didn't just hide the code—he disguised it. We'll have to isolate the trigger chains manually."

"There's no time to do that now," Lena advised. "Can you download the code?"

"To what?" He sounded frustrated. "Coda's chip is practically full."

"What about–"

"Hang on," he snapped. Alexis looked away from the temperature gauge long enough to see him pull up the holo-keyboard for his wrist device and set to work.

"Okay," he said a minute later. "I set up a relay to the *Black Jack.*"

"What?" Lena sounded alarmed.

"It's the only way to get the data."

"Is that a problem?" Alexis asked. Lena's tone had worried her.

"The computer has to work harder to transfer the data to the ship," Lena explained. "Which could cause the temp—"

Suddenly—beep-beep-beep.

The digital screen of the thermometer lit orange. "Temperature's rising!" Alexis warned.

Jack cursed.

The thermometer's tone shifted to a faster beeping, rising in pitch. Red warning lights pulsed on the device.

"Temperature's spiking," Alexis warned. "Two degrees above threshold. If it hits three, we trigger the fire protocol."

"We're not done yet," Jack said, still punching commands into his wrist device.

Alexis wireless synced her wrist device to the thermometer, took off the locket and set it on the nearest computer. Then, she spun on her heel. "I'll fix it. I saw something back in the maintenance closet."

She bolted to the ventilation grate, pulled herself up, and disappeared into the shaft, crawling as fast as her elbows and knees would let her.

Back at Utility Closet K-22, Alexis dropped down and immediately yanked open a supply crate she'd noticed earlier. Inside sat a cluster of CO_2 canisters, clearly labeled with fire-response warnings.

"Come to mama." She grabbed a canister and wedged it into the vent shaft opening. She twisted the nozzle. The idea was to use the carbon dioxide to lower the temperature of the air flowing through the shaft into the room. The trick would be making sure she didn't use so much that Jack and Lena suffocated, which was sure to happen if the room's fire protocol was triggered

The canister hissed violently, venting into the duct-work. Cold fog rolled along the shaft. She checked her wrist-device which she had previously set up to mirror the thermometer's display and saw the temperature dip a fraction.

Then she heard a noise and turned—too late.

The maintenance worker, now awake and looking angry, stood beside the wheeled cart. His adhesive bonds hung in shreds from his freed wrists and ankles. His eyes were wide, and he lunged at her with a snarl.

They crashed into a tool rack, metal clattering to the floor. Alexis grunted as his elbow clipped her jaw, but she twisted beneath him, slamming her knee into his side. He reeled back, giving her room to reach for a plasma spanner—but he batted it away and went for her throat.

She rolled, slamming him into the wall, but he was strong.

He grabbed a length of wire and looped it around her wrist, trying to pin her arm.

She snarled and head-butted him, dazing them both. He stumbled, and she sprang up, grabbing Jack's bag of tools, and swung it full-force into his ribs.

He went down with a gasp—but surged back up, blood at the corner of his mouth. "You're not getting out of here—"

Alexis pivoted, driving her elbow into his jaw.

CRACK.

The man collapsed, finally unconscious.

A second later, Jack climbed out of the shaft, holding the still hissing carbon dioxide canister. He saw Alexis standing over the body, chest heaving and his eyes widened slightly. "I can't believe you took that guy down by yourself."

"Yeah, so?"

"I'm not going to lie," he said, voice a little breathless. "That's hot."

She shot him a look, lips twitching. "Next time, you can wrestle the angry maintenance guy."

"Nah," he said, stepping over the unconscious man to go to her. "You clearly had it handled." Taking her wrist, he looked down at her temperature display. "Room's back in the green."

She leaned against the wall, sucking in air like she hadn't breathed for hours.

"You sure you're okay?" Jack stepped closer.

She gave him a tight smile. "Adrenaline's still doing laps. But yeah. I'm good. Asshole ripped my mask, though. And I think my cheek is cut." She touched the mask where it was ripped, hoping the cut beneath it wasn't too bad.

He reached out and gently touched her cheek, thumb brushing just below the cut. "You keep surprising me."

"I thought you already had me figured out," she said, voice soft.

"Not even close."

His hand lingered a beat longer than necessary before he dropped it.

They stood close—too close. The air between them crackled with unsaid things, with what might have been said if they weren't seconds away from fleeing for their lives.

Alexis looked up at him, the adrenaline still surging, this time for a different reason. She didn't know what might have happened next because at that moment, they heard movement coming from the air shaft. Then Lena appeared.

"We're done." She climbed into the room and looked around, eyes widening when she saw the unconscious man. "Everything okay in here?"

"Yeah, but not for long. That interface I set up to transmit data to the *Black Jack* is going to set off alarms, so we need to get out of here and go directly to the shuttles. With luck, we'll be planet-side before the alarms go off."

They took a moment to resecure the unconscious man's bindings, brush themselves off and check that their masks were still holding. Then they exited the closet and walked briskly toward the shuttle bay.

Having encountered no problems along the way, they approached Pad 3, where the planet-bound shuttle, visible through the transparent bulkhead, sat idle. It was the same one that had brought them here. Jack, Alexis and Lena crossed the loading floor, avoiding eye contact, and boarded the shuttle—slipping into separate seats. Jack chose one near the front, while Lena and Alexis took seats on either side of the center aisle.

The shuttle was half-full, occupied by a handful of workers finishing their shifts. Everyone looked exhausted. No one noticed anything off—yet.

The pilot's seat remained empty.

Lena leaned over and whispered to Alexis. "Pilot's probably grabbing a stim-coffee. Let's hope he hurries."

The longer they waited, though, the more anxious Alexis became. When a station alarm sounded, she mimicked the other passengers, looking around, pretending to be curious though she knew what it was. Someone had discovered their infiltration of the server room.

Moments later, she heard the clomp of boots on metal. A half-squad of station guards entered the far end of the hangar, scanning the area, weapons still holstered, but eyes sharp. One of them pointed toward Pad 3.

"Time to go," Jack muttered, already moving.

He ducked through the small bulkhead door and into the cockpit. The controls were familiar enough—similar model to an older scout skiff he once stole near the Orbis Belt.

He strapped in and powered the shuttle. Engines whined to life.

In the back, passengers looked up, confused.

Jack activated the shuttle's PA system. "Everyone remain calm. This is a nonviolent commandeering of this shuttle. Sit tight, stay quiet, and no one gets hurt."

The guards broke into a sprint as the shuttle lifted off with a bone-jarring surge of G-force. The docking bay's blast doors were only halfway open. With a sick sense of déjà vu, Jack tilted the shuttle hard, fed power to the thrusters and scraped through with centimeters to spare.

We're out!

Lena left her seat and, taking the co-pilot's seat, studied the control panel display. "No tracking tags, no pursuit shuttles launched. We're clear—for now."

"What's the plan?" Alexis asked, coming to stand by them, but keeping watch on the passengers, making sure no one tried to be a hero. "Back to the shuttle station?"

Jack's jaw tightened. "No. Too risky." He punched in coordinates. "Heading for the *Black Jack*."

The shuttle dipped into the upper atmosphere, rattling as it burned through the cloud canopy. Below, the lowlands stretched gray and green, mist curling above large bodies of water.

In the distance: a black shape sat half-concealed beneath camo-netting and rock outcroppings. Their ship.

Jack brought the shuttle down hard onto the uneven terrain, kicking up dust and debris. The passengers in the back clutched armrests and stared wide-eyed.

"We're making a brief, unscheduled stop," Alexis announced dryly. "Complaints can be submitted later."

The ramp hissed open. Lena was already on her feet. "Go!"

They bolted down the ramp and sprinted for the *Black Jack*. Mid-run, Jack activated the ramp control on his wrist device. It dropped and he sprinted up it, Lena and Alexis following close behind him.

Jack made a beeline for the cockpit. "Start-up sequence now!"

Lena hurried to her engineer's console. "Diverting power to primary thrusters—stand by!"

Outside, dust was clearing—and far off in the distance, several fast-moving sky-chasers glinted in the sunlight, incoming from the shuttle station.

Jack opened the throttle and the *Black Jack* roared to life, rattling as it lifted from the rocks. The camo-netting tore away, fluttering like a ghost in the wake.

"They'll try to lock missiles," Alexis warned, eyeing the bogeys closing in.

"Let them try." Jack's voice was low, gaze focused on the horizon. "We're punching through."

With a seismic shudder, the *Black Jack* blasted into the sky, slicing through the atmosphere at full burn.

A transmission lit up the console—an urgent hail from planetary security.

Alexis flipped the switch and let it go silent.

Behind them, the surface disappeared beneath the clouds. As they reached the outer atmosphere, the planetary security ships slowed. They weren't equipped for deep space flight.

Jack exhaled slowly. "That was close."

"Where to now?" Alexis wondered aloud.

"Someplace where we can analyze all this data," Lena said, coming up to join them.

Jack smiled. "I know just the place."

Chapter Twenty

THE *BLACK JACK* FLOATED in the silent void, systems on passive mode, lights dimmed to a soft amber glow. Outside the starboard viewport, stars twinkled across the dark canvas, distant suns casting cold fire. They were far from any trade route, adrift on purpose—untraceable.

Inside, in the dim-blue glow of the command console, the trio were now mask-free and in their own clothes. Lena sat at the galley table, her fingers flying across the keyboard of her computer, eyes locked on lines of cascading code. Jack stood behind her, looking over her shoulder, arms crossed, brow furrowed. Across the table, Alexis hunched over a data pad, scanning data with sharp eyes, a steaming mug of stim-root tea forgotten on the table in front of her.

"It's like sifting through dry grass," Lena muttered. "Ninety-eight percent of this is legitimate code—routine comm relays, navigation protocols, internal diagnostics."

"Means we're looking for the two percent that could destroy the galaxy," Jack said dryly.

She gave a humorless snort. "Yeah. No pressure."

A soft chime sounded—another program complete, another sweep returned.

Nothing.

Alexis got up and went to stand beside Jack, looking over Lena's shoulder. "It has to be there—"

"I know," Lena interrupted. "But it's cloaked. Whoever wrote this knew what they were doing. It's not only buried—it's wearing camouflage."

Jack tapped the console beside her. "Let's keep digging. Check anything that loops irregularly. Watch for duplicate authorization headers."

"Yeah, yeah." Lena expanded the search parameters.

Silence stretched between them, broken only by the hum of the life support system and the occasional chirp of an analysis cycle completing.

Then—

"Wait." Lena straightened slightly, eyes narrowing. "Hold on—let me run that line again."

Jack leaned closer to the screen. "What is it?"

Working at the keyboard, she isolated a single subroutine buried between lines of code regulating the wormhole's flux calibration—a place no one would ever think to look.

It was a line of authorization—legitimate on the surface, but tagged with a recursive checksum that shouldn't have been there.

Lena began unfolding it, her eyes growing wider. "This ... this is it. A backdoor protocol."

Jack's voice was tight. "Control override?"

She nodded slowly. "Layered access. Command injection. It uses a modified version of the Galactic Connectivity Enhancement kernel. Someone embedded it into the system and disguised it with outdated sub-headers. If we hadn't been looking for it—"

"We'd never have seen it," Alexis finished grimly. "So, someone can issue commands to the wormhole station remotely. Lock access, reroute traffic, disable safety protocols."

"Crash transits," Jack added darkly.

"Collapse wormholes," Lena muttered.

A beat of silence.

Then Jack said, "And this confirms what we suspected. Someone's trying to control the wormhole network."

"But it doesn't tell us who," Alexis pointed out. "There are no ID tags, no signatures."

Lena's brow wrinkled. "But we have the trace program Coda installed—remember? Besides downloading data, it was pinging the transmission path. Tagging IP jumps."

She pulled up a side window and started the trace results. For several long seconds, the screen remained blank.

Then a single red icon blinked into existence—an endpoint address.

"Got it." Lena's voice was tight with tension. "One origin node. A massive server core ... located on Veridian Prime."

Jack's breath caught.

"Coordinates?" Alexis asked.

Lena entered a command. A map of Veridian Prime appeared on the holo-display. The coordinates triangulated.

The image zoomed in.

The holo-rendering sharpened—a sprawling estate, nestled in the emerald hills outside Veridian Prime's central city of Galathea. Fountains, courtyards, private shuttle pads.

"Son of a bitch!" Alexis couldn't believe it. "That's Simon Rourke's estate."

"How do you know?" Jack asked.

"Eight years working for Galathea PD, you get to know who owns the palatial estates." She stared at the image. "It all fits. The access, the power, the money. He's the only one with the infrastructure to run a supercomputer capable of interfacing with a wormhole core remotely."

"But it's not proof," Lena said softly. "That server could be routing for someone else. It could've been hijacked. There's no direct fingerprint tying Simon to the code."

"We need something irrefutable," Alexis agreed. "Something we can show to the intergalactic council—or the press—something that forces their hand."

Jack straightened. "The only way to do that is going to be to physically access the supercomputer—and you can bet Simon's got it heavily guarded."

"We wouldn't necessarily have to access it ourselves," Lena suggested, drawing both of their attentions. "We can use my nanobots. They'll be able to bypass any security he has by accessing the data from inside the computer. We'll only need to get close enough to deploy the bots."

Alexis was already shaking her head. "No way. That estate has orbital sensors, ground-to-air auto-turrets, perimeter drones, a private security team, and probably some mercs on retainer. We'd set off a dozen alarms before we even reached the front door."

A heavy pause followed.

"Unless ..." Frowning, Alexis reached for her tablet again, flicking through news updates, public feeds, and private chatter.

She scrolled.

Paused.

Scrolled again.

Then stopped.

Her finger tapped the screen. "This is it! This is how we can get in." She turned the tablet to face Jack and Lena. On the screen was a bright, glossy society article from Veridian Vogue with a headline that read:

Galactic Tycoon to Host Star-Drenched Charity Gala on His Private Estate. All Eyes on Simon Rourke!

Below it were images of the mansion lit with floating lanterns, a guest list of elite politicians, artists, and dignitaries. The article promised "a night of elegance, rare vintages, and exclusive access to the technology wizard himself."

Lena turned her gaze on Alexis. "You've got to be kidding me."

Jack grinned slowly. "No. She's not."

Alexis swiped through to the event details. "Security will be on alert, but it'll be spread thin. Focused on guarding people, not the computer. A gala is the perfect cover for us."

"We need invitations," Lena said.

"And disguises," Jack added.

"We need a plan." Alexis tapped the tablet thoughtfully. "The gala is being catered by Flavura, a high-end catering company with a mobile crew system. Staff are rotated in from different branches depending on where the event is taking place and the number of guests. Their uniforms are standardized. Most guests won't recognize the help."

"You're saying we go in as caterers?" Lena asked.

"Yes," Alexis replied. "All we have to do is secure uniforms, bypass the hiring rotation, upload our names to the crew manifest, and walk right through the front gates—trays in hand."

Jack rubbed a hand down his face. "That's crazy."

"It could work," Lena said, nodding slowly. "Simon's not expecting anyone to go after his supercomputer. We'll be background noise."

They fell silent, each lost in their own thoughts. Then Jack blew out a breath and grinned.

"Let's go crash a party."

Later, after dinner, they sat in the galley, where a holo-projected layout of Simon Rourke's estate, pulled from public records, hovered above the central table. Jack had dimmed the ship lights, and now the only glow came from the map and Lena's wrist device as she annotated sections in red and blue.

"I've never worked security for one of Rourke's events," Alexis said, "but I've sat in on the briefings for them. In the past, the gala is held in the west ballroom and courtyard." She used her finger to draw a circle around the designated areas. "Guest access will be here," she pointed to the front door and the doors leading from the courtyard to the ballroom. "And main security will be posted along this perimeter wall."

"Unless he has a room we aren't seeing here," Lena said, "the most likely location of the server core is the East wing, lower level."

Alexis nodded. "We enter as catering staff, wearing ChromaMorph outfits that will transform into evening attire. Blending with the rest of the guests, we can explore Simon's estate and locate the computer."

Jack frowned. "ChromaMorph isn't cheap."

"Not a problem," Lena said, grinning. "I was very lucky at the games the other night. But we'll need a central base in Galathea to operate from. We can't stay on the Black *Jack*."

"I have a house there. We can use it," Alexis volunteered.

The three shared a look.

It was the beginning of the endgame.

They were walking into the home of the man who might be engineering galactic control, armed with nothing but disguises, wit, and the hope that the evidence they needed existed on that supercomputer.

"Alright," Jack said, finally. "It's time to set course for Veridian Prime."

Much later, sitting in the kitchen inside Alexis's house in Galathea, Lena's sleeves were rolled to her elbows, her hands steady despite the caffeine-fueled buzz behind her eyes. The air smelled faintly of solder and coolant. Before her, in a transparent bio-seal chamber, a capsule of nanobots shimmered with an iridescent light in the suspension fluid, awaiting programming.

Modular panels displaying diagnostic data encircled the kitchen table, casting a faint glow on Lena's concentrated expression. The surface of the table was a chaos of micro-cables and circuits, their clutter an engineer's paradise. This corner of Alexis's house had become a makeshift lab, its tidy domesticity upended by Lena's invasion of tech. Everything they needed for the mission sat in this room, either half-assembled or a few keystrokes from completion.

"These little guys are going to break into the brain of the most secure computer on Veridian Prime," Lena murmured, half to herself, half to the bots. "Let's make sure they don't screw it up." She tapped at her holo-keyboard, lines of code streaming across the display. She'd spent hours tweaking Coda Varek's infiltration program, modifying the adaptive replication protocol so the bots could survive the physical interface with Simon Rourke's isolated network. The program was meant to piggyback off the core's maintenance cycles—enter quietly, transmit everything to a shadow server, then fade quietly into the background. She paused, fingers hovering, considering whether to have the bots self-destruct. They were too expensive for that. She decided, instead, to retrieve them. A problem for later. She watched as they floated, a small, silent universe under her control.

Jack's voice broke her concentration. "You sure they won't get caught by any security sweeps?" His shadow fell across the table, joining the clutter and noise.

Lena didn't look up. "Unless Rourke's running predictive AI that hasn't been patented yet, no. These bots mimic heat signatures and magnetic pulses. They'll just be part of the background noise." She continued to type, her focus splitting between Jack's presence and the task at hand. The air felt charged, as if the slightest spark might set off a chain reaction.

Jack folded his arms, unconvinced. "And you're sure the program will work?"

"I should ask you that," she interjected, smirking. "After all, you wrote it. I just added some fine-tuning to allow it to adapt faster than any security system can." Her confidence was infectious, a necessary antidote to the doubt that lingered over their plans. She flicked a switch, and the display flashed green. The sight was as satisfying as a cold drink on a dry planet.

Jack watched the swirling specks. "They're creepy."

"They're brilliant." She sealed the capsule containing the nanobots with a hiss and locked it into a hardened carrying case. "Besides, they're our only shot." She gave him a look. "And they're ready to go."

He leaned against the wall, eyes narrowing as if weighing something heavy. "We're taking one hell of a risk. If this doesn't work—"

"It'll work." She cut him off, her tone leaving no room for argument. "When we get the data, we'll have the proof we need. We'll be able to shut down Rourke and clear Michael's name."

The mention of his friend's name seemed to pulse in the air like a beacon, drawing their shared silence around it. He moved closer, his presence a reminder of the gravity pulling at them all. "And you're sure they'll transmit everything before they go quiet?" His gaze drifted over the setup, the tangle of electronics, the faint glow of monitors. "Rourke has eyes everywhere."

"Not inside his own systems. Not if we do this right." She placed the case on the table with a thud, the weight of it as real as their gamble. "The *Black Jack's* relay will pick up the data the moment it hits the atmosphere."

Jack nodded, the seriousness of their undertaking mirrored in the taut lines of his expression. They exchanged a look, a moment suspended between fear and hope. Jack turned away, and Lena watched him go, her heart pounding a beat that matched the urgency of their mission. They had twenty-four hours before the gala. The clock had already started ticking.

In the bedroom, Alexis adjusted the collar of the black-and-gold catering uniform, turning before the mirror. The uniforms had arrived via dead drop, courtesy of a forger Lena knew. She eyed the outfit critically, tugging at the fabric as if she could reshape its destiny through sheer will. The sleeves and seams lay snug against her frame, tailored to perfection. Her expression held a flicker of amusement, imagining Simon Rourke's face when they infiltrated his gala. The room around her was sparsely furnished, a reflection of the pragmatic life she led—everything in it had a purpose, like the uniform she wore.

She held her arms out to the sides, testing the range of motion. *You'd never know this wasn't legit,* she thought, examining the embroidered Flavura logo stitched over the chest. She reached for a chroma-adaptable panel embedded in the collar and tapped twice. The uniform shimmered, color and fabric morphing into the visual texture of a high-end cocktail dress. Her reflection wore a self-satisfied grin, the kind that rarely found its way onto her face. This mission would be different; she could feel it in the way the dress transformed, fluid and seamless, around her.

Jack's knock on the door was followed by his voice. "Hey, can I come in?"

"Yeah," Alexis called, still admiring the way the dress clung to her form in the mirror.

Jack entered, the edge of uncertainty in his gaze heating when he saw her. "Wow! You look stunning. You'll fit right in with Simon's high-society guests."

"That's kind of the point." Her mind was already racing through the details of their plan, visualizing herself blending into the gala's opulence, extracting information while the party thrummed around her. Then she tapped the panel again, and the fabric flickered back to the catering uniform. "Clothes like these could sure cut down on wardrobe clutter."

Jack stepped closer, his presence filling the room. "Tonight could be dangerous. I don't suppose there's any way I can talk you out of going?"

"Not a chance," she assured him, searching his face and noting the lines of worry etched across it. His concern was a double-edged sword, cutting through her defenses while fortifying her resolve.

"Figured you'd say that." His resignation was tinged with admiration, his voice a mixture of fondness and frustration. "I don't want anything to happen to you." His hands went to her arms, grasping her gently in a connection he was afraid might break.

"Nothing will." Her tone held a confidence that bordered on defiance. She stepped back slightly, creating a space between them that only emphasized the gulf of emotion.

They stood in silence, and she was aware of the razor-thin line they walked.

"I should leave." But instead of walking away, he pulled her gently toward him.

His lips met hers with a tenderness that surprised her. The kiss was long and passionate, a moment suspended outside of time, outside of consequence. She kissed him back with the same intensity, the same need to feel something real before they both had to disappear into the parts they were playing.

When they finally parted, they were both breathless and quiet, the echo of what had just happened filling the room more completely than any words could. For a long moment, he simply rested his forehead against hers, saying nothing. Then he pulled away slowly, a reluctant smile playing at the corners of his mouth.

He walked to the doorway, but lingered there for a moment, casting one last look that made her heart trip over itself, and then he was gone.

The emptiness he left behind was as profound as his presence had been, leaving Alexis with emotions that felt unguarded and raw.

She touched her fingertips to the lips he'd left tingling as a single tear slipped down her cheek. She let it fall, knowing she couldn't let herself feel this way tomorrow. Not if they were going to make it out of this alive.

Chapter Twenty-One

Twin moons glinted above the hills, casting silver shadows across a sea of green. Their soft light spilled like ink over the mirrored surface of the lake. Simon Rourke's mansion rose like a crowned jewel on the far bank, the walls of pale stone and alloy reflecting an aura of invincibility. Hover-limousines drifted like predators to the main gates, releasing their passengers—shimmering guests clad in luxury—into the heart of indulgence.

Behind the fortress of power, the service road offered a different face of the estate—hidden in obscurity, tangled in the gnarled embrace of overhanging trees. This route, reserved for less prestigious deliveries, lacked the grandeur of the main gates, but pulsed with its own brand of energy as the catering vans approached. They rolled forward in careful formation, unobtrusive and utilitarian, toward the gate where the lone guard waited.

Inside the second van, the space resembled a cargo hold designed for service, not comfort. Dim lights flickered overhead, casting a detached glow over metal surfaces. Alexis sat in the back, her breath misting in the chilled air, hands steady as she checked the forged IDs. Around her, silence pressed in, broken only by the faint mechanical hum of the refrigeration unit.

Jack drove, his hands firm on the wheel, though his clenched jaw betrayed his tension. They all wore their catering uniforms—dull, matte black—designed to make them invisible among the throng of wait staff.

Before them, the mansion loomed—gorgeous, threatening, full of secrets. Her thoughts churned, reviewing every scenario, every potential point of failure.

Slowly, Alexis inhaled, letting the cold settle into her lungs. *Breathe. It's just nerves.* The thought steadied her, even as her heart raced beneath her calm facade. She adjusted the straps of the small evening purse in her lap. Hidden inside was the nanobot vial. The purse was small enough to slip inside the pocket of her server's jacket.

Feeling Lena's gaze on her she glanced over.

"If the bots work as well as this fridge, we're golden." Lena's attempt to lighten the mood made Alexis smile.

Outside, the van slowed to a stop. Glancing out the window, Alexis watched the guard approach, the glow of the ID scanner reflecting off the van's window. If their credentials didn't work, the game was over before it had even started.

The tension from the others bled into her like static, invisible, but unmistakable.

Jack lowered his window and held out their credentials. The guard leaned forward so he could peer inside the van. Alexis and Lena smiled back at him. Then the guard scanned the cards.

Time slowed.

Then came the flash of green.

Jack gave the guard a nod when he gestured them forward and then raised his window. His grip noticeably eased on the steering wheel, and Alexis felt the tightness in her chest begin to ease.

"We're in." Jack's voice was low, as if he was wary of tempting fate. He eased the van forward, past the guard, and into the shadow of the estate. Silence returned, but it pulsed now with anticipation, edged in fear.

Jack brought the van to a stop near the back of the house and, for a moment, none of them moved. Alexis looked at Lena, and their eyes met in quiet solidarity. Then she glanced toward the mirror, meeting Jack's gaze. He held her stare, something unspoken passing between them—a shared understanding. Then Jack gave them a nod. It was time.

Moving with calculated haste, they emerged from the van and regrouped at the rear, where they removed various catering supplies.

Jack took the lead, maneuvering a delivery crate past the last of the security detail, into the house. Alexis came next, carrying a tray of food, while Lena brought up the rear, pushing a cart carrying cleaning supplies—and a concealed drone within.

They reached the maze of service corridors and vanished among the similarly dressed staff and servers, hurrying about in an orchestrated blur.

Lena turned down a hallway that led to the utility room, while Alexis and Jack continued toward the main kitchen. No one was watching when she found the closet they'd identified while studying the house plans and ducked inside.

She was glad to discover that the closet was, as it had appeared on the schematics, big enough to accommodate both her and the cart. While it had a ceiling light, she left it switched off. She didn't need it. She had excellent night vision. And the last thing she needed was for someone to spot a light coming from beneath the door and open it to investigate.

Pushing the cart to the back of the closet, she wrinkled her nose at the smell of dust and the various cleaning supplies lining the shelves. It was unpleasant, but it wasn't like she hadn't been in situations with tighter quarters and worse smells.

Reaching for the large box of cleaning detergent on the bottom level of the cart, she set it on the upper level, where it would be easier to reach. If anyone had opened the tabs of the box and looked inside, they would have found powdered detergent. Lena felt along the bottom seam of the box and pressed a small, nearly invisible lever. Then she lifted the upper portion of the box to reveal a secret bottom. From inside, she withdrew her tablet to reveal a layer of foam beneath. Nestled in the foam was the drone: a small, matte-black device shaped like a housefly. It even had membranous forewings which it used for flying.

She picked it up, admiring its design, then flicked her tablet on. The drone sprang to life, its wings buzzing. Its eyes blinked a soft faint red and when she glanced at the screen of her tablet, she saw an image of herself, looking down. The resolution of the image was surprisingly clear and she couldn't help but smile. The drone design wasn't unique, but she'd built this one herself and allowed herself a moment to gloat over the fine work she'd done. But only for a moment, because it was time to play hide and seek.

The words had barely formed in her head when the closet door rattled. She ducked instinctively behind a stack of storage bins, her heart thudding in her chest. Then the rattling stopped, and she heard footsteps walking away.

That was close.

It was a reminder that they didn't have time to waste.

As if conjured by her thoughts, she heard a whisper in her ear. Alexis's voice, letting her know she and Jack were heading down to the lower-level East wing where they suspected the computer was located. When they found it, they would release the nanobots, currently stashed in Alexis's purse, signal Lena the job was done and the three would quickly rendezvous outside by their van and leave.

Of all the scenarios they'd planned for, this one was best-case.

So, Lena waited, the drone hovering nearby.

The signal from Alexis came moments later. Disappointing, but not unexpected.

"Deploy the drone." The computer wasn't there.

Responding to Lena's navigation commands, the drone slipped beneath the closet door and into the main corridor, its tiny wings as quiet as a whisper. The image on Lena's tablet was crystal clear as it flew, hugging the walls and corners until it reached the main ballroom. Lena had to focus as she piloted the drone through the crowded room, darting past the cuffed pants and sharp heels of the city's elite. She had made the bug as small as her skills would allow, but even the smallest speck could seem huge when the wrong eyes noticed it.

As soon as she had an opening, she piloted the drone upwards, flying over the heads of the people mingling in the ballroom, taking advantage of the high ceilings and bright lights to keep the drone hidden.

Across the audio-feed, the guests' voices sounded more like a flock of squawking geese than multiple distinct conversations. The sound grew fainter the further away the drone flew.

It took only moments to confirm the computer wasn't on the main level, so Lena guided the drone up the stairwell, flying past gold-framed portraits of Simon Rourke standing with various members of the galaxy's top brass. Reaching the next level, she guided the drone swiftly forward, toward the more intimate areas of the house.

Reaching the first closed door, Lena hovered there for a moment, studying it. There was a small gap between the top of the door and the door jamb, so Lena carefully guided the drone through it. Once the drone was inside, she checked her tablet and adjusted her earpiece. According to the schematics, this was a guest bedroom. The drone flitted past an expensive-looking dresser, and Lena saw a woman's blouse tossed carelessly on top. On the floor in front of the dresser lay a tangle of a man's pants and socks.

Using the controls on the tablet, she scanned the room with the drone's camera. The king-sized bed sitting against the opposite wall was occupied by two entwined bodies. Lena stared at the screen in disbelief, her mind processing the figures: a man's naked body lying on top of a woman with fiery red hair.

Lena blinked hard, trying to eradicate the image burning into her mind. This was clearly not the computer room, so she piloted the drone back through the gap above the door and along the hallway to the next room. The soft, reassuring hum of the drone's wings on her tablet was the only sound in the otherwise silent closet.

She wondered what Alexis and Jack were doing.

On the lower level, after telling Lena to deploy the drone, Jack and Alexis stepped out of sight into a small alcove. When they were sure the coast was clear, they each tapped the button on their collar. Jack's server's garb shimmered and shifted into a sleek midnight tuxedo. When he turned to Alexis, she was dressed in a backless crimson gown that accentuated her figure and revealed hints of glowing skin beneath the deep neckline. Her fingers brushed the skirt of her dress, testing the fabric with a look of awe that matched his own. The fabric shimmered red as it caught the light. Jack felt mesmerized.

"You really do look beautiful."

"Thank you." She looked both surprised and pleased. "You look very handsome in your suit."

Grinning, he adjusted his newly formed cufflinks. "Thanks." The tuxedo fit perfectly, and the deep black fabric seemed to absorb all the light in the narrow space. He hadn't worn anything this formal since—well, maybe since ever.

He pushed off the wall and gave a mock bow, the perfect gentleman in his newly minted tuxedo. "Shall we join the party?" he suggested, offering her his arm.

With the band playing something bold and strange, the noise upstairs was a roar of voices, music, and laughter, bright and dizzying as it flowed across the wide-open ballroom. Jack guided Alexis through the crowd of people like a shuttle navigating an asteroid belt.

No one paid attention to the couple moving group to group, nodding in interest, and picking up bits of conversation. Jack grabbed two drinks from the tray of a passing server who looked momentarily confused at the sight of them. For half a heartbeat, Alexis worried he recognized them from earlier, when they were pretending to be part of the catering staff, but then he quickly schooled his features and continued on his way across the room.

Alexis swirled the liquid in her glass thoughtfully, wondering if it was too expensive to taste good. Someone bumped into her and she turned, recognizing the thickset man as the Galathean mayor. He mumbled an apology before turning back to the man he was talking to. At that moment, a server appeared with a tray of small plates and hors d'oeuvres. He stopped beside the mayor and his companion, who helped themselves to plates. As the server moved away, Alexis stepped into his path, which brought her a step closer to the mayor. As she slowly helped herself to a plate of food, she listened closely, trying to follow the thread of conversation between the men.

"I'm surprised to see you," the younger man said to the mayor. "I thought you were boycotting Rourke's party."

The mayor shook his head as he finished chewing his food. After he visibly swallowed, he said, "The City Council members made it clear they expected me to be here. Rourke may be an asshole, but he's a major player in our city, don't you know."

"Don't let him hear you," the young man quickly advised. "You don't want to be on his bad side. Once he implements his wormhole enhancement project, he'll be virtually untouchable."

After a minute, the men split up, each going in a separate direction. Alexis turned back to Jack.

"Learn anything?" he asked in a whispered voice.

She shook her head. "Nothing we didn't already know."

By silent agreement, they kept walking, blending into the next group with ease. The plan was to mingle, picking up any intel they could, until Lena told them she'd found the computer room. Then they would slip away, simply another couple looking for a quiet place to be alone, and head to the computer room. There, they would deploy the nanobots, currently stashed in Alexis's purse.

Back in the utility room, Lena sat on the floor, eyes glued to the tablet as the drone's soft whirring filled the air. The camera was scanning the master bedroom, the last room on the second level, confirming Lena's worst suspicions. She called Alexis and Jack, hating what she was about to tell them.

"It's not here." No computer. Nothing. Maybe they'd been wrong from the start.

Jack's voice came through the earpiece; a low murmur wrapped in disbelief. "You're sure? You checked everywhere?"

Lena sighed. "Of course. I'm in the utility room and it's obviously not here. With the drone, I searched the kitchen, ballroom, family room, a study, and three bathrooms on the main floor. Plus the four bedrooms, two bathrooms, and the master bedroom with ensuite on the second floor. I saw a couple of small devices, but no supercomputer."

She paused, letting her words hang in the air, feeling defeated. She wanted to suggest it was at one of Simon's other locations, but she knew that wasn't true. The search program had traced the supercomputer's IP address to this location. Her mind raced through other possibilities, quickly rejecting each one as implausible. However, it was hard to argue with the obvious. They'd missed something.

Jack was quiet, but she could practically feel his doubt, hear it in the silence coming across the earbud.

Then Alexis cut in, her voice sharp and certain. "Wait a minute. There should be nine."

"Nine what?" Jack sounded confused, but Lena could hear the spark in Alexis's voice, sharing a moment of clarity Lena hadn't yet caught up to.

"The schematics showed six rooms and three bathrooms on the main floor, not five rooms and three bathrooms."

Lena felt her pulse quicken as she mentally ran the list again, ignoring the bathrooms: kitchen, utility, ballroom, family room, study.

Alexis continued, the confidence back in her voice. "Six rooms. You only searched five. Check the schematics. He wouldn't want anyone easily accessing his computer, so he's concealed the room. Just because we can't see it, doesn't mean it's not there."

Lena was already keying commands into the tablet. Soon, the schematics appeared on her screen. Lines and labels shifted as she zoomed in, and there it was. Next to Simon's study, a blank space without a label, large enough to be the hidden room. Her breath caught in her throat, then released in a rush of relief.

"Alexis," she whispered, her excitement barely contained, "I think you're right. There's an unmarked room in the schematics, next to the study. I'm sending the drone back downstairs to check it out."

Bringing the camera feed back up on her screen, Lena guided the drone out of the master bedroom and down the hallway. The camera feed was steady, clear, showing a hallway with few guests and fewer distractions. She relaxed, watching its smooth progress toward the stairs.

Suddenly, the feed went blank. The sound of wings was replaced by static. Lena's fingers hovered over the screen; her breath caught in her chest.

"Come on." She pressed her ear closer to the speaker. The static was deafening, drowning out her thoughts, but she was sure she'd seen something right before it hit: the blur of a hand, a swift motion, too close for comfort. She tried to recalibrate, switching frequencies, tapping the screen until her fingers throbbed. Nothing. She switched again. And again. "Damn it. Don't do this to me."

She hadn't realized she'd spoken aloud until she heard Jack's concerned voice in her ear. "What's wrong?"

"We've got a problem." She tried to sound calm, but the pressure was building in her chest, an overwhelming tightness that made it hard to breathe. "I lost the feed."

The black screen mocked her. She fought back the rising panic and scanned the other frequencies, the precision of her fingers deteriorating as the tension ramped up. She took a deep breath and forced herself to think clearly. Forced herself to look at the facts.

"Lena?" There was a sense of urgency in Jack's tone.

"Give me a second." She had to think. It wasn't random interference, not from the ballroom or the scanners. She'd accounted for that, set up every contingency she could. It wasn't dead batteries or system failure. The new cells had promised at least two hours of stealth time, though she'd hoped they would get out in less than one.

Her fingers flew across the tablet, working to restore the feed. It took a few tries before it clicked back on. The image wavered, showing exactly what she had feared: a narrow strip of marble flooring, several dozen meters closer than it should have been. The perspective tilted and righted itself, showing the bottoms of shoes standing much too close.

Had someone seen the drone? Mistaken it for a housefly and swatted it?

She closed her eyes and exhaled as the certainty settled in. It was only a matter of time before someone stepped on it—unless she got there first.

"The drone is down," she hissed, already hurrying from the utility closet. "I repeat, drone is down. Bottom of the stairs. We have to get it before someone steps on it."

She reached the kitchen and snagged a towel off the counter. Every instinct urged her to hurry, but she had to force herself to move at a normal human speed.

Reaching the ballroom, she focused her gaze on the base of the stairs. When there was a momentary parting in the gathered crowd, she scanned the floor. If she'd been human, she wouldn't have been able to see the drone, but she spotted it on the floor, mere centimeters from where a man stood, his back to the drone as he spoke to friends.

The man rocked forward a step, laughing at something a companion said. Then, like a pendulum completing its oscillating movement, the man's body began its backward motion. As if in slow motion, Lena watched his foot lift, knowing that when he stepped back, he would crush the drone. Still too far away to save it, she watched in horror as his foot came down.

Chapter Twenty-Two

THE GLINT OF THE drone's shattered casing caught Alexis's eye just as a man's foot arched downward, threatening to destroy it. She sprang into motion, moving so quickly that she almost collided with him, sacrificing her plate of hors d'oeuvres with a fumbled and loudly exclaimed "Oops!"

Shrimp and crackers scattered like dry rain on the polished floor. The man looked furious at first, and then his face softened when he saw her, surprise and then something else relaxing the set of his jaw.

"Butter fingers, huh? Well, no harm done."

He leaned down to retrieve the food, but never got the chance.

"I'll clean this right up." Lena appeared from nowhere with a cloth and wiped up the food, and the damaged drone. Then she hurried away.

A strange mix of emotions went through Alexis's mind as she watched Lena vanish—impatience, gratitude, annoyance. The urge to follow was so strong that she almost forgot she was being watched.

She turned back to the man, forcing a laugh. "I hope I didn't ruin your boots." He was still staring, and it was pretty clear he wasn't too worried about his footwear. He said nothing, just looked at her legs and smiled a knowing smile. She felt a surge of irritation but let it pass, shrugging as she moved on.

Back in the utility closet, Lena locked the door. Then she grabbed several cleaning towels, rolled them up and laid them on the floor, against the door. She needed the lights on now and hoped the towels would prevent errant light from slipping out beneath the door. Then she hurried over to her cart, slid to the floor, yanked the lid off the cleaning bin, and rescued the broken drone. Her fingers worked with speed and skill, opening the casing and spreading out the delicate insides like surgical tools on a tray. She felt the seconds slipping away as she assessed the damage, the breath tight in her chest.

One cracked wing rotor.

Bent leg.

Fried cam-link.

You're a mess, bug. She bent a fine piece of wire back into place. *But I've seen worse.*

Whether she was trying to convince the drone or herself, she didn't know. Time. Time was the problem. She wondered how long Jack and Alexis could hold off inspecting the study themselves.

She studied her supplies as she laid them out. Everything she needed was here—at least in theory. Her thoughts moved quickly as she replaced a damaged capacitor with a part that was designed for something else entirely. *Should do the trick.*

She didn't need to look at her chrono to know how long it had been, but the sense of urgency grew with every passing second. The frame wasn't perfect, but it was functional. It would have to be enough. She bit her lip and moved on.

The new cam-link came together easily, and Lena took her first easy breath. Maybe she really could do this. *Last adjustment.* She hooked up the wires and swapped in the last tiny part. Her breath caught in her throat as she closed the casing and snapped the cover in place.

Moment of truth.

She powered the drone up and set it on the floor. The tiny motors hummed. Then a sharp click sounded, and the drone launched awkwardly into the air. She watched it buzz and wobble, her heart beating as fast as the rotors. She took a deep breath and tapped her earbud.

Several tense minutes had passed since Lena disappeared with the drone. Jack paced the perimeter of the ballroom, eyeing the door she'd gone through and wondering whether he should follow. He was still debating it when Lena's voice crackled in his ear.

"Back online." Jack nearly sighed with relief when he heard Lena's voice. "Flying erratic, but functional." Her voice held an edge of pride. "I'm going to send it to check out the study—see if I can find the door to the computer room."

Jack caught Alexis's eye and saw her subtle nod. She'd heard Lena's transmission. He tapped his chin, signaling her to stay put. They would wait until Lena reported back.

Though he couldn't see the drone, he imagined it flying through the air, wobbling as it avoided ceiling fans and dodged through the crowd. "No need to impress anyone with your flying skills. Just make sure it gets there."

"What's the fun in that?" Lena's voice was playful. He had to remind himself that she knew what she was doing, even with a damaged drone. "Almost there."

Jack stayed focused, listening to the buzz of conversation around him and keeping his gaze on Alexis.

Then came Lena's voice. "Drone just slipped into the office."

Once again, an image of the study appeared on the tablet's screen. Lena imagined the little bug hovering near the ceiling, capturing every detail of the well-appointed study lined with dark wood, the massive desk dominating the space and the monitors embedded in the walls.

Then, suddenly, the study door opened and Simon Rourke stepped into the room.

"Shit!" Lena felt her stomach lurch and hurriedly guided the drone up higher. Simon was tall and sharp-eyed; she couldn't let him see the drone. She maneuvered it to the top shelf of the nearest bookcase, where she settled it.

"Lena?" Jack's voice sounded nervous across her earbud.

"Rourke walked into his study. We're okay, though."

Perched on the bookcase, the drone's tiny lens focused on Simon. Lena watched through her tablet as he crossed the room and opened a drawer. She held her breath. He flipped through papers, his expression as composed as ever, and tucked them back in. Then, with a glance at the closed office door, he turned and pressed his palm against the wall.

The soft click was barely audible through the drone's mic. Lena felt the tension unravel in a long exhale. She almost cheered as a hidden panel slid open, revealing a concealed chamber beyond.

Gotcha!

"Found the room," she announced softly. "Hidden door in Simon's office. Behind the desk."

On the tablet screen, Simon peered into the hidden room, but didn't go in. Then, he closed the panel, picked a tablet up from his desk and turned to go. He stopped short of the office door and seemed to eye the bookcase with suspicion. Lena froze as if she was perched on the bookcase shelf. Then the moment passed, and he left the office.

Relief. "He's gone," she whispered, feeling a little lightheaded.

Back in the ballroom, Jack and Alexis had moved to stand near the entrance of the hallway leading to Simon's study. They exchanged discreet congratulatory smiles when they heard Lena's message.

Moments later, Jack watched Simon appear and re-join the party. "Now's our chance."

"Wait." Alexis's voice sounded through his earpiece. "What if he goes back? One of us should stay and distract him if that happens."

Jack frowned, not liking the idea, but he couldn't argue against it. "I'll stay."

"Don't be ridiculous." Across the room, he though he saw Alexis roll her eyes. "I don't know anything about computers. Lena, go with Jack. Pick up the nanobots on your way."

"On my way." Lena's voice replied through the earpiece. Jack shifted impatiently. He wasn't happy about splitting up, but they were committed now.

"Be careful," he muttered, wanting to say more.

"This will work." Alexis spoke as though she knew exactly what was going through his head. Maybe she did. She had a knack for reading him.

She caught his eye as she turned away and it was the way she looked at him, the way she grinned with so much confidence that convinced him she'd be okay. He thought of Michael and how proud he'd be of his sister. Then he thought of how screwed he'd be if anything went wrong, and he steeled himself for what he had to do. Taking a steadying breath, he slipped around the corner, into the East hallway, to wait for Lena.

In the closet, Lena hit her chroma-morph button. The catering uniform shimmered and reformed, silver fabric snaking over her shoulders like liquid metal. She tucked her tools and tablet out of sight, then opened the door and slipped out. Two loitering catering staff gave her a curious glance but said nothing as she walked confidently past them. She started making her way through the gathered guests while Alexis, several meters away, moved to intercept her. They passed each other, seamlessly transferring the purse from Alexis to Lena. Lena kept walking without breaking stride.

At the hallway's entrance, she turned to find Jack already there. "Let's do this."

"Alexis?" Jack looked tense.

"Stop worrying. She can handle it."

"Who says I'm worried?" He was moving ahead of her as he said it, avoiding looking at her.

"Right," Lena teased.

Reaching the study, they both looked back up the hallway to make sure it was clear before Jack tried the doorknob. Finding it unlocked, he pushed it open enough to peek inside. Then he went in.

Taking a deep breath, Lena followed him, gently closing the door behind them.

While Jack monitored the doorway, she moved behind Simon's desk, trying to remember the exact spot where Simon had stood when he'd opened the panel.

Placing her palm against the wall, she pressed gently on various spots, trying to mimic Simon's movements. It took several tries before she felt the panel depress beneath her fingers. *Click.* She heard the sound, and even though she'd expected it, she still jumped, but then turned to give Jack a triumphant look. "Got it."

The panel swung open, revealing a small, hidden room glowing with crystalline light. A sleek supercomputer dominated the space.

"Look at that." Jack sounded awed as he came to stand beside her. "I've never seen anything like it."

She started to step forward, but Jack held out a hand to stop her. She gave him a questioning look until he pointed to the retinal scanner beside the frame, and then to the faint shimmer of security beams. No one was walking through that threshold.

But they didn't need to. Retrieving the vial from the purse, she opened the lid and poured the nanobots onto the floor. They buzzed softly as they activated and moved into the room, easily slipping beneath the security beams.

She waited for a beat, then reached out and closed the panel. It had just shut when the door to the study swung open—

A guard stepped inside.

For a nano-second, Jack's mind went blank. They'd been caught. He only saw one way out of this. He stepped forward, readying himself to tackle the guard, when Lena stepped in front of him and slapped him, hard, across the face.

"Don't you ever try to kiss me again, you arrogant bastard," she snapped. Then she stormed past the stunned guard and out of the office, leaving Jack standing, dumbfounded.

The guard smirked. "Guess it didn't go well, huh?"

Jack rubbed his cheek, forcing a sheepish grin. Then, as inspiration struck, he purposely slurred his speech. "You could say that. Thought the study was empty ... I—" He hiccupped, swaying slightly. "Got a little too much vintage in me tonight."

The guard chuckled. "Yeah, well, better luck next time, but pick another place to try your luck. This room is off-limits."

Jack moved to step past the guard, deliberately staggering and placing a hand on the guard's shoulder for balance. "Thanks, pal. You're a lifesaver."

Under the guise of shaking the man's hand, Jack awkwardly grabbed the guard's wrist instead, his palm covering the security terminal strapped there. A subtle click sounded from the scanner strapped around Jack's wrist—a sleek, matte-black metal band hidden beneath his cuff. After the click, he felt the faint vibration of the band against his wrist

A fraction of a second later, the scanner silently pinged completion and Jack corrected his grip, grabbing the guard's hand and shaking it.

"Try to sober up before you embarrass yourself again, huh?" The guard laughed as he extricated his hand from Jack's grip and gently, but purposefully, turned Jack to face the open doorway and gave him a slight shove to get him moving.

Jack smiled back at the guard. "No promises." Then, giving the guard a sloppy salute, he continued out into the hallway.

As he strolled leisurely and a little unsteadily toward the ballroom, he palmed the van's remote, subtly triggering its start sequence. The device vibrated in response, a reassuring signal that it was up and running.

Stepping into the ballroom, the chaos of the party swallowed him. The buzzing conversations, clinking glasses, and loud music created an almost impenetrable wall of noise, perfect for remaining invisible. From across the room, he caught Alexis's gaze and held it a moment, then he moved swiftly, sliding past clusters of finely dressed guests without drawing a single curious glance.

Outside, he felt the night air, thick and humid, embrace him as he stepped away from the mansion. He touched the button on his collar. The sophisticated fabric of his tuxedo shimmered, shifted, and morphed back into the catering uniform he'd worn earlier in the evening.

He glanced back once at the glow of the ballroom's chandeliers filtering through the window curtains, then hurried across the expansive lawn. Anyone watching would see a member of the catering staff headed to his van, not the man who had just been in Simon Rourke's private study.

Reaching the vehicle, he climbed into the driver's seat and exhaled. He maneuvered the van until it faced the driveway, its engine whisper-quiet in the evening stillness. He didn't have to wait long before Lena appeared in the driveway behind him, once again in her catering uniform and carrying a bag which he assumed carried her micro-tools and tablet. She climbed into the front seat beside him.

"How's your cheek?"

He thought she might have smiled, but couldn't see her face well in the dim lighting of the van.

He rubbed his cheek, even though it no longer smarted. "I haven't decided whether to be thankful or mad. But if I'm being honest, that was smart thinking."

"Thank you." She turned to look over at the mansion and he followed her gaze, waiting in silence for Alexis to appear. He hoped she didn't run into any problems.

Alexis had moved closer to Simon, knowing that from this position she would more easily be able to distract him if it looked like he might return to the study. The other advantage, she'd hoped, would be that maybe by standing this close to him, she might overhear his conversation and learn something new.

She feigned interest in the idle chatter of nearby guests, letting their words wash over her while she remained acutely aware of Simon's every movement. He seemed unaware of her presence, absorbed in his conversation with a sharp-dressed man who looked like he belonged to some upper echelon of power. Alexis strained to catch fragments of their dialogue—something about a shipment, timing, profit margins. Her instincts screamed they were important, but without context, she couldn't be sure. She tried to hold her impatience at bay, reminding herself that even a hint could prove valuable.

She waited a couple of beats, using the time to finish her drink while giving Jack and Lena plenty of time to reach the van. Then, setting the empty glass on a passing server's tray, she turned toward the door.

She'd only taken a step when a hand gripped her arm, pulling her to a stop.

"Not so fast," a now all-too-familiar voice said. "Where do you think you're going?"

She looked from the hand holding her to the man it belonged to.

Krauk.

Simon Rourke.

Chapter Twenty-Three

ALEXIS'S HEART KICKED AGAINST her ribs. She quickly adopted an expression of polite confusion and turned slowly, the hem of her gown brushing the floor. Simon Rourke stood there, drink in hand, his predatory smile razor-sharp.

His attention was clearly on her and she forced herself to stay poised, forcing the tension out of her limbs, the anger out of her eyes. When she faced him, she widened her gaze, tilting her head in a pretense of curiosity.

"Excuse me?" Her thoughts raced. Had her disguise faltered, given her away? Had she been too bold, trailing him around the room, inserting herself into random conversations? She held her breath, unsure if it was adrenaline or dread that coursed like fire through her veins.

Rourke's eyes glinted with cold amusement. "I don't believe we've met." His voice carried over the clink of crystal and hum of conversation. "And I make it a point to know everyone worth knowing."

Alexis knew how to play this game. It was one she had practiced, perfected. Her stomach twisted with anticipation and a touch of revulsion, but she stayed in character. She would endure this and more if it brought her closer to the truth about Michael.

With a carefully constructed innocence, she smiled, a demure tilt of her lips. "I'm sorry, Mr. Rourke. I was about to step out for some fresh air."

Rourke's eyes flicked over her with something like satisfaction. "A beautiful woman like you shouldn't leave without introducing herself. And certainly not without sharing a dance."

His voice carried that same confidence, the sense of entitlement that ran like poison through everything he said. The charm that came from knowing he was in control. She felt her skin prickle, a visceral reaction that urged her to run, to escape. Instead, she steeled herself against the revulsion that clawed at her insides. She wasn't there for her own comfort. She was there to unravel the truth behind the stolen crystals, and, more importantly, behind Michael's death.

Mustering a smile that seemed both demure and defiant, she gave a breathy laugh that landed light and careless. "How could I refuse?"

In a gesture as arrogant and assured as the man, he held out his hand, palm up. Her skin crawled at the thought of touching him, but she did it anyway, placing her hand in his.

With a slight tug, he led her onto the dance floor, effortlessly twirling her into a waltz. The orchestra's music swelled. All eyes seemed to brush over them, casual, uninterested. A safe audience.

Outside in the van, Jack and Lena sat, listening through their earpieces.

Jack muted his microphone. "I should go back inside." The thought of Alexis alone with Rourke, of her in danger, twisted Jack's insides like a knife. His fingers drummed a restless tattoo on the steering wheel, matching the beat of his heart.

Lena sighed, tapping her earpiece to mute her microphone. Then she leaned back in her seat, watching Jack with the kind of patience only she could muster. "She's got this, Jack. Alexis is tougher than she looks."

He didn't answer, but kept his gaze focused on the house. The windows were lit up like small deep-space beacons. Every second felt like an eternity.

The connection crackled, and he tensed, listening, but unable to make out the words. "Damn it. What's going on in there? Why isn't she leaving?"

Lena put a hand on his arm, her grip surprisingly strong for someone so small. "Give her some credit. She knows what she's doing."

Jack exhaled sharply, a breath he hadn't known he was holding, but the worry didn't ease.

"She'll leave as soon as she can," Lena continued. "When she can do it without raising suspicion."

He wanted to believe that. Needed to believe it. But Jack had been in too many situations where the worst-case scenario wasn't a possibility—it was inevitable. He couldn't shake the feeling that something would go wrong, that Rourke would see through Alexis's disguise and she would pay the price.

Lena released his arm, her smile meant to reassure. "Relax, would you? You're making me nervous." She settled back, trying to project a calm that Jack couldn't absorb.

Inside, Simon pulled Alexis closer, and the press of his hand on her back made her stomach twist with anger and disgust.

"You never did tell me your name," he pressed her.

"Liora Vex. Investment acquisitions." It was a name and role she'd used while working undercover two years ago. If Simon tried to investigate her on the galactic web, her name and credentials would check out. The police department left undercover profiles active for years after they'd stopped using them.

"Liora Vex ..." he repeated. "Sounds exotic. I pride myself on knowing everyone with influence. Yet you almost slipped past me."

"I'm afraid my firm is small; it's hardly worth the notice of a man of your means and accomplishments."

"Well, Liora Vex, it's nice to meet you. I must admit that, at first, I thought you might be a reporter."

"A reporter?" She laughed, feigning embarrassment. "Hardly, although I'm sure there must be a few reporters here under false pretenses." As they continued to turn across the floor, Alexis tilted her head, affecting curiosity. "Rumor has it, you have something ... very big in the works. Wormhole enhancement technology? Sounds like it could change everything."

Simon chuckled, low and smooth, the sound rich with self-satisfaction. "You flatter me, Miss Vex. I can't divulge too much tonight, of course. But let's just say the future of intergalactic travel will be rewritten—with my help."

Built on deception and the blood of innocent people is more like it.

She kept her thoughts to herself and returned his indulgent smile with a sweetness that almost sickened her.

He leaned in conspiratorially, lowering his voice as if this small act of inclusion would bind them together. "There's a press conference in Galathea's main plaza in three days. That's when the universe will learn what I've built."

The news rattled her because it meant Simon was further along with his plans than they'd anticipated, but she never missed a beat of the dance. "I look forward to it."

Simon watched her for a beat, then spun her again. The grandiosity of his movements was an homage to his own ego.

Her pulse raced, each beat louder than the last. He thought he had her in his thrall, thought she was another insipid fan. He didn't know how much of a threat she really was. It was that knowledge that kept the smile on her face.

She watched the surrounding guests, the swirl of satin and sequins, the curious eyes that regarded them as nothing more than a man and his newest conquest. It made her smile wider, knowing Simon believed it, too. She willed him to believe the lie, willed him to underestimate her.

As the song ended, Simon dipped Alexis in an extravagant gesture, drawing polite applause from a few nearby guests. Alexis straightened, fluttering a hand against her chest, feigning flustered nerves.

"You're quite the accomplished dancer, Mr. Rourke." She let the tremor in her voice suggest breathless admiration. "I—I believe I need a moment to catch my breath."

Simon gave her a wolfish smile, his certainty as overwhelming as his arrogance. "Of course. Allow me to fetch you a drink."

She knew this was her chance. "That would be wonderful. While you're doing that, I believe I'll use the powder room to freshen up."

He released her with the assurance of a man who was confident his charms had won her over. Alexis felt the rush of impending victory, the exhilaration that tasted like freedom, like triumph. She slipped through the crowd of guests, careful not to draw too much attention. Her pulse hammered as she moved into the hallway, away from Simon's too-keen eyes.

"You know this is the worst part for me," Jack said to Lena out in the van, his admission edged with frustration. "The waiting. The not knowing."

The connection over their earbuds crackled again, and he straightened, suddenly alert. But all he could make out was the muffled echo of voices and music. It wasn't enough to satisfy the anxiety gnawing at him, but it was enough to let him know Alexis was still there.

He knew Lena was right, knew Alexis had more skill and nerve than he'd expected. The knowledge did nothing to allay his worry.

His fingers resumed their rhythm on the wheel, an outlet for the energy he couldn't contain. Then the connection crackled again, and this time, Jack heard the clear, familiar tones of Alexis's voice.

"On my way."

Inside, Alexis breathed deeply, steadying herself, keeping the smile on her lips as she disappeared into the powder room.

The moment she was out of sight, she locked the door and pressed the ChromaMorph collar at her throat. The elegant gown shimmered and changed, dissolving into the familiar catering uniform she'd worn earlier in the night.

She cracked open the door and checked the hallway. Coast clear. She slipped back into the hallway and, keeping her face averted from the ballroom, hurried for the nearest door, the one that led out into the gardens.

No one stopped her and soon she slipped outside. The garden stretched dark and empty before her, the path illuminated only by landscape lights. She had nearly reached the opposite end when she heard footsteps behind her. Instinctively turning, she momentarily froze when she saw Simon standing on the patio.

His gaze traveled over her, and she held her breath, waiting for him to call her out. Instead, his gaze continued past her like she was invisible. Like she was nothing. Like she was exactly what she needed him to see: another member of the catering staff, one of a hundred nameless faces at his disposal.

Along with the relief, a sense of urgency crept back into her limbs. She turned and hurried away, her feet pounding the earth in time with her pulse.

When she reached the far edge of the garden, the outline of the van appeared like a beacon, a lifeline. She ran toward it, flung open the van door and climbed inside, breathless and elated.

"Go!" she gasped. "Before he realizes I'm—"

Jack gunned the engine, the van lurching forward, cutting off the rest of her sentence. Alexis tumbled into the seat, laughter breaking through the gasps. Lena was grinning at her, clinging to the door frame as they sped away from the mansion, from Rourke, from danger.

Alexis burst through the door of her house, Jack and Lena close on her heels. "I don't think anyone followed us."

"Agreed," Jack said. "Now, let's find out if the risks we took were worth it."

The trio moved with purpose to the kitchen table, where Jack and Lena took seats before their computers.

"How long before we get data?" Alexis was feeling too anxious to sit.

"First, we have to make sure the nanobots haven't been detected." Jack typed away at the holographic keyboard.

"And how are we going to do that?" Alexis asked.

Jack stopped typing long enough to give her a quick smile. "You remember when that guard walked in and caught Lena and me in Simon's study?"

Alexis scowled at him. "Of course. I'm pretty sure my heart stopped beating for a minute."

"Well, I saw an opportunity to scan his security device and took it."

"How?" Lena asked.

Jack stood to take off the catering jacket and hang it on the back of another chair. Then he unbuttoned his shirt sleeve and rolled it up, revealing the thin black metal band wrapped around his wrist.

Alexis grew alarmed when Lena gasped. "What is that?"

"It's a scanner," Lena told her, but her gazed continued to drill into Jack. "You should have told us you were walking around with a scanner strapped to your arm. In case you got caught."

"Yeah, well, that's exactly why I didn't tell you. We already had enough to worry about. I didn't want you worrying about me getting caught." He shrugged before sitting back down. "Besides, it's a moot point now. I didn't get caught and—" He placed the band next to his computer and continued typing. A minute later, he swept his hand up his computer screen so the display switched to a holographic display they could all three easily see.

The screen was divided into six separate images, aligned in two rows of three images each.

As Alexis peered more closely, she realized she was looking at different rooms of—

"Is that Simon's house?"

"It is," Jack replied. "Using the information I scanned from the security guard's device, I'm now able to access the various security camera feeds.

They watched the feeds for several long minutes. There were still plenty of guests in the ballroom, chatting, dancing, eating, and drinking. Guards were positioned around the room, looking bored. Then Alexis, standing behind Jack's chair, noticed Simon Rourke dancing with a young woman he was holding much too close. As the couple moved about the dance floor, Alexis glimpsed the woman's expression and immediately felt sorry for her. She didn't look like she was happy. Alexis could empathize.

Jack tapped another key, and the images changed to six new images of different rooms in Simon's house.

"No image of the study," Lena observed.

"He doesn't want his own people spying on him," Jack tapped another key and this time only a single image appeared, one featuring a massive computer and dozens of ...

"Luminite crystals," Alexis breathed. "So Coda's right? Simon's using the stolen crystals to power his computer?"

"Not just any computer. That's definitely a super-computer," Jack said, "but we couldn't get close enough to the crystals to see whether they have registration numbers on them. Maybe..." He pressed several keys, and the image zoomed in closer on one of the crystals. "Gotta give the guy credit for having the best tech available. Look at the clarity. Even if we'd been able to get into the computer room, we wouldn't have been able to see the crystal this clearly without picking it up." As the image got closer to the crystal, the image blurred before Jack could correct it.

Alexis placed her hands on his shoulders to balance herself as she leaned closer to the image floating in the air before them. "I don't see a registration number, do you?"

"No," Lena confirmed.

Alexis straightened. So, they'd confirmed that Simon had access to stolen crystals, which he was using to power a supercomputer. They still didn't know what he was up to. "Lena, how long will it take for the nanobots to infiltrate his computer and start sending us data?"

"They were programmed to infiltrate the computer and then remain dormant until I activate them."

"Do it," Jack directed her.

Lena pressed a sequence of keys and then sat back. "Now we wait."

Alexis walked over to the nearest empty chair at the table and sat. "Tell me again why Simon's computer won't detect them?"

Lena smiled. "They're coated with electromagnetic shielding materials specifically designed to avoid triggering electronic security measures like the computer's intrusion detection system."

"I still don't understand how they'll access the data we need."

"It's simple, really. Their size allows them to move through the gaps around circuit boards and along cable pathways to the storage device. Then they'll send out electrical impulses which will induce the storage device to transmit data, which the nanobots will capture and immediately transmit to the *Black Jack* using the latest spread spectrum techniques to avoid detection and interference. Then we'll use our link to the *Black Jack's* computer system to access the data from here."

"How will the nanobots know which information to send?"

Jack sighed. "We didn't have time to program them on what to look for, so they'll send back everything they find. I'll run the incoming data through a keyword search program. Those files and documents in which a keyword match is found will be prioritized over the others. After that, it'll be up to us to sift through the data."

Alexis felt a rush of unease. "That could take a long time."

"It could," Jack agreed. "Which is why we should all try to grab some sleep and then start fresh in the morning."

Alexis secretly hoped Jack would suggest the two of them share a bed, but instead, he offered to sleep on the couch while Lena took the guest bedroom. Though disappointed, Alexis told herself it was for the best. If she and Jack shared a bed, the last thing she would want to do is sleep, but it had been a long day and she was exhausted—they were all exhausted. So, after making sure both Jack and Lena had fresh linens and towels, Alexis retreated to her bedroom where she quickly fell asleep.

Chapter Twenty-Four

The next morning, Alexis thought about the events from the night before. With sunlight filtering through the kitchen windows and the smell of the breakfast they'd recently finished still lingering in the air, their infiltration of Simon's gala felt distant, like she hadn't lived through it but was only reading about it in a report.

The only evidence it had been real was the massive amount of data that had been transferred to Jack's computer overnight while they slept.

Now, a dizzying array of screens floated above the kitchen table, each one filled with complex schematics, encrypted messages, and classified reports.

Alexis leaned forward, her gaze darting from screen to screen as she tried to make sense of the deluge of information. Beside her, Jack's fingers were dancing across a haptic interface as he started cross-referencing the files.

Simon had apparently documented every transaction and interaction, clearly not worried that anyone but him would ever access the data. For the next couple of hours, they read documents and emails and listened to audio files.

Finally, needing a break, Alexis got up and went into the kitchen, where she prepared lunch for them. She carried the food over to the table and set it down. Jack stopped what he was doing to reach for a sandwich.

"Thanks," he said. "All this digging was making me hungry."

"Have either of you found anything we can use?" Alexis asked.

"Not specifically," he admitted. "At least not yet, but it looks like Simon's been in communication with someone in an influential position with the Galactic Assembly."

"You can't tell who it is?" Alexis asked.

"Not yet but look at these financial transactions. Simon's been paying this person a lot of credits for something. What about you, Lena? Find anything?"

When Lena didn't respond, Alexis looked over at her. She had earbuds in and was listening to something. Feeling their gazes on her, she slowly looked up.

From her expression, Alexis knew something was wrong. "What'd you find?"

"Lena?" Jack pressed her when she didn't respond.

She breathed in a heavy sigh and plucked the earbuds from her ears. She looked at Alexis. "Sit down." As soon as Alexis complied, Lena pressed a button, and the audio crackled to life. Simon's voice, unmistakable in its cold authority, filled the room.

"I trust you understand the importance of tying up loose ends. Michael Mattix has become a liability neither of us can afford."

"What are you suggesting?"

Alexis felt her blood turn to ice at hearing the all too familiar voice.

"Liabilities need to be removed. Permanently. And without suspicion," Simon replied. "Make it look like he's gone rogue, caught stealing Luminite crystals."

"I'll have to take those crystals into custody," the other man said. "Even with the evidence, there will be ...people ...who question his death."

"See that they don't," Simon barked. "I'm paying you to make problems like Michael Mattix go away. If you can't do that, then you become a liability."

There was a heavy sigh from the other man. "I'll see that it's done. When?"

"The evening of the fourteenth," Simon replied. *"Michael will be at the warehouse on Main and Fifth."*

The other voice could be heard agreeing, then the call ended.

The room seemed to tilt. If Alexis hadn't already been sitting, she might have toppled to the ground. Her brother had been shot on the fourteenth while supposedly stealing crystals from a warehouse at Main and Fifth. And if that wasn't bad enough—

"I recognize the other voice," she told Jack and Lena. "That's Chief Townsend, the head of Galathea's law enforcement."

Her former boss and mentor.

The betrayal hit like a physical blow. Townsend, a man she had trusted, respected ... had been responsible for her brother's murder.

"Alexis?" Jack's voice seemed to come from far away, laced with concern.

She shook her head, unable to speak past the lump in her throat. The grief, the anger, it all came rushing back, threatening to overwhelm her. She pushed away from the table, stumbling towards the doorway that led to the bedrooms. "I ... I need a moment."

Jack watched her go, his heart aching for her. He understood all too well the pain of betrayal, the scars it left behind. He wanted to go to her, to offer comfort, but he knew she needed space to process this.

With a heavy sigh, he turned back to the screens, his jaw set with determination. They had to keep digging to find the proof they needed to bring Simon and his accomplices to justice.

The wealth of information Simon had stored in his computer was staggering.

"Simon Rourke is a piece of work, isn't he?" Lena commented, echoing his thoughts. "I found his calendars. Check out the names of the government officials he met with regularly." She put the list of names up on the screen so Jack could see. "He's got contracts with these same people, either directly or through their shell corporations. The contracts are vague on what services these people are providing, but check out what he's paying them." She pulled up a financial ledger showing the payout of billions of credits. "And that's only their monthly fee. He's also paying them large bonuses each time the Galactic Connectivity Enhancement Project progresses to the next stage of development. And the regulatory approvals are a joke. I'm not finding any evidence that the GCEP's actually been audited."

"Someone's been testing the system. Check this out." He pulled up test results that were never meant to be public, showing successful trials where wormhole pathways were altered or hijacked using the new systems developed under the guise of the project.

"Simulated overrides?" Lena asked.

"Looks like it to me," Jack confirmed. "And that's not all. I found a backdoor algorithm buried in the program that allows remote access to the wormhole network's controls without going through standard security measures."

"That's it, then," Lena breathed out a sigh of relief. "We have him."

Jack wasn't feeling as confident. "There are still some gaps in proving that Simon is behind all of this. I'd feel better if we could find something directly implicating him." His gaze strayed over to the doorway through which Alexis had disappeared, and he couldn't help worrying about her.

"Go." Lena gestured with her head toward the doorway. "Go check on Alexis. I'll keep digging and see what I can find."

He hesitated, wanting to go, but he felt guilty leaving all the work to Lena.

She nodded, understanding in her dark eyes. "Go. I've got this."

He squeezed her shoulder in silent thanks, then headed for Alexis's room.

Alexis sat on the edge of her bed, her gaze fixed out the window. The sky beyond was a kaleidoscope of purple and pink hues, the setting sun painting the city in a surreal, almost dreamlike light. It was a serene backdrop, a stark contrast to the turmoil swirling inside her.

A soft knock on the door broke the silence. "Alexis? It's me." Jack's voice was gentle, tinged with concern.

"Come in." Her own voice sounded distant to her ears.

The door opened, and Jack stepped into the room. Seeing her, he crossed the room and sat beside her, the mattress dipping slightly under his weight.

"Are you okay?"

She let out a shaky laugh. "I don't know. I'm not sure I know what 'okay' is anymore." She turned to face him, her eyes glistening with unshed tears. "My own boss, a man I've looked up to and respected for years, killed my brother." She sighed. "It makes me so ... angry"

Jack moved closer, nudging her shoulder with his. "I know. And we'll see that he's brought to justice. Both him and Rourke."

"Then what? Finding the truth has been my single focus for so long; now that we're close to doing just that, what happens afterwards?" She leaned her head against his shoulder. "I feel lost, Jack. Like I don't know my purpose anymore. I don't think I can go back to the force."

He reached over, his hand finding hers, his fingers intertwining with hers in a gesture of comfort, of connection. "Your purpose, Alexis, is to live. And ... and to find happiness. You deserve that."

She raised her head to look at him, really look at him, and she saw the depth of emotion in his eyes. The care, the understanding ... the love. "And what if I said my happiness was with you?"

Jack's breath caught. "Then I'd say ... be sure, Alexis. I don't live the easiest life, constantly flying around, working jobs that skirt the gray area between legal and illegal. I never know where I'm going or what trouble I'll find when I get there. But there's one thing I know for certain. I love you, Alexis. I have for a long time. And if you'll have me, I'll be by your side, every step of the way. We'll figure this out together. The future, the fight ahead ... all of it."

As Alexis gazed into Jack's eyes, she felt her heart swelling with a warmth that spread through her entire being. Despite the chill of grief and uncertainty that still lingered, his presence was like a comforting blanket, wrapping her in safety and love.

"I love you too, Jack," she whispered, her voice barely above a breath. She remembered the moment he had saved her from Raxon Flux and never betrayed her to her parents. In that defining moment, she had known that he was the one for her.

With the iridescent sky casting its ethereal glow just outside the window and the weight of their shared past and future hanging in the balance, they locked eyes once more. When Jack leaned towards her, she instinctively moved to meet him halfway. Their lips met in a kiss that was at once exhilarating and tender.

She gave a soft moan of pleasure when he threaded his fingers through her hair and deepened the kiss. She felt like he was pouring every ounce of his love and longing into that embrace, and she clung to him, her hands fisting in his shirt, desperate to close any remaining distance between them. The kiss grew heated, a fire igniting between them as their pent-up desires were finally unleashed.

In a tangle of limbs and breathless whispers, they fell back on the bed, lost in each other. Clothes were slowly shed as hands roamed and explored every inch of each other's bodies. Every touch was a promise, every kiss a declaration of their love. The rest of the world faded away, leaving only the two of them intertwined as they surrendered to the passion that had been building for so long.

In the kitchen, Lena rubbed her tired eyes, the soft glow of the computer screens the only illumination in the now dimly lit room. She had lost track of time, her focus solely on unraveling the complex web of data before her. The implications were staggering, the depths of Simon's manipulation and cruelty seemingly endless.

The sound of footsteps drew her attention, and she looked up to see Jack and Alexis entering the kitchen, hand in hand. There was a new intimacy between them, a closeness that went beyond mere physical proximity. Lena smiled softly, a knowing look in her dark eyes.

"Well, look who finally rejoined the land of the living," she teased, her voice carrying a note of warm affection. "I was thinking you two had gotten lost in the Quantum Realm."

Jack chuckled, running a hand through his tousled hair. "Sorry, Lena. We ... needed a moment."

Alexis squeezed his hand, a small smile playing on her lips. "But we're back now, and ready to dive into whatever you've found."

Lena nodded, gesturing to the screens before her. "Oh, I've found plenty. Simon's plans go deeper than we ever imagined. It's not just about control; it's about domination. And if we don't stop him …" She shook her head, the gravity of the situation weighing heavy in the air.

She laid out all the evidence she had found prior to his checking on Alexis, as well as the correspondence she'd found after he left—communications between Simon and his closest advisors, discussing the actual intentions behind the Galactic Connectivity Enhancement Project. It was clear now that the project's public goals of improving connectivity and safety were nothing more than a façade for testing and implementing control mechanisms.

Jack leaned forward, his brow furrowed as he studied the data Lena had compiled. "We can't trust the authorities with this," he said, his voice low and urgent. "Simon's got his hooks in too deep. If we go to them, he'll bury the evidence before we can even blink."

Alexis nodded, her eyes gleaming with determination. "We need to expose him publicly, somewhere he can't control the narrative." She paced the room, her mind racing with possibilities. "Somewhere with too many witnesses for him to silence."

Lena smiled. "Wait a minute." Her fingers flew across the holographic keyboard. "While you two were … occupied, I found something interesting. Simon's holding a press conference in two days."

"That's right," Alexis exclaimed. "He mentioned something about that at the party. He's holding it right here in Galathea."

"Not just any press conference," Lena clarified, pulling up a new set of data. "He's announcing the go-live launch of the GCEP. What if we hijack the press conference—"

"And broadcast the evidence to every corner of the galaxy," Alexis finished for her, sounding excited. "We can show the people the truth."

"Exactly," Lena agreed. "I can hack into the network, splice our data into the feed. They'll never know what hit them."

"I like it," Jack said, throwing in his support.

"We'll only have one shot at this," Alexis warned. "We need to make sure our plan is solid."

They set about planning, working through every nuance until every detail was mapped out, and then they discussed it again. Finally, as the first hints of dawn painted the sky in hues of lavender and gold, they stepped back from their work, exhausted but resolute. Jack ran a hand through his disheveled hair, his gaze sweeping over the intricate diagrams and lines of code that held the key to their success.

"We're as ready as we'll ever be." His voice was rough with fatigue but laced with an undercurrent of strength.

"I have to ask you again. Are you both sure you want to go forward with this? If we get caught, Simon will make sure we don't live long enough to share our side of the story."

The three sat in silence for a long moment as they contemplated the consequences of what they were about to do. Finally, Lena broke the silence.

"Then that's the plan. We slip in, slip out. No cuffs, no body bags."

Chapter Twenty-Five

ON THE DAY OF the press conference, Alexis stood amidst the restless crowd, the air thick with anticipation and the low hum of conversation. Her gaze was fixed on the temporary stage erected outside Rourke Enterprises, where Simon Rourke was moments from his grand entrance. She shifted her weight, trying to relax. She, Jack and Lena had arrived earlier that morning and had parked their rental van a few blocks away from where Alexis now waited.

Several city blocks had been cordoned off to accommodate the hundreds gathered for what the media had dubbed a "historic announcement." Alexis scanned the surrounding faces—journalists jockeying for position, eager civilians, polished executives. She wondered if any of them suspected the truth.

Applause erupted as Rourke strode onto the stage, his presence commanding instant attention. He wore a confident smile as his ice-blue eyes swept over the audience. Alexis studied his every move, wishing others could see past that charismatic exterior to the ruthless, power-hungry man beneath the facade.

"Friends, esteemed colleagues, visionaries of the galaxy," Rourke began, his voice amplified across the plaza by hidden speakers. "Today marks a momentous leap forward in interstellar travel. Thanks to my groundbreaking technology, wormhole travel will be faster, safer, and more efficient."

He paused, letting the words settle. Alexis narrowed her gaze, quietly seething. Simon Rourke was a ruthless, ambitious predator, cloaked in a veneer of charisma.

"Imagine," Rourke continued, "being able to fly safely from Prime Veridian to Zephyr in half the time it takes today!"

At his gesture, security personnel rolled out two towering vid-screens behind him. They flickered to life as he pressed a button. A dizzying array of data and graphics filled the displays, showcasing the intricacies of the GCEP's functionality. The crowd *oohed* and *aahed* as digital ships soared across simulated wormholes, clocks ticking down transit times with dazzling speed.

"Today, it is my pleasure to launch the Galactic Connectivity Enhancement Project," Rourke proclaimed. "The single greatest software achievement of our time."

The audience, swept into his vision, erupted into another round of applause. Alexis stayed still, her pulse quickening beneath her composed exterior, while Rourke stood basking in the crowd's adoration.

Three blocks away, sitting in the back of the van, Lena sat hunched over a dashboard of glowing screens and blinking lights.

Almost there.

Her fingers danced across the keyboard, lines of code racing across the monitors as she prepared to intercept the demonstration signal.

Just a few more seconds ...

She had spent hours studying the media's system architecture, identifying vulnerabilities, and crafting the perfect exploit. Now, with the demonstration underway, she had a narrow window to hijack the broadcast and expose Rourke's true intentions.

With a final keystroke, she initiated the hack sequence. The van hummed with the whir of the powerful computers, and the screens flickered as the program wormed its way into the demonstration's feeds.

Come on, come on. Her gaze focused on the progress bar. *Just a little more ...*

Back at the plaza, the vid-screens flickered. The clean graphics stuttered, glitched, then vanished into static. Murmurs stirred the crowd. Rourke's confident smile faltered.

The static cleared.

Financial records rolled across the massive displays—shell company payouts, bribes disguised as consulting fees, vast sums funneled into shadow accounts linked to government officials.

The screens transitioned to a series of consultancy agreements and contracts. The documents, rife with vague descriptions of services rendered by entities connected to government officials, contained clauses for substantial bonuses and additional payments tied to the project's progression.

Whispers turned to gasps as detailed calendars and meeting logs materialized on the screens, revealing a pattern of private meetings between Rourke and influential government figures at critical junctures. The dates of these encounters aligned perfectly with the regulatory approvals and the inexplicable acceleration of the project's timeline.

Then came the messages: text logs, emails, and voice transcripts. Each more damning than the last. Rourke's private correspondences with intermediaries, implicating him in efforts to manipulate wormhole regulations, sidestep oversight, consolidate control.

The crowd shifted uneasily, faces tilting up, expressions hardening from awe into something darker.

But the most damning revelation was yet to come. An audio recording crackled to life, filling the assembly with the unmistakable voice of Simon Rourke. His words, cold and calculating, echoed through the stunned crowd:

"I trust you understand the importance of tying up loose ends. Michael Mattix has become a liability neither of us can afford."

"What are you suggesting?" The voice of Chief Townsend could be heard asking.

"Liabilities need to be removed. Permanently. And without suspicion. Make it look like he's gone rogue, caught stealing Luminite crystals."

Then the news clip covering Michael's death played, showing Chief Townsend announcing the death of Michael Mattix, shot stealing Luminite crystals. Lena had found the clip in her earlier searching, and she zoomed in on Simon Rourke, standing in the background. The flash of satisfaction in his eyes and the brief smile that touched his lips would normally have been missed by any onlooker, which was why Lena froze that image until she was sure everyone had seen it.

The plaza fell into stunned silence as the implications of what they were seeing and hearing became clear to the audience

"Shut it down!" Rourke barked to his aides. "Shut it down—now!"

But the data held, unrelenting, playing its revelations for all to see.

In the chaos, Rourke's security team closed ranks, hustling him toward the side exit. He disappeared into the Rourke Enterprises building as the crowd surged forward, a wave of angry humanity crashing against the barricades.

Alexis pushed her way through the crowd, fighting against the flow. "Don't let his words deceive you." She pressed disposable data drives into as many hands as she could, distributing copies of the damning evidence. "Verify this information for yourselves."

Behind her, the vid-screens blinked off, but the damage was done.

The crowd was no longer an audience.

It was an uprising.

Across town, Jack strode into the Solaris Dominus Intelligence Agency's secure conference room, his boots echoing softly against the polished floor. The dim lighting cast the room in shadow, punctuated by the eerie blue glow of holographic displays reflecting off the faces of the three high-ranking SDIA officials seated at the long table.

"Thank you for meeting with me." Jack moved to the front of the room to stand before them.

"Marsden," the eldest official replied gruffly, "the only reason we're here is because you claimed to have evidence of a threat against the government."

"I do." He held up a data chip. "On this chip is evidence that Simon Rourke is planning to take full control of the entire intergalactic wormhole network." He strode over to the computer console, inserted the data chip and hit play.

The room darkened further as the same data files and audio and video clips interrupting Simon's press conference played across the screen. The montage ended with the audio clip of Simon Rourke ordering Chief Townsend to kill Michael Mattix.

A heavy silence hung over the room like a lead blanket. Jack slowly met each official's gaze, his voice low and steady. "Michael discovered Simon's illegal Luminite crystal smuggling ring, and he was getting close to discovering why Simon was stealing those crystals. Simon couldn't let that happen, so he had Michael killed."

The youngest official shook his head in disbelief. "I knew Michael couldn't have betrayed us. He was too damn loyal."

Jack nodded solemnly. "Michael was a good man who got too close to the truth and paid the price. He made a mistake by keeping what he knew to himself because he wasn't sure who he could trust. That's why I asked to meet with you three. Because there is no record of Simon having you on his payroll."

"Chief Greenwood." Jack addressed the only female. "You're head of the cyber division. I'd like to direct your attention specifically to this code my team and I found embedded in Rourke's GCEP program."

He found the file with the programming code and pulled it up. Chief Greenwood gazed rather casually at the screen for a moment and Jack was afraid she wouldn't give it her full attention, but then her expression changed from bored to curious and she slowly rose from the table to move closer to the vid-screen. After five long minutes, she stepped back, her lips pressed thin, her face pale beneath the flicker of the display.

"Joan, what is it?" one of the other officials asked.

"This ... bypasses every safeguard in the wormhole system," Greenwood said grimly. "It grants unilateral control to a single operator." She turned her gaze to Jack. "Presumably Simon Rourke is that operator?"

He nodded once. "We need to act fast. Simon's announcing the launch of this program right now. Once it's active, he controls everything. Travel, commerce, military movement—all of it."

The oldest official stood, his face etched with resolve. "We'll send a team immediately to bring Rourke in for questioning. If what you're saying holds up—" his gaze hardened, "—he won't escape justice."

At that moment, Jack's comm-device chirped. With a flick of his wrist, he activated the device.

Alexis's holographic image materialized before him. "Jack, we've got a problem. Simon's on the move. He headed into his building a short while ago with his security team."

"Damn it. Hang on." He turned to the others. "Simon's on the move. We need to get a team there now."

The youngest official, Agent Briggs, tapped his own comm, barking rapid orders. "Dispatch a tactical response team to Rourke Enterprises. Tell your people to hold position and observe until we get there."

Jack nodded, adrenaline sharpening his focus. "Alexis," he said, reopening the comm as he strode toward the door, "listen carefully. Go back to the van. Have Lena access the building's systems. Lock down the elevators. Lock down the damn stairwells if she can. Stall him."

Alexis's hologram tilted her chin in determined affirmation. "I'm on it. You be careful."

Jack's lips quirked faintly. "You too."

He snapped the comm closed and followed the officials up the spiral stairs. He burst out onto the roof of the SDIA building, the bright sunlight momentarily blinding him. In the distance, he could see the gleaming spire of Rourke Enterprises piercing the skyline.

Nearby, a fleet of SDIA shuttles took off, sirens blaring and lights flashing. Jack jumped onto the nearest shuttle with the other SDIA officials. The flight to the press conference only took a couple of minutes. Soon they were setting down outside the building. Armored officers were already pouring out of another shuttle and taking up positions around the perimeter. They were quickly followed by the arrival of additional shuttles.

Jack descended the ramp, hitting the pavement with a purposeful stride. Around him, SDIA agents fanned out, their weapons gleaming in the bright sunlight, forming a tightening perimeter around the building's main entrance.

Jack waited outside with the other officials as the agents breached the lobby, sweeping inside. A flicker of hope bloomed in his chest that they'd find Simon cowering in this office.

Minutes dragged into tense silence until an agent finally emerged, helmet visor lifted. "He wasn't in his office. We're sweeping the building now. So far, there's no sign of Rourke."

Jack cursed under his breath, the frustration coiling tighter in his gut. He pressed his comm. "Alexis, status?"

Her voice crackled back, tense. "Lena accessed the security systems and was able to lock the elevators and emergency stairwells like you said, but we just caught him on camera using the internal stairs."

Jack's mouth pressed into a grim line. "Tell Lena to buy us whatever time she can. Every second counts." He turned as the senior SDIA official approached, his gray hair catching the glare of the floodlights. "Rourke's still inside?"

The man nodded and then gestured to Jack. "You're with me."

Together, they entered the building, the lobby eerily quiet beneath flickering security lights. The polished marble gleamed beneath their boots, eerily pristine.

The elevator doors stood ajar, locked, thanks to Lena's override.

"Stairwell," Jack muttered.

They climbed swiftly, the echo of footsteps bouncing up the metal stairwell in steady rhythm. At the fourteenth floor, they emerged into a hall of frosted glass and pale tile, lined with minimalist furniture and polished chrome fixtures. The place exuded money—clean, cold, expensive.

Simon's office loomed at the end of the corridor, the tall double doors thrown wide. Inside, the authorities meticulously comb through everything. Gloved hands rifled through drawers, searching for any shred of evidence that could further implicate Rourke. The soft hum of scanning devices filled the room as they swept for hidden data drives or concealed compartments. A thin man with wire-rimmed glasses kneeled by a hidden panel, prying open a concealed safe.

"Find anything?" Jack asked, stepping inside.

The agent glanced up. "Encrypted drives. Destroyed computer. No physical traces of Rourke."

Jack's jaw clenched. His gaze swept the room—leather chairs arranged around a sleek glass desk, a view that overlooked the glittering sprawl of the city. A whiskey decanter sat untouched beside a pair of crystal tumblers, as if waiting for a toast that never came.

His comm chirped.

"Jack," Alexis's voice came through, breathless. "He's gone."

Jack froze. "Gone? Gone where?"

"He took the stairs down to the lower maintenance levels, but there aren't that many cameras down there. We don't know where he's going."

He turned to the SDIA commander. "He's moving. We need to check sub-levels."

The man nodded, signaling to his team. "Two squads, with us. Let's move."

They exited fast, boots pounding down steel steps into the bowels of the building. The polished luxury above gave way to bare concrete walls, flickering halogen bulbs, the hum of power conduits snaking along the ceilings. Water dripped somewhere unseen. Pipes hissed in quiet protest.

At the maintenance level, the team spread out, weapons raised. Jack's footsteps slowed, senses alert. The silence on this level was oppressive. Wrong. Something felt off.

"Eyes sharp," he murmured.

Then, a faint scuff of footsteps ahead.

Jack swung his blaster up. "Simon—!"

A figure darted between pillars—a blur of black coat and silver hair. Shots rang out. Sparks bloomed off the concrete by Jack's head as Simon vanished down a side corridor.

"He's here!" Jack took off at a sprint.

The agents followed, pounding through winding service halls lit only by emergency beacons. Jack's breath roared in his ears as they turned corner after corner, chasing shadows.

Ahead, a steel door hissed closed.

Jack skidded to a halt, slamming his palm against the locked access pad. "Override it!"

An agent shoved forward, hacking into the panel with rapid keystrokes. "It's shielded!"

Jack's comm buzzed, Alexis's voice cutting through the static. "Jack! Lena just got a ping on the security system. Someone just accessed the building's private hangar!"

Jack's blood ran cold. "He's escaping."

"We're trying to jam his clearance codes, but he's got redundancies," Alexis warned.

Jack turned to the team. "We need to breach that door. Now."

The agent slapped an explosive charge onto the lock. "Stand clear!"

The blast rang sharply in the confined space, the door groaning before crashing inward in a spray of sparks and smoke.

Jack charged through.

On the other side, empty shadows greeted him. Only the faint rumble of a departing shuttle echoed through the vast subterranean hangar. Across the tarmac, a sleek black transport was lifting skyward, thrusters casting long flickering shadows across the metal deck.

"He's gone." Jack's chest heaved, his hands curling into fists. Simon had slipped through again.

A quiet chime buzzed from his comm. Alexis's voice came through, softer now. "Jack?"

"I'm here."

Her relief was palpable even across the line. "We're locked out of his systems, but Lena pulled one last data fragment before he severed the link."

Jack closed his eyes. "Where did it go?"

"It pinged off the supercomputer."

He stared up at the disappearing shuttle, its engines burning like falling stars as it vanished into the night sky. "He's headed back to his estate."

The game wasn't over.

Not yet.

Chapter Twenty-Six

Jack sprinted down the street, dodging pedestrians and weaving between parked transports. He spotted the van's familiar outline up ahead. His heart was pounding by the time he finally reached it and wrenched open the back door.

Inside, Alexis and Lena looked up, tense anticipation etched on their faces.

"If he gets to his computer before we can stop him …" He left the sentence hanging. They all understood the consequences.

"Even if we fly an SDIA shuttle to his estate," Alexis said, "he'll get there before we do."

"And if he uploads the computer program to another location, there'll be no stopping him," Lena added.

"Could we use the nanobots?" Alexis asked. "I mean, they're still inside the computer, right?"

Jack turned to Alexis, his eyes shining with admiration as he leaned in and brushed his lips against hers in a brief kiss. "Pure genius."

She smiled, a faint blush coloring her cheeks.

"*Krauk—yes*!" Lena's words were accompanied by the rapid clacking of keys as her fingers flew across the computer keyboard. Her eyes narrowed in concentration, the glow of the screen casting an eerie light on her pale skin. "I'm accessing the nanobots now. Just need to establish a secure connection and bypass the encryption protocols."

Alexis frowned. "So, what's the plan? Erase the program?"

"No, erasing isn't a permanent solution," Lena said, not pausing in her work. "We need to destroy it. I'm programming the nanobots to turn off the cooling system and then introduce a simple virus into the operating system. As soon as it's activated, the virus will replicate and spread like wildfire. Simon's computer will work overtime trying to destroy it, which will overheat the crystals, causing them to become unstable."

"How unstable?" Alexis asked.

Jack offered a grim smile as he raised his fisted hands and then opened them wide, spreading out his fingers to mimic an explosion.

Alexis frowned. "What about the people at the estate? Won't the explosion kill them?"

Lena's eyes flicked to another monitor. "I ran a bioscan. Guards at the gate. Minimal staff in the house. We can tap into the security cameras and use the audio to warm them."

"The timing needs to be just right," Jack said. "We can't give them time to stop the nanobots."

Alexis hesitated, then nodded.

Jack turned back to watch Lena work, her expertise evident in every keystroke. The way she navigated the complex systems with such ease and precision never ceased to amaze him.

As the seconds ticked by, the tension in the van grew palpable. Jack's mind raced with possibilities, his heart pounding in his chest. What if Simon arrived home and discovered their plan? What if he managed to transfer the wormhole software before they could prevent it?

"How's it looking?" he finally asked Lena, unable to control his anxiety.

"Almost there." Then, with her final keystroke, she sat back. "Done. The virus has been introduced and is replicating. At three hundred-fifty degrees Celsius, we'll lose the nanobots. The crystals are good up to about fifteen hundred degrees Celsius. After that, they enter a state of thermal runaway beyond which it will be impossible to cool them. Their continued heating will cause their containment systems to break down, triggering a violent reaction that causes them to explode."

"How long?" Alexis asked.

Lena shrugged. "I don't know."

"Pull up the security cameras," Jack directed.

Alexis studied the images, making note of only one or two staff members present. Knowing Simon's ego, he'd probably given most of his people the day off so they could attend the press conference. "I wish we had eyes on the study."

"Oh my stars!" Lena exclaimed. "I totally forgot. The drone. It's still in Simon's study." She dug in her backpack and pulled out the tablet. A few keystrokes later and an image of Simon's study appeared on the tablet's screen. She turned back to her computer and studied the display showing the nanobots' progress. "Multiple system failures detected," she reported, her words measured and precise. "Cooling systems offline, core processors overheating. The virus is executing exactly as programmed. It won't be long now."

"Activate the security audio," Jack directed. Once Lena had complied, Jack leaned down to make sure the computer mic picked up his voice. "Attention. There is a bomb located someplace on the Rourke estate.

Please vacate the premises immediately, for your own safety." When he finished, he looked at Alexis and Lena and shrugged. "Trying to explain the computer was about to blow would take too long. Telling them there was a bomb seemed the most expedient."

Alexis turned her attention back to the security camera images and was relieved to notice that, after a moment of confusion, the few staff members they'd spotted were moving toward an exit. She leaned forward so she could peer at the tablet's screen displaying the live feed from Simon's study.

Suddenly, a figure appeared on the screen.

"Simon," Alexis gasped.

Jack's breath hissed between his teeth. "Damn it."

"The crystals are close to overload," Lena warned. "If Simon is still there when they explode—"

"He'll be killed." Alexis didn't particularly care if Simon lived or died—after all, he'd had her brother killed—but she wasn't a murderer. "We have to warn him."

Jack's jaw clenched because, in that frozen second, a choice hung between them.

They watched Simon open the panel to the hidden computer room, his figure pausing mid-stride as his gaze landed on the supercomputer's flashing red alerts. His body momentarily stiffened, then, abruptly, he lunged forward, his hands flying across the keyboard in a frantic blur.

"What's he doing?" Alexis asked of no one in particular. "Is he trying to neutralize the virus?"

Lena's eyes narrowed, fingers already dancing across her own keys as she zoomed in on the drone's camera. "It's too late for that. Look at his input. He's transferring files."

"Audio," Jack ordered, his voice clipped. Lena tapped a command, and sounds of Simon's computer room filled the van; sterile echoes of mechanical hums and Simon's shallow, rapid breaths.

Jack stepped forward, his voice rising as he addressed the camera. "Simon! This is Jack Marsden. It's over. You've lost. The virus has already compromised your system—there's no stopping it now. And there's no time to transfer your program before those crystals go critical. Get out. Save yourself. Surrender to the authorities."

On the screen, Simon paused, his head tilting slightly, as if listening to Jack's warning. For a moment, Alexis allowed herself a glimmer of hope. Maybe he would listen, maybe he would see reason ...

Then he shook his head, a dismissive gesture that sent a chill down her spine. He turned back to the supercomputer, his fingers resuming their frenzied dance across the keys.

Jack cursed again. "Simon, this isn't a trick! The cooling system is down, and the crystals are destabilizing. When they go, everything in that room will be vaporized. Including you if you don't leave!"

Alexis's hand found Jack's arm. "We need to warn the SDIA."

He nodded grimly and pulled out his comm-device, keying in a direct call to Agent Briggs. "This is Jack Marsden," he said when the call was answered. "The supercomputer at Simon's estate is about to blow. Keep everyone at a safe distance!" he warned, his voice strained.

"How much time do we have?" Briggs's disembodied voice asked.

"None!"

Through the comm-device, they heard the agent's panicked shout: "Everyone pull back! Fall back now!"

Jack ended the call, turning his focus back to the feed. He leaned toward the microphone, voice urgent, pleading. "Simon! Please—get out of there!"

Alexis held her breath, gaze locked on Simon's face. She could see the conflict playing out on his face, the hesitation in his movements. For a long, agonizing moment, she thought he might choose to save himself.

Then his expression hardened, a steely resolve settling over his features.

Jack sighed heavily, a look of defeat etched onto his face. "He won't listen. He still thinks he can win."

"Maybe we could—" Alexis's words were swallowed by a sudden burst of static. The camera feed jittered, glitched, then went black.

A cold silence enveloped the van, pressing down like a physical force.

Alexis reached out, gripping Jack's hand tightly in her own. She could feel the tension in his muscles, the frustration radiating off him in waves.

And then she heard a distant boom, muffled but unmistakable. "The crystals exploded," she said quietly, releasing Jack's hand. She stared at the static-filled monitor, a numbness spreading through her limbs.

The weight of the moment pressed down on her like a physical force. She stared at the blank monitor, her mind reeling as she tried to process the implications of what had just happened. Beside her, Jack and Lena were motionless, their faces a mix of shock and disbelief.

"Did we ..." Lena's voice trailed off, her eyes wide and haunted. "Did we kill him?"

The question hung in the air, a stark reminder of the gravity of their actions. Alexis swallowed hard, her mouth suddenly dry. "We don't know that for sure." Even to her own ears, the words sounded hollow and unconvincing.

Jack ran a hand through his hair, his expression grim. "We all knew the risks. Including Simon."

Alexis nodded, but the knowledge did little to ease the guilt that gnawed at her insides. They had taken every precaution, done everything in their power to minimize the risk of casualties. But in the end, it hadn't been enough.

She thought back to their earlier discussions, to the hours they had spent agonizing over the ethical implications of their plan. They had all agreed that Simon's control over the wormhole network was too dangerous to ignore, that the consequences of inaction were far worse than the risks of intervention.

Now, faced with the possibility that their actions had led to the loss of a life, those arguments felt flimsy and insubstantial. Alexis closed her eyes, trying to reconcile the conflicting emotions that warred within her.

"What about the SDIA agents?" Lena asked suddenly. "Was anyone hurt?"

Jack called Agent Briggs, activating the comm-device's speaker.

Seconds dragged into endless minutes.

Then a burst of static cracked through as the call was answered, followed by distant shouting.

"Marsden, you there?" The voice was faint, barely audible over the background noise. It was Agent Briggs.

"I'm here," Jack replied. "Casualties?"

"None. All SDIA personnel are safe and accounted for. And, as far as we can tell, Rourke's security personnel and staff are all safe as well. Thanks for the heads up."

Alexis let out a shaky breath, relief flooding through her, but it was short-lived.

"What about Simon?" Jack asked. "He was in the computer room seconds before the crystals blew."

"No idea," Briggs responded. "Fires burning too hot to go inside, but I can't imagine anyone surviving that blast."

"I understand," Jack said quietly.

"We'll secure the site," Briggs added. "And keep you updated."

The line clicked off.

Silence reclaimed the space. They sat together, lost in separate thoughts. Alexis stared at the console, exhaustion settling deep in her bones. It felt surreal—the end of a chase that had defined her every waking moment since Michael's death.

She exhaled slowly. "Right now, I just want a drink. And maybe a bathtub deep enough to drown in."

Jack gave a tired smile. "You've earned both."

"Definitely." Lena leaned back in her seat and rubbed her eyes. "Tomorrow's problems can wait. Let's go celebrate our win."

The next evening, after a good night's sleep and a relaxing day, laughter echoed through Alexis's living room, the sound a stark contrast to the chaos of the past few days. The lights of Veridian Prime glittered beyond the window, the city stretched out like a jeweled tapestry beneath a velvety indigo sky. From where she sat, curled into the oversized armchair by the fireplace, Alexis could see the faint flicker of airship beacons winking among the stars.

Across from her, Jack lounged on the couch, his long legs stretched out, his boots kicked off and forgotten under the coffee table. His hair—thick, dark, unruly—was pushed back from his face in lazy waves that caught the glow of the fire.

Beside him, Lena perched on the arm of the couch, swinging one booted foot idly. Her short, violet hair caught the light in flashes of indigo and wine, framing her pale face and the slight, mischievous smile that never quite left her lips. Beneath the hem of her rolled-up sleeves, her luminescent skin glimmered faintly.

In their hands, three mismatched glasses, filled with amber liquid, were raised in a toast.

"To putting an end to Simon's twisted plan," Alexis declared, her voice steady, though a quiet undercurrent of disbelief trembled beneath the words.

"And to clearing your brother's name," Lena added, raising her glass higher, the amber liquid catching fire-light as she smiled—proud, weary, luminous.

Jack raised his glass, a crooked grin spreading across his face. "And to us. We made one hell of a team."

As their glasses met in the center, the sharp chime seemed to seal something between them. Jack savored the burn of the whiskey as it slid down his throat, the warmth settling in his chest. He couldn't believe it was finally over.

"I couldn't have done this without you two," Alexis said, her tone softening. "Thank you, for everything."

Lena reached over, her small hand squeezing Alexis's shoulder. "It was one hell of a ride, wasn't it?"

Jack watched both women, his heart unexpectedly full, his chest tight with a strange ache he couldn't quite define. He opened his mouth to speak, but the sharp, insistent beep of Lena's communicator cut through the moment.

She frowned, glancing down at the device on her wrist. Her black eyes scanned the message—widening as a mixture of shock and worry flickered across her delicate features. Her already pale skin seemed to drain of color entirely.

"It's my father," she said quietly. "My mother ... she's got Morvain's Syndrome."

Alexis blinked, confusion knitting her brow. "What's that?"

Jack straightened, his expression darkening with immediate understanding. "It's bad. It's a neurodegenerative disease—rare, but aggressive. Mostly hits Lyrans or anyone with bioluminescent genetics."

Alexis's eyes darted between them. "I've never heard of it."

"You wouldn't," Lena said softly, her voice tighter than usual. "It comes from exposure to unstable quantum radiation. It attacks your nervous system ... your light cells start to fail first. Then the rest of you follows. It's... fast."

"How fast?" Alexis asked.

Lena's jaw clenched. "Weeks. If that."

Jack's chest tightened further. He already knew the answer to the next question, but he asked anyway. "What are you going to do?"

Lena's fingers danced over her comm, tapping out rapid commands. Her posture was calm, but the tension in her shoulders betrayed her. "I don't have a choice. The meds she needs—neural stabilizers—aren't available on Lyra anymore. They're too tightly regulated. But I know where I can get them."

Jack's stomach sank. "Purgo-Max."

She nodded. "My father's expecting me there. He's got contacts ... maybe a lead on where I can find what she needs." Her short purple hair shifted as she glanced between them. "But it won't be easy."

Alexis's brow furrowed. "Then we'll go with you. Watch your back."

Lena smiled, but the sadness in it pulled at Jack's chest. "Thanks. But this is something I need to do alone."

Jack hesitated. Part of him wanted to argue, to insist, but he knew that look on her face. The stubborn set of her jaw, the determined gleam in her eyes. She wasn't asking permission.

"I'll give you a ride to the intergalactic port, at least," he offered.

"No need." Lena glanced at her comm. "I already booked a shuttle. It'll be here soon." Her gaze softened, but only for a heartbeat. "There's time for me to pack and then finish our drinks."

Lena left the room to pack her few belongings into the duffel bag she'd brought with her from the *Black Jack.* When she returned, silence settled over them like a heavy blanket. Jack stared at Lena, memorizing the shape of her silhouette against the firelight, the slight tilt of her head, the stubborn lift of her chin. He'd known their partnership wouldn't last forever, but he hadn't expected it to end like this. Abrupt. Heavy with unspoken things.

They slowly finished their drinks in silence, their celebratory mood now dampened. Finally, a soft chime sounded from Lena's comm. She checked it, exhaled, and nodded once. "Shuttle's here."

She crossed to the sink, setting her empty glass down with a quiet clink. Jack and Alexis stood as she returned.

"I guess this is it." Jack rested his hand on her shoulder. "We had a good run."

Lena looked up at him, her black eyes shimmering. "Hell yeah, we did, but all good things come to an end." Her gaze flicked toward Alexis. "Besides—" her grin turned teasing, "—you two deserve a little alone time."

"Promise us you'll be careful out there," he said. "And if you need anything, anything at all, you know how to reach me."

Lena's hand covered his, her skin cool against his own. "I will. And the same goes for you two. If you ever find yourselves in trouble, call."

With a last squeeze of Jack's hand, Lena turned to Alexis, pulling her into a tight embrace. "Keep your eye on this one," she whispered loud enough for Jack to hear, her tone teasing despite the weight of the moment.

Alexis laughed, the sound muffled against Lena's shoulder. "I'll do my best."

As Lena pulled away, she fixed Jack with a pointed look. "And you, try to stay out of trouble."

A grin tugged at the corners of his mouth. "No promises."

With a final wave, Lena made her way to the door, her steps determined. Jack watched her go, a sense of unease settling in the pit of his stomach. He knew Lena could handle herself, but the thought of her venturing into the heart of Purgo-Max alone sent a chill down his spine.

The door clicked shut behind her, the sound echoing in the sudden stillness of the room. Jack turned to

Alexis. "She'll be okay." He wasn't sure if he was trying to convince her, or himself.

Alexis stepped closer, laying her head against his shoulder. "I hope so."

A silence stretched between them, soft, fragile. Jack's arm curled around her waist, anchoring them both in that shared, uncertain peace. "How are you holding up?"

She shrugged, a wry smile tugging her lips. "I'm fine. Now that it's over, I feel a little lost."

He pressed a kiss into her hair. "I know what you mean. It's like the ground beneath your feet has shifted, and you're not quite sure where to stand."

Alexis leaned into him, resting her head on his shoulder. He pulled her closer. "Let's take a break, just the two of us. We'll go somewhere far away from all of this."

She pulled back, her eyes widening with surprise. "Are you serious?"

He nodded, a grin spreading across his face. "Totally. It'll be a chance for us to get to know one another better."

A slow smile bloomed on her face, her eyes sparkling with a mix of excitement and something deeper, something that set Jack's heart racing. "I like the sound of that," she murmured, her hand coming up to cup his cheek.

Their lips met, the kiss soft and sweet at first, then deepening as they melted into each other. The world fell away, the worries of the past and the uncertainties of the future fading into the background. In that moment, there was only the two of them, lost in the promise of what could be.

Chapter Twenty-Seven

Jack set the *Black Jack* down on Veridian Oasis 4, the smallest of the tropical islands scattered across the Empyrean Sea. The ship settled onto the landing pad like a bird folding its wings, engines powering down with a quiet hum. Just beyond the ridge lay a white sandy beach and beyond that, the turquoise ocean glittered beneath a sky so clear it seemed unreal.

For the next four days, the island, the beach, and the only cabin would belong solely to them. For Alexis, who had literally waited years to spend such alone time with Jack, it was the perfect vacation.

She stepped out of the hatch and stopped dead, her senses overwhelmed by the riot of colors and scents. Wildflowers dotted the landscape in bursts of magenta and gold. A warm breeze carried the sweet aroma of jasmine and salt. To one side, the ridge sloped gently down toward a beach so white it glowed against the deep blue of the sea.

Jack came to stand beside her, his hand brushing against hers. "This place ... is incredible."

"I can't believe we're actually here." She drank it in like something fragile that might disappear if she blinked.

"Believe it, sweetheart." He offered her a grin as he reached for her hand.

Alexis closed her eyes, tilted her face to the sun, and let herself exhale the tension she hadn't realized she'd been holding since the day Michael died. Standing there—Jack's warmth beside her, the scent of salt and wildflowers in the air—it felt like peace for the first time in too long.

"Let's check out the cabin." Jack suggested after a few minutes.

She nodded, and they collected their bags from the ship and then made their way along the dirt path winding up through the trees.

When the cabin came into view, nestled between palms and hibiscus, Alexis felt a soft laugh bubble up in her chest. Weathered wood, a wide porch, a hammock strung between two posts—it was simple, perfect.

Jack keyed in the code, and the door swung open into a space that smelled of cedar and sea salt. Stepping inside, they looked around. To the left, a cozy kitchen and dining nook. To the right, a sitting area with mismatched chairs and an enormous window overlooking the sea. A large bed waited down the short hallway, promising lazy mornings.

Jack pulled her into his arms, grinning down at her. "What do you think?"

She smiled, resting her forehead against his. "I couldn't ask for anything more."

They unpacked quickly, trading boots and jackets for swimsuits. When they stepped back outside, hand in hand, Alexis felt a giddy lightness settle into her bones. They made their way down the path to the beach, pausing at a small wooden boat resting at the base of the ridge.

"We're taking that out later," Jack promised, and Alexis laughed, nodding.

The sand was warm underfoot as they reached the water's edge. Alexis wiggled her toes into it, sighing in contentment. "I could get used to this."

"Me too." Jack squeezed her hand.

They walked along the shore in silence, the waves brushing their ankles, their footprints trailing behind them and the gentle crash of waves the only sound. Alexis's mind wandered, the events of the past few weeks playing out in a dizzying montage. The dangers they had faced, the secrets they had uncovered—it all seemed so far away, like a half-remembered dream.

When they rounded a bend in the shoreline, a secluded cove came into view, its clear waters sparkling in the sun.

Alexis let out a delighted gasp. "I can't believe how gorgeous it is."

"The water looks inviting, doesn't it?" Jack gave her a mischievous grin. "Come on, let's check it out." He peeled off his shirt and started jogging toward the water.

Grinning, she stood there and admired his nearly naked form. The longer she watched, though, the harder it was to ignore the lure of the water. Soon, she was peeling off her shirt and shorts, which she'd put on to cover her swimsuit, and was racing into the water.

When she was deep enough, she stooped down, letting the cool embrace of the waves wash away the last of her worries. Sunlight danced on the rippling surface, casting shimmering patterns on the soft white sand below.

Swimming further out, she noticed the water transitioning from a bright aquamarine to a rich, hypnotic blue, still so clear she could see the colorful schools of tropical fish darting among the vibrant coral formations below. Exchanging excited glances, Jack and Alexis took deep breaths and dove beneath the surface.

A wondrous underwater world greeted them. Sunbeams filtered through the water, illuminating the brilliant coral reefs stretching out before them, teeming with life in a dazzling array of shapes and hues. Neon-colored fish flitted in and out of the intricate structures, while sleek silver fish glided gracefully by. Sea anemones swayed gently in the currents, their tentacles undulating like delicate underwater flowers.

As they explored deeper, the reef gave way to sandy expanses dotted with seagrass. A curious sea turtle swam by, its wise eyes seeming to appraise them before it glided off into the blue. Alexis pointed excitedly as a pod of playful ripplefins appeared in the distance, their sleek forms cutting through the water with effortless grace.

From below, a glint caught her eye—a shiny, bright rock nestled among the coral. Intrigued, she swam closer and reached out to pick it up. As her fingers closed around the object, a sharp pain jolted through her hand. Bubbles escaped her mouth in a surprised gasp.

Clutching the rock, she kicked towards the surface, Jack following close behind. As they broke through the waves, Alexis held up her hand, wincing at the sight of crimson blood mingling with the seawater.

"Let me see." Jack gently took her hand in his and examined the cut, his brow furrowing with concern. "How'd you cut it?"

She uncurled her fingers, revealing the culprit—a jagged fragment of coral, its vibrant colors belying its razor-sharp edge. "I thought it was a rock. Guess I should have known better."

"The cut's not too deep," he told her, his gaze soft with affection. "Let's get back to shore and patch you up. We don't want to attract any unwanted attention from the local sea life."

Together, they swam back towards the beach, the crystal waters caressing their skin. As they emerged from the waves, their feet welcomed the sun-warmed sand. Jack led Alexis further up shore to where their clothes lay and then, once again, gently examined her hand.

"We should go back to cabin and take care of this," he suggested.

"It's not that bad. See? The bleeding has already stopped. I'd rather stay out here a little longer." She was enjoying their time together too much to want it to end so soon.

He agreed, a bit reluctantly, and they spent the afternoon swimming and lounging on the beach, talking and laughing as the sun made its lazy arc across the sky.

As the sun began to dip toward the horizon, they made their way back to the cabin, sand clinging to their skin and salt drying in their hair.

Once inside, Alexis turned to Jack, stepping close, her arms winding around his neck. "Thank you, for everything."

He gently brushed a strand of hair from her face, his fingertips lingering, as though committing the feel of her to memory. His throat tightened with everything he felt for her—gratitude, awe, love that scared the hell out of him—and yet he still managed a crooked smile. "There's no place I'd rather be." His voice was rough with emotion. "You're the best thing that ever happened to me, Alexis."

Her eyes shimmered, and she leaned in, close enough that he could feel her breath against his skin. Her voice was barely a whisper, but it struck him like a bolt to the chest.

"I have a confession," she breathed, searching his eyes. "I didn't just recently fall in love with you. I've loved you for as long as I can remember. But now? It's more. It's everything."

A quiet, disbelieving laugh escaped him as he pulled her into his arms, holding her like she was the only solid thing in the universe. He pressed his forehead to hers, eyes drifting closed. His voice dropped, rough and steady with the weight of truth. "You're my heart. My safe harbor when everything else falls apart. I didn't even realize how lost I was ... until you. You make me whole. Wherever you are? That's home."

Then he kissed her, slow and deep, pouring every unspoken promise into that moment. The world faded away. The danger, the scars, the uncertainty—none of it mattered. It was just them, tangled together, exactly where they belonged. And for that moment, everything was perfect.

Later, they leisurely showered and, when they were done, Jack bandaged Alexis's hand. Then they set about making dinner.

Soon, the gentle clink of utensils against plates filled the air as Jack and Alexis savored their intimate dinner. The warm glow of candlelight cast a soft, romantic ambiance over the cabin's rustic dining area. Jack's eyes met hers across the table, a smile playing at his lips as he opened his mouth to speak.

Suddenly, the sharp trill of his comm device shattered the tranquil moment. His brow furrowed as he glanced at the screen. "It's Agent Briggs," he told her before tapping the screen and bringing the device to his ear. "Marsden here."

He listened intently to the voice on the other end, then, "Understood. Keep me informed." He ended the call.

"What is it?"

He ran a hand through his hair, his gaze fixed on the flickering candle flame. "They found skeletal remains in the wreckage, but the body was burned beyond recognition. It's probably Simon, but it's going to take some time to make a positive ID."

A heavy silence settled over the room as they finished their meal and then worked together to wash the dinner plates and utensils.

Finally, when the work was done, Alexis went to sit on the couch while Jack excused himself for a moment. When he joined her, he was holding two glasses and a bottle of Solarian ice wine; rare and very expensive.

He set the bottle and glasses on the coffee table, but instead of joining her on the couch, he remained standing. "I've had this bottle tucked away on the *Black Jack* for ten years now, waiting for the perfect moment—and the perfect person—to share it with. I know now that you're the perfect person and I'm hoping that this might be the perfect moment."

She gasped when he dropped to one knee before her. "Alexis, I want to spend the rest of my life with you. Will you have me?"

Tears pricked her eyes as the depth of her feelings for this man welled up inside her and overflowed. She gently cupped her hands on either side of his face, holding him in place. "Yes, Jack. I'll have you, for now and for always." Then she kissed him.

It was several long minutes before Jack could open the bottle of wine so they could celebrate.

After finishing their first glass, he set his glass down and stood up from the couch, a mischievous glint in his eye as he extended his hand to Alexis. "May I have this dance?" His voice was laced with a playful formality.

She laughed, the sound like music to Jack's ears. "You may." She placed her hand in his and allowed him to pull her to her feet.

With a few taps on his wrist-mounted device, Jack queued up a slow, romantic melody that filled the room. As the music swelled, he drew her close, one hand resting on the small of her back while the other held hers, their fingers intertwined.

They swayed together, their bodies moving in perfect synchronicity as if they had been dancing together for years. Jack gazed down at Alexis, his heart swelling with love and adoration for the woman in his arms.

As the music continued, their bodies drew closer, the heat between them building with each passing moment. Jack's hand slid up her back, tangling in her hair as he lowered his head, capturing her lips in a searing kiss.

She responded with equal fervor, her arms winding around his neck as she pressed herself against him. The kiss deepened, their tongues tangling together as passion ignited between them.

Without breaking the kiss, Jack scooped her into his arms, carrying her towards the bedroom. As they tumbled onto the bed, their hands roaming each other's bodies, their evening was only beginning.

Jack and Alexis lay tangled together, their bodies warm beneath the rumpled sheets, moonlight casting pale silver stripes across the bed. The windows were open to the sea breeze and the rhythmic hush of the waves had lulled them to sleep.

Suddenly, the serene silence was disrupted by the sound of shattering glass. Alexis bolted upright, her heart pounding in her chest. Beside her, Jack was already slipping from the bed.

"Stay here." His voice was low and urgent as he slipped on the shorts that he'd discarded earlier that evening.

Alexis shook her head, her eyes flashing with determination. *Not a chance.*

She slipped from the bed and quickly dressed in her own discarded clothes. Then she retrieved her weapon from the nightstand drawer. Years on the force had hardwired certain reflexes.

Jack tossed her a quick glare over his shoulder, but he didn't argue. He was checking the charge on his own weapon, every muscle coiled and ready. "Stay close."

They crept toward the bedroom door, their footsteps soundless on the wooden floor. Jack pressed his ear against the door, listening. Alexis mirrored him on the other side. Nothing. Silence, thick and unnatural.

After a moment, Alexis shook her head to indicate she'd heard nothing. Then Jack slowly opened the door. After a quick peek to make sure it was clear, they moved into the hallway, covering opposite sides to avoid being surprised.

Then they crept down the hallway toward the main room. When they reached it, Jack turned on the overhead light. The two intruders froze as light flooded the room, but their paralysis was only momentary. Recovering, they open-fired, the sizzling sound of blaster bolts filling the air.

The room erupted into chaos as Jack and Alexis dove for cover behind the couch and returned fire. Then someone swore as their blaster clicked, indicating its charge was dead. That left at least one armed intruder against the two of them.

Exchanging looks with Jack, Alexis knew what he was thinking and nodded. He held up one finger. Then another. When he held up the next, they would open fire.

Then, suddenly, the cabin lights cut out, plunging them into a darkness so complete they would have been totally blind except for a few anemic beams of moonlight filtering in through the window.

Jack's hand on her arm kept her in place, their plan aborted. They were up against at least three intruders. The two in the main room and one other. The person who'd cut the lights—and whose location was unknown.

She tapped Jack's arm to get his attention. "We need to split up," she breathed into his ear, her voice barely audible.

She didn't need to see his expression to know he didn't like the plan; his silence told her as much, but after a moment, he gave her hand a squeeze. He knew as well as she did it was their best chance of coming out of this alive.

Giving herself a moment to savor his touch, just in case it was the last time she felt it, she eased away from him, moving quietly on all fours into the darkness, using the back of the couch to guide her.

When she reached the end, she took a moment to get her bearings. The room was open concept, with the couch dividing the sitting room from the kitchen and dining areas, which now lay behind her as she faced the back of the couch.

Holding still, barely breathing, she listened. The silence in the room was oppressive, broken only by the occasional creak of a floorboard or the rustle of fabric as someone moved. The problem was, she wasn't sure if that someone was one of the intruders or Jack.

Suddenly, a floorboard creaked to her right. She swung her blaster up, finger tightening—

A figure lunged, a glint of metal in their hand.

She fired. Light flared, illuminating the attacker's shocked face before he dropped, his weapon clattering to the floor.

Across the room, she heard a scuffle, followed by a muffled grunt and the thud of a body hitting the floor. Had it been Jack?

With her heart in her throat, she went back the way she'd come, along the back of the couch, moving towards the sound.

When she reached the end of the couch, she saw Jack standing over the prone form of another attacker, his blaster trained on the unmoving body. He looked over as she approached, his gaze meeting hers.

"You okay?" he whispered.

She nodded. "I'm good. I shot the other guy." She hesitated. "Jack, I don't think they were alone."

No sooner had the words left her mouth than a figure emerged from the hallway shadows.

"Drop your weapons," the man ordered in a voice that sounded eerily familiar. As Alexis toyed shooting him, a shot rang out. She winced, feeling a searing pain across her upper arm so intense, her grip loosened on her weapon and it fell to the floor. "Drop it, Marsden," the voice growled. "Or the next shot won't be in her arm."

Jack bent and placed his blaster on the floor and then straightened to stand beside her. Together, they stepped back as the figure moved forward.

Simon Rourke stepped into the faint moonlight filtering through the window, his ice-blue eyes gleaming with malice. "Oh, I'm sorry. Did you think I was dead?"

Alexis's stomach turned at the sight of him alive, whole, and still dangerous.

Simon tossed a length of cord at her feet. "Tie him."

She hesitated, glaring.

"Now."

"Do it, Alexis," Jack said quietly. "It's okay."

She moved in front of Jack, her back to Simon, as she tied his wrists together. When she was done, she stepped away so Simon could inspect her work. Keeping his weapon focused on her, he reached out and gave the cord a tug, then smiled when it held firm.

"Now!"

Alexis was confused. Who was he talking to?

Then she felt a sharp pain at the back of her head and everything went black.

Chapter Twenty-Eight

Jack roared in anger when he saw Alexis crumple to the floor, praying she hadn't been hit hard enough to kill her. He then turned that anger on the man standing behind her, the man who'd hit her with the butt of his blaster. It was the intruder he'd scuffled with earlier who must have come to while Jack was being tied up.

"Pick her up," Simon ordered the man. "We're going for a walk." He pointed the blaster at Jack and then gestured that Jack should start walking toward the door. "Don't think about running when you get outside; I have people stationed out there who will shoot on my orders."

Not feeling like he had a choice, Jack did as he was told. Simon followed behind him and the man carrying Alexis brought up the rear.

As they started along the path toward the beach, Jack asked Simon, "You obviously got out of the computer room before the crystals exploded, but how'd you make it off your estate without the SDIA agents spotting you?"

Simon chuckled. "Quantum Leap Device. Their range isn't much, but they're very handy to have. You know, for when you need to quickly get from the fourteenth floor of an office building to the basement without taking the stairs. Or when you need to move from inside the house to the far edge of one's property."

That explained a lot. "Whose body did the SDIA find?"

"Sam Hollis. My valet. He came to offer his assistance. Sadly, my QLD can only transport one person at a time. I was forced to leave Sam behind."

"You're despicable."

"Perhaps, but I'm not a fool." He gave Jack a smile. "Did you really think I'd trust everything to a single server? For all your troubles, you only destroyed a copy of my work. My back-up server doesn't have the latest program updates, but it shouldn't take long to install them."

Jack felt a bolt of frustration shoot through him.

By now, they'd reached the small boat at the base of the ridge.

"Grab that rope and drag the boat to the water," Simon told him.

Once again, he did as he was told; all the while, he frantically searched for a way to save Alexis and himself.

Reaching the water's edge, Jack let go of the rope and turned to face Simon.

"What I don't understand," Simon began casually, as if they were old friends relaxing on the beach. "I'm quite sure we've never met before, so this can't be a personal vendetta. And I was extremely careful about covering up my project, so I doubt you discovered what I was doing. And yet—here we are? I'd like to know why." Before Jack could respond, Simon shrugged. "But it's not really that important anymore."

He motioned for the man carrying Alexis to set her into the boat.

So he's going to dump us in the water and let us drown. Now that he understood the plan, Jack's thoughts raced. He was a powerful swimmer, so maybe once they were on the water, he could tip the boat over. It would be harder for Simon to kill them if he were fighting to keep himself afloat.

He had only a fraction of a second to realize that plan wouldn't work as the man came toward him. In the next instant, pain shot through his head and everything went black.

Jack came to at the cold shock of saltwater enveloping him. Then came the crushing realization that his wrists were still bound and his legs were now tied to a heavy anchor that was slowly dragging him downward. Instinctively holding his breath, he strained to see underwater.

He wasn't the only one in the water. Alexis, still unconscious, was tied to the same anchor.

Then came a thunderous splash as something fell into the water a short distance away. After the bubbles cleared, Jack saw the body of the man who'd hit him slowly descending to the sea floor, his leg similarly tethered to an anchor. He wasn't unconscious, though. Judging from the burn marks, he was dead, killed by a blaster shot to the head. And he wasn't alone. There was another body tied to the same anchor, equally dead.

Simon was getting rid of loose ends.

Jack fought to loosen the cord around his wrists, but it held tight. He kicked his legs, hoping to jettison himself toward the surface. The rhythmic pull of the anchor, however, was both powerful and relentless. For a long, heart-stopping moment, his only thought was: *This is it. This is the end.*

But in that abyss of despair, a stubborn spark of survival flared. Even if he couldn't save himself, he had to save Alexis.

Alexis.

Feeling a wave of despair, his gaze went to her, this time noticing the white bandage around her hand. The bandage he'd applied earlier that evening because she'd picked up a piece of coral and cut herself!

Gritting his teeth, he clawed at the rough fibers of the rope, pulling himself down toward the anchor, toward the ocean floor. Every movement was agony, but adrenaline helped numb the pain. With trembling determination, he reached the bottom and grabbed the anchor with one hand to keep himself from floating up while he searched the ocean floor for a piece of coral.

When he couldn't see one, he used his free hand to fan the ocean floor, sending up waves of sand that momentarily blinded him.

He nearly cried out, releasing what little breath he had left, when his hand found a piece of coral. He picked it up and, locating the sharp edge, he grazed it against the rope connecting his leg to the anchor, sawing through the fibers, one painstaking slice at a time.

As he worked, his heart pounded in time with the slow, oppressive drag of the anchor. He stole a glance at Alexis. Her body would instinctively hold its breath under water, but for how long? He had to work fast.

With a final, desperate tug, the rope frayed and snapped, freeing him from the anchor. He rose to the surface, dragged in a lungful of air and then dove below.

He focused on slicing through the rope tying Alexis to the anchor.

Time wasn't a luxury they had, and it felt like it was taking forever.

After a few more passes of the coral, the rope frayed and snapped. Then Jack was hauling Alexis to the surface, praying he wasn't too late.

Looping his arms around her to hold her head above water, he set off for shore.

Again, time seemed to stand still and by the time his heel hit the ocean floor, letting him know he was close enough to shore to stand, he was exhausted.

With what little strength he had, he dragged Alexis up onto the beach and began administering CPR along with breathing air into her lungs.

Her gurgled cough moments later was music to his ears. He quickly turned her on her side so she could throw up the water in her lungs, relieved when very little came up. She'd been able to hold her breath longer than he'd expected.

Her eyelids fluttered open, dazed and glassy.

"Jack ..."

Relief crashed over him so hard he nearly collapsed. He gathered her in his arms, pressing his forehead to hers. "You're okay. I've got you."

She clung to him, trembling.

The gentle crash of waves against the shore seemed almost mocking in its tranquility, belying the life-threatening danger it had posed mere moments ago.

Jack's arms tightened around Alexis, his heart still racing with the adrenaline of their narrow escape. He buried his face in her damp hair, inhaling the briny scent of the sea mingled with the familiar, comforting scent that was uniquely her.

She clung to him, her breaths coming in short, shuddering gasps as she fought to regain her composure.

They sat in silence for a long moment, their hearts gradually slowing to a more normal rhythm as the reality of their survival sank in. Jack's mind raced, trying to piece together the events that had led them to this point. Simon Rourke's reappearance, the ambush at the cabin, the desperate struggle beneath the waves—it all seemed like a surreal, waking nightmare.

Eventually, Alexis pushed herself upright, scanning the shore. "Do you think he's still here?" Her voice was tight with apprehension, her eyes scanning the dark tree line that bordered the beach.

Jack followed her gaze, his own senses on high alert. There was no sign of movement, no sign that Simon had lingered on the island. Still, he knew better than to let his guard down. Until they were far away from this place, they couldn't afford to assume they were safe.

"I don't know," he admitted, his jaw clenching with determination. "But we can't stay here."

With a groan, Jack pushed himself to his feet, his muscles protesting the sudden movement. He reached down, offering Alexis his hand. She took it, her fingers cold and clammy against his skin as he helped her up. Hands still bound, they leaned on each other, their steps unsteady as they made their way up the beach, the sand clinging to their wet clothes and hair.

"Back to the ship?"

He nodded. "The *Black Jack's* our best shot."

They headed toward the ridge, each step heavy with fatigue. The ship gleamed above them, solid and waiting. Reaching it, they stumbled up the ramp, the metal cool beneath their bare feet. The ship was a welcome refuge and as soon as they were inside, Jack sealed the hatch, slumping against it.

Then, noticing how Alexis trembled, he led her to the small living quarters, helping her sit on the edge of the bed before locating a knife and cutting her bonds. Then she took the knife and cut the ropes around his wrists.

As soon as he was free, he rummaged through the drawers for dry clothes. He tossed her a soft T-shirt and a pair of sweatpants, grabbing similar items for himself. They changed in silence, the rustle of fabric the only sound in the room.

Once they were dressed, Jack crossed to the weapons locker, his movements purposeful as he retrieved their spare blasters. He handed one to Alexis, watching as her fingers curled around the grip, her knuckles white with tension. The weight of the weapon was a grim reminder of the danger they still faced.

Jack sat beside her on the bed, his shoulder brushing against hers. "We need a plan," he said, his voice rough with exhaustion.

Alexis nodded, her expression grim but determined. "We need to know if Simon is still on the island. We can't risk him coming after us again."

Jack ran a hand through his damp hair, his mind racing. "We could take the *Black Jack* up, do a sweep of the area from the air. But if Simon's watching, he'll spot us in a heartbeat." A flicker of memory sparked in his mind—the brief mention of a short-distance hovercraft in the cabin's amenities description. "Wait. There's a hovercraft at the cabin, meant for exploring the island."

Leaving the ship, Jack and Alexis crept cautiously along the shadowy path, the towering trees forming a dense canopy overhead that blocked out the moonlight. The damp leaves underfoot muffled their footsteps as they made their way back toward the cabin, Jack in the lead with his blaster drawn.

As they approached, they slowed their pace, senses on high alert. The night seemed unnaturally still, the usual chatter of nocturnal insects and the rustling of small creatures eerily absent. Somewhere in the distance, a mournful bird call echoed, sending a shiver down Alexis's spine.

The cabin came into view through a break in the trees, the weathered wooden structure dark and foreboding in the gloom. Jack motioned for Alexis to stay low as they crept closer, taking cover behind the dense foliage that bordered the clearing.

Alexis's heart pounded in her chest as they inched their way around the perimeter, each step measured and deliberate. When they were close enough, they approached the cabin and ducked beneath a window, their backs pressed against the rough logs of the exterior wall.

Jack raised himself up slowly, peering over the window ledge into the dimly lit interior. Then he straightened.

"Jack?"

He glanced at her. "It looks empty. Stay here while I check it out."

She nodded, and he took off. She raised herself enough to peek through the window and saw when Jack entered the cabin. He looked around the main room before heading down the hallway. Seconds later, he reappeared and, catching her gaze, motioned for her to join him.

"He's not here," he told her when she walked into the cabin. "But we should check the rest of the island to be sure."

She nodded. They left the cabin and searched the back shed, locating the hovercraft. Jack climbed onto it and started the engine. Then, rightly assuming she wouldn't wait behind while he checked out the island alone, he held out a hand to help her climb aboard. As soon as she'd settled in the seat behind him, he took off.

It took them only twenty minutes to search the entire island and confirm they were alone once more. During their search, they'd found a large patch of crushed foliage where Simon's ship had obviously landed. The ship—and Simon—were gone.

"Now what?" Alexis asked, already knowing the answer.

"Now, we go find him—and end this."

Chapter Twenty-Nine

Returning to the cabin, Jack and Alexis packed up their belongings and hauled them to the *Black Jack*. Their vacation was over. Simon had to be found. Jack had contacted Lena, who had recently arrived at Pur-go-Max, to let her know about Simon. They'd talked for a long time, brainstorming ideas for dealing with Simon. At one point, they'd even had Coda on the call, offering his ideas. When Lena had suggested she fly back to help them, Jack told her no. He and Alexis would deal with Simon. Lena had her own problems to deal with.

Now, sitting at the table in the *Black Jack's* galley, Alexis beside him, Jack used his computer to place a call to Agent Briggs.

After a couple of rings, the screen flickered several times and when it finally cleared, Agent Brigg's face appeared on the display.

"Hey Jack, if you're calling for an update on the body we found, I don't have one. I told you it might be a couple of days before we make a positive ID."

"The body belongs to Sam Hollis. He was Simon's valet."

Agent Briggs frowned. "How could you possibly know that?"

"Simon told me, right before he tried to kill me and Alexis."

The stupefied expression on the agent's face would have been humorous under less dire circumstances. Then, finally, "Oh, *krauk*."

"Yeah. And that's not all," Jack went on. "He's got a back-up server and program."

"He's rebuilding everything," Alexis said, her voice sharp with frustration. "And if we don't stop him, he's going to take control of the wormhole network."

"Any chance he's bluffing?" Agent Briggs asked.

Jack exchanged a quick look with Alexis before replying. "Are you willing to take that risk?"

Another long silence. "No. I'll get a team started on tracking him down, but it's a big universe. He could be anywhere."

"We'll help."

Before he could continue, Agent Briggs interrupted him. "No. You and your team have done enough. I need for you to stand down; let the SDIA take it from here."

"Roger that," Jack said, his expression grim. Then he ended the call.

The galley felt small and claustrophobic in the dim blue light of the blank display screen. Jack leaned back in his seat, rubbing a hand over his face. There was a time when he would have said to hell with the potential danger and gone after Simon anyway, but he was no longer alone and last night, he'd almost lost Alexis forever.

He turned to her, sitting beside him with her arms crossed and a steely determination in her gaze.

"What now?" she asked.

He studied the tightness around her mouth, the tension in her body. She was like a spring wound to the point of snapping, ready to uncoil at any moment. He knew that feeling all too well. Knew, too, how she would answer his question before he asked. "I don't suppose you'd stay behind this time. Wait for me to come back once I've dealt with Simon?"

Her gaze was unflinching. "Not on your life."

He'd known that would be her answer, but part of him was still worried for her. Not that she couldn't take care of herself; he knew she was more than capable of holding her own in any fight. But he couldn't help wanting to keep her safe, and he couldn't ignore the little voice in his head that said the best way to do that was to take her back to Galathea. Of course, if he did that, she'd hate him for it. Maybe forever.

He exhaled slowly, letting the doubt drift away. Alexis was strong and stubborn. And she wasn't the only one at risk. Simon was out there somewhere, a threat to the billions of beings living in the tri-galaxy area. He gave her a crooked, tired grin. "Well, then, let's go find Simon."

"But Briggs told us to stand down."

Jack furrowed his brow, feigning confusion. "Are you sure? With all the static coming across the transmission, I couldn't make out his words."

"Right." She tried to smile, but didn't quite manage it as the weight of the situation fell over her, pushing the banter aside. "How are we going to find him? He could be anywhere."

Jack gave her a reassuring smile. "Thanks to Lena and Coda, I've got a few ideas." She arched an eyebrow, urging him to continue. "Before Simon had his man knock me unconscious, he said his back-up program lacked the latest updates and I know, from studying his program, that some of those updates involved the interface with the wormhole system. Simon knows we found his backdoor, so he won't try to use that again, but he's all about redundancies, so he'll have another way in. He'll want to test the system before going live. That's how we find him."

She bit her lip, looking confused. "How exactly?"

"I'll show you." Gesturing to the computer screen, his fingers moved in quick, silent commands across the keyboard. Streams of data bloomed on the screen—communications logs, satellite telemetry, anomaly scans. He tapped into the deep-traffic network he'd once used to smuggle information past military firewalls.

He opened a secondary window, overlaying it with a map of the quadrant. Dozens of wormhole nodes lit up like tiny stars.

"If he rebuilt the program," he continued, more to himself than her, "then somewhere out there, it's running tests. Ping protocols, data pulses. Anything that might mimic network activity. Even dormant, that code will reach out. It has to." They studied the display, watching as the star map shifted and changed as, one by one, false pings dropped away.

"Do you think he'll keep the same code signature?" Alexis was watching the screen intently.

Jack shook his head. "Not exactly. Simon's not stupid, but he's vain, so the new code signature should be close enough to the old one for us to spot it."

"Won't the SDIA be looking, too?"

Jack gave a grim smile. "Yeah, but the SDIA will have to wait for approval before they can start their data mining. We don't."

Alexis nodded, and he saw the flicker of understanding in her eyes. "And if we find Simon first, what then?"

He reached over, brushing a stray lock of hair from her face. "Then we stop him, once and for all."

"Okay. What can I do to help?"

Jack turned back to study the computer display. "Look for anything that pings multiple systems at once," he explained, his gaze flicking between the display and her face, waiting for her to nod in understanding.

"What are you going to do?" she asked when he pushed back from the table and stood.

"It doesn't take two of us to watch this display." Retrieving another computer from a lower cabinet, he set it up next to her at the table. "While you do that, I'm going to work on a little surprise for Simon in case we find him."

Hours passed with the two of them sitting side-by-side at the table. The only sounds were that of Jack's typing, the quiet hums of both computers and the rhythmic pulsing of ocean waves washing up the beach.

Then, suddenly—

"Jack, look at this." She turned the display toward him and pointed to where multiple pings lit the same location on the star map.

Taking a closer look, Jack recognized the location as being deep in the shadow of a radiation field near the Ignus Nebula.

"What is that?" she asked. "A relay station?"

"Not exactly. Old asteroid lab, decommissioned years ago. No registered traffic. But it's still got a comm array ... and that," he pointed, "is Simon's code. Masked, but it's there."

She frowned. "Why there?"

"Nebula interference masks the signal. Perfect for hiding a supercomputer while testing the new wormhole code. He thinks no one's watching. It makes sense. Damn it, he's smart."

"But we found him." Her gaze met his with a look of triumph. "We actually found him."

"Yeah, we did," Jack replied, sounding pleased. "Let's go get him." When he glanced at her, he saw she was biting her lip. "What?"

"Maybe we should let Agent Briggs know? He could send a tactical team."

He thought about it, but then decided she was right. "He's going to tell us to stand down again," he told her. She only smiled.

He placed the call and quickly explained to Briggs what they'd found and provided him with the exact coordinates. After a few more minutes of discussion, Briggs signed off, saying, "Thanks for the info. You—stand down. Let us handle it."

He and Alexis exchanged glances. "No static that time," she noted.

"You know what that means?" A teasing smile played at the corners of his mouth.

She nodded. "It means we'd better get going if we plan to get there first."

The Ignus Nebula loomed ahead of them, a swirling mass of scarlet and gold gases that pulsed like a living heartbeat in the void. Jack piloted the *Black Jack* through the thickening currents of radiation and debris, eyes locked on the silhouette of a lone orbital platform up ahead. Its structure was skeletal and dark, a black stain against the fiery canvas of the nebula.

Alexis stood behind him, one hand braced on the back of his chair, her gaze scanning the jagged outline of the station. "You're sure this is it?"

He nodded grimly. "Signal's coming from that central node. That's where he's hiding the other server."

The platform had long been abandoned—once a mining hub, now forgotten by nearly everyone. Everyone except Simon Rourke, apparently. She wondered if he was here—or was he running his program remotely?

As they neared the docking ring, Jack killed the external lights and powered down everything but life support and sensors. If Simon was here, they didn't want to alert him to their presence until it was too late for him to run.

They suited up quickly—tactical gear, compact blasters, knives strapped to thighs, and comms linked to private channels. Jack accessed the old entry codes through a bypass loop and triggered a soft magnetic clamp to dock the *Black Jack* against the hull.

"Ready?" She nodded. "Keep your breathing filter handy. According to the station's diagnostics, the air is breathable, but just in case ..."

She followed him to the floor hatch, where he bent to access a floor panel. He pressed a button, and the hatch hissed open. Jack went first, dropping into the darkness. Alexis followed, working to keep her breathing slow and steady.

Inside, the station smelled of stale air and corrosion. Gravity generators were functioning enough to provide a sluggish sense of weight. Emergency lights flickered fitfully, casting long shadows between the beams and wiring. Twisted cables ran along the floor like writhing snakes. Alexis, her senses on high alert, kept close behind Jack as they started down the corridor, their footsteps barely making a sound on the cold steel floor. Every turn, every intersection they approached, felt like a potential trap.

The glow from Jack's handheld scanner lit the immediate area around them, but beyond its reach, the shadows appeared darker, more ominous.

"Anything yet?" Alexis asked softly.

"Cables, and rust," he replied. They continued walking until the signal blipped. Jack immediately raised a fisted hand, signaling her to stop. Then he pointed toward the junction. Quietly, Alexis slipped past him, scanning for movement until she reached the junction, peering first to the left, then to the right.

All clear.

She signaled Jack, who came forward to join her. Then, checking his scanner, he turned left, once again taking the lead.

Their path led deeper into the labyrinthine structure, past hatches and doors welded shut. At each one, Jack hesitated, half expecting the flash of a gun, but nothing happened. The scanner flashed more insistently, and, with every step, the distant hum of a server intensified.

Then suddenly, the corridor ended, and they were standing at the opening of a massive circular chamber, its walls lined with power cores and conduit streams. At the center stood a supercomputer identical to the one they'd found on Simon's estate, right down to its crystalline cores glowing a pale violet.

And in front of it, Simon.

Chapter Thirty

SIMON WORE DARK UTILITY armor, his silver hair swept back. When he turned to face them, his ice-blue gaze appeared calm and his expression cool, unruffled. The blaster he held was leveled at them.

"Aren't you two dead yet?" His voice was like a cold handshake.

"Sorry to disappoint," Jack lowered the scanner to reveal his own blaster aimed at Simon. "But we couldn't let you finish what you started."

Simon gave a slow, easy smile. His eyes were like glaciers—pale, cutting, patient. "Looks like I underestimated you," he said, his tone edged with admiration and something else.

Jack took a step forward, his aim unwavering. Alexis moved up to stand beside him, and Jack noted out of his peripheral vision that the hand holding her blaster was steady.

They were close enough now to Simon that Jack could see the calculated look in his gaze and it set off alarm bells.

"This ends now," Jack warned, hoping to end things quickly, peacefully.

"All right. You win." Giving up much too easily, he slowly bent and placed his blaster on the floor. Then, straightening, he raised his hands. "I surrender. Are you planning to shoot me now? Or are the authorities on their way?"

"The SDIA will be here shortly," Jack told him.

"I see. Then, while we wait, perhaps you can explain to me—why?" He watched them carefully, his eyes searching for answers.

"We didn't know about your plan," Jack admitted. "Not at first. Not until we found the stolen Luminite crystals on your ship."

An expression of new understanding crossed Simon's face. "You were the intruders aboard the *Nebula Marauder.*"

Jack nodded. "We were looking for the stolen crystals."

"Not even the mines knew crystals were being smuggled out before they could be registered. How did you?"

When Jack hesitated, not knowing how much Alexis wanted him to share, she stepped forward. "You remember Michael Mattix?" she asked. Simon's brow furrowed slightly and a flicker of confusion crossed his features. "You ordered Chief Townsend to kill him while he was allegedly stealing Luminite crystals from a warehouse in Galathea."

A flicker of recognition lit Simon's gaze. "Ah, yes. I remember. Mattix had a unique skill set which made him a valuable employee. Except he started asking too many questions, a sure sign he was going to be a problem. But how does that concern you?"

"Michael Mattix was my brother," she told him. "I knew he'd never be involved with stealing Luminite crystals. So, I decided to investigate his death and get answers. Being a detective with the GPD gave me access to the evidence taken from the crime scene. That's when I realized the crystals were unregistered and I set out to find who was behind the crystal thefts."

"Ah," Simon said, finally understanding everything. "I'm sorry for your loss, but really, you should have left it alone." While he'd been talking, his hands had been moving slowly together in front of him. Now, suddenly, he used one hand to tap a sequence into the control pad around his other wrist.

Jack lunged forward as the lights surged, throwing the chamber into harsh relief. Behind them, the large doors slammed shut with a clang. Jack and Alexis spun around, realizing too late that their only exit was sealed.

"Seriously?" Jack barked at Simon, frustration gnawing at him. "You think locking us in will stop us from taking you prisoner?"

Simon's smile widened, smug and knowing. Then he pulled a breathing filter from his pocket and shoved it into his mouth. A fraction of a second later, gas began pouring from the ceiling vents, curling like ghostly tendrils through the air.

"Suppressant," Alexis shouted, recognizing it instantly. Moving swiftly, she pulled her own filter from her pocket and shoved it into her mouth. She cast a quick glance at Jack to make sure he'd done the same.

"That's not going to stop us," Jack growled around his filter.

"No," Simon said. "But these might."

A large panel in the wall slid open and two humanoid security drones stepped forward. Their sleek black chassis gleamed with menace, and their red optics flared like demonic eyes. They stood silent for a moment, presumably assessing their targets, then powered up in unison with a chilling whir.

"Let me introduce you to my friends," Simon said from his new hiding place behind a wall of cabinets, his voice smooth as ice.

The drones raised their arms, revealing plasma blasters instead of hands. Jack and Alexis dove for cover as the drones open fired. Plasma blasts sizzled past them, searing holes in the floor and wall. Jack rolled, popped up, and fired a round into the head of one drone. It sparked, staggered, but didn't fall.

Jack spit his breathing filter into his open palm. "Aim for their power core!" he shouted over the chaos. "Base of the neck." The gas filled his lungs like acid, and he choked it back before reinserting his filter.

Alexis fired a volley and her shots slammed into the second drone's chest, leaving scorch marks and showers of sparks, but not the crippling damage they needed. She mentally swore as the drone advanced, relentless; its targeting systems locked on, firing plasma bursts that forced her and Jack to retreat.

They hit the floor and rolled, coming up to crouch behind the support beams as plasma fire chewed through the floor where they'd stood moments before. Alexis felt her heart pounding in her chest but did her best to control her fear. This was not her first blaster fight, and she prayed it wouldn't be her last.

Next to her, Jack steadied himself, gritting his teeth as he fired another shot. His aim was true, the bolt of energy striking the base of the neck. The drone reeled but stayed upright, its systems refusing to give in.

Alexis didn't have a clear shot from her current position, so, taking a deep breath, she stood, letting the drone find her.

"Get down!" Jack shouted as plasma sprayed past her, catching the side of her suit in a shower of sparks. She didn't flinch, but pulled the trigger of her blaster in a single smooth motion. The bolt cut through the gas like a knife, slamming into the drone's power core with a precision that surprised even her. The drone jerked violently, a puppet with its strings cut, and crashed to the floor.

Jack drew fire from the second drone, diving into the open as it locked onto him. The air sang with heat and ozone, plasma scoring the ground at his feet. He moved with the grace of instinct, leading the machine away from the supercomputer, away from Alexis, giving her the space to line up the shot.

Despite the danger, she couldn't help but be impressed by his actions as he pulled the drone's attention in a deadly dance across the room, leaving it exposed. She took a breath and held it.

She fired once. Twice.

The drone turned too late, sensing the threat but unable to adjust in time. Her third shot punched through the power core with a sound like breaking glass. Systems cascaded into failure, the glow of red optics dimming as the drone shuddered and fell.

She barely had time to catch her breath before Simon's voice cut through the aftermath.

"Congratulations," Simon drawled as he stepped from behind the cabinets, beginning a slow, disdainful clap. "You exceeded expectations. I genuinely thought the drones would make quick work of you. Perhaps I underestimated your recklessness."

He gave a theatrical sigh, as if disappointed in a group of underachieving students.

"But surely even you realize how futile this little disruption is. You're too late."

He gestured lazily toward the supercomputer. The crystalline cores pulsed with increasing intensity, throwing sharp light across the room. On the monitors, code streamed so rapidly it resembled vertical waves of static, too fast for the eye to follow. In the center: **WORMHOLE ROUTING OVERRIDE ENABLED** pulsed in red.

"You see," he continued, adopting the tone of a bored professor lecturing first-years, "while you were playing tag with my security systems, I activated the final phase of the protocol. Elegant, isn't it?" He approached the console, fingers gliding across the controls with infuriating ease.

A tri-galactic star map filled the screen—crimson lines webbing across entire sectors, each labeled with system tags and encrypted route codes.

"This—" he said, sweeping one hand toward the glowing map, "is control. Every wormhole in the tri-galactic corridor. Trade. Surveillance. Smuggling. Military logistics. I own it all. Do you understand what that means?"

He turned to face them, tilting his head as if addressing especially slow pupils.

"With one directive, I can reroute cargo meant for border colonies into deep space. Collapse supply chains. Strangle economies. Or simply ... delay medical transports until they arrive too late. The Galactic Assembly built this network to maintain order. And now," he smirked, "they've handed me the keys."

He let that hang in the air, then added with quiet triumph:

"Game over. You lost. All that effort—so admirably naïve."

Then the map on the display flickered. Lines of code froze. Alerts popped up. Warnings flashed. FATAL ERROR. VIRUS DETECTED.

"What—what is this?" Simon's expression showed alarm as he turned to the computer and quickly entered commands.

Jack stepped forward slowly, his weapon still raised. "That would be my virus." Simon's head snapped up. "You remember your signature wormhole protocol? The one so sophisticated only you could trigger it? It inspired me to make something similar—a virus with a single purpose: to eat your override alive the second it was activated."

Simon snarled. "I don't believe you. There's no way—"

"You're right," Jack told him. "I wasn't smart enough to write a code like that myself. So I enlisted the help of a friend. You remember Coda Varek, don't you?" Jack smiled. "He remembers you."

"But how is this possible? There are government security protocols in place."

"Oh, that part was easy," Alexis said. "When we told the SDIA that we wanted to insert a retaliatory virus into the main wormhole array, they were skeptical, at first. We told them the virus would sit dormant until someone tried what you just did and then it would follow the override command right back to the originating computer, obliterating the code along the way, thus destroying the override program and rendering the originating computer inoperable. They gave us the go-ahead."

"You bastards—" Simon lunged for them, but Jack shot the floor in front of his feet, causing him to jerk to a halt.

On the screens, the last of Simon's code crumpled. Then the screen went blank, and the computer fell silent, except for the hum of the cooling fans.

"Game over," Jack said, his tone sounding final. "Your code's gone. You lost."

Simon stood frozen before the dead console, the glow of the crystals tinting his face a sickly blue. For a split second, his expression was as blank as the monitor—then it twisted into something raw and feral. His eyes darted to the blaster lying where he'd abandoned it earlier.

"Don't." Jack raised his own weapon in a fluid motion. Alexis mirrored him, her gun sighted in the dead center of Simon's chest. "You can't shoot your way out of this."

Simon hesitated, sweat breaking out across his brow. Then, from the corridor outside, heavy footsteps echoed, rhythmic and sure. Simon's eyes widened in a silent, last-second calculation, but Jack saw the recognition there ... Simon knew who was coming.

In the next instant, the large doors opened and Agent Briggs entered, flanked by six armored SDIA agents, weapons at the ready.

"Simon Rourke," he called, voice steady as stone. "You're under arrest. Step away from the weapon and raise your hands. Now."

With the fight in him draining from his posture, Simon slowly raised his hands. The movement was almost graceful, as if he wanted to preserve some last scrap of dignity.

The SDIA agents closed in, two keeping their weapons trained on Simon while the others fanned out to secure the chamber.

Briggs approached, cuffs already in hand, face expressionless. "You're charged with conspiracy, murder, and a laundry list of other offenses." He snapped the cuffs around Simon's wrists. "If you're lucky, you'll be allowed to rot in a cell somewhere cold and dark for the rest of your life."

Simon didn't answer. His gaze remained locked on the dead console, on the ashes of his great ambition.

Jack and Alexis lowered their blasters, but neither took their eyes off Simon until Briggs gestured to the waiting agents. "Take him."

The SDIA squad moved as one, gripping Simon's arms and guiding him toward the exit. The rubber soles of their boots thudded on the metal floor in time with the hum of the supercomputer's cooling fans.

Before reaching the exit, Simon craned his head back, meeting Jack's gaze one last time. There was no smugness in his expression now—only the stark, desperate fury of a man who thought he was too clever to lose.

"This isn't over," Simon said, his voice low and venomous. "If it's not me, it'll be someone else."

Jack shrugged, the gesture small but definitive. "I know, which is why the virus Coda and I created will exist in perpetuum—always backtracking and destroying any unauthorized program that tries to override the wormhole network." He smiled. "I guess we should thank you. Not only did the government clear Coda of all charges related to his alleged cybercrimes, but they gave us each a tidy sum of credits for the use of our virus."

A bit more of the color drained from Simon's face before the agents hauled him out of the room.

Briggs lingered, turning back to Jack and Alexis. "Nice work," he said, the words clipped but weighted with meaning. Then his gaze shifted to Alexis. "And I thought you'd want to know—Michael's name will be cleared. Officially."

Alexis blinked. "What?"

Briggs gave a slow nod. "When we combed through the files Simon had stored, we found the data Michael sent him. It wasn't what it looked like. The SDIA confirmed that the so-called 'internal registry' Michael gave Simon was a dummy. It was filled with embedded trackers and ghost beacons—every access point, every protocol he gave Simon was tagged."

Jack straightened. "So he was baiting him."

"Exactly," Briggs said. "He used the fake registry to map Rourke's entire smuggling network—trade routes, drop points, contact logs. The whole damn thing. He built the trap from the inside out."

Alexis stood in stunned silence, her hand slowly falling to her side.

Briggs's voice gentled slightly. "He knew the risk. That he might not live to see it work. But he made sure you would."

He gave them a final nod, then turned to follow his agents, his boots echoing down the corridor.

Jack and Alexis were alone. A heavy silence settled over the chamber like the last breath before a storm breaks. For the first time in what felt like forever, Jack allowed himself to exhale.

He turned to Alexis. Her posture had relaxed a little, the gun now resting at her side. Her expression was unreadable at first—then it shifted into something softer. Something painfully proud.

"You were right," Jack said gently. "He never stopped being the good guy."

A small, wavering smile touched her lips. "It's really over," she said, letting out a breath. "We cleared Michael's name and caught his killer."

Jack nodded, feeling the truth of it in the bone-deep weariness spreading through his limbs. "Yeah. We did."

They stood for a while, watching the Luminite crystals dim one by one as the cooling fans shut off. The room was no longer a battleground or a tomb. It was just another dead end on the edge of the galaxy.

"You know what Michael would say to me after I cracked a major case?" she asked, her breath barely above a whisper.

Jack tilted his head. "Tell me."

She gazed up at him. "He'd say, 'I knew you'd find the truth. You always do. Now let it set you free.'"

Jack wrapped his arm around her shoulders, giving her a gentle squeeze before steering her toward the exit. "Sounds like good advice."

Chapter Thirty-One

THE SUN STRETCHED LONG golden fingers across the veranda, bathing everything in a honeyed glow as Jack stepped outside carrying two steaming mugs of coffee. The gentle breeze stirred the curtains at the open window behind him, ruffling his hair as he approached.

They were at another island resort, similar to the one they'd been at two days ago, but without all the memories of Simon.

Alexis sat curled up on the cushioned bench, her feet tucked beneath her, her face tilted toward the sea. The soft, oversized shirt she wore—the same one Jack had tossed on the bed last night—slipped off one shoulder, exposing sun-kissed skin. When she turned, her violet eyes caught the sunlight, glowing warm and sleepy.

"You're a sight I could get used to," Jack said, handing her the mug.

She smiled lazily, wrapping both hands around the ceramic, inhaling the rich aroma. "That's the general plan."

He settled beside her, one arm draped across the back of the bench, fingers brushing her shoulder. Before them, the ocean glittered like scattered diamonds beneath the rising sun, the tide rolling in steady, rhythmic waves that matched the slowing beat of her heart.

"I still can't believe it," she murmured. "We're here. Nobody's chasing us. No one is trying to kill us."

"For now," he added, his lips quirking.

She laughed softly, tipping her head against his. "I'm serious. This ... us ... it feels real. Face it." She leaned into his warmth, savoring the solidity of him beside her, the steady rise and fall of his chest. "You're stuck with me, Marsden."

"I wouldn't have it any other way."

A bird trilled somewhere in the canopy of trees, its call blending with the crash of distant surf. Palm fronds swayed lazily in the breeze, casting dancing shadows across the worn wood of the porch. In the distance, the *Black Jack* gleamed where it rested near the edge of the trees—a silent sentinel waiting for its next adventure.

Alexis sipped her coffee, then gazed at him over the rim of the mug. "I've been thinking."

He groaned playfully. "That never ends well."

She ignored him. "Maybe I'll start a little investigative firm, right here on the island. Nothing big. Missing persons, lost heirlooms, maybe catch the occasional cheating spouse."

"You'd be bored in a week."

"Probably." She tilted her head to look at him. "But you'd be here. And for the first time in years ... that's enough."

Jack's gaze softened, his thumb brushing the edge of her sleeve where it drooped down her arm. "I have a better idea." She set her mug down and twisted toward him. "Let's not limit ourselves to one tiny island. Marsden and Mattix Investigations services the entire tri-galaxy area."

"That could be interesting," she agreed. "But Marsden and Mattix Investigations? It doesn't sound quite right. What about Mattix and Marsden Investigations?"

He dipped his head closer to hers. "What about Marsden and Marsden Investigations?"

She smiled up at him. "I do like the sound of that."

"Me, too." He sealed the vow with a kiss.

For a long, perfect moment, they simply sat together, their silhouettes outlined against the shimmering sea, two souls finally at peace.

Far across the galaxy, the toxic storms howled overhead, a distant, muffled roar above the rock and rust shell of Purgo-Max. Down in the depths, beneath the planet's desolate surface, the black market throbbed with life. Glowing fungi lit the edges of the narrow passages, their faint green-blue haze staining every face with the same sickly hue.

Lena adjusted the strap of the crate across her shoulder, keeping it tucked tight to her side. The medical supplies inside were worth a small fortune—and more importantly, worth her mother's life. She had them. She was almost home free.

Almost.

The vendor had taken longer than expected. Negotiations on Purgo-Max always did, especially when Lyran blood was involved. Half the smugglers wanted to cheat her. The other half wanted to proposition her. She'd dealt with both, but time had slipped away.

She rounded the last corner toward the docking bay and came to an abrupt stop. A cluster of Starlashed enforcers loitered near her ship—the sleek, patched-together shuttle she'd flown in on. The e-SAM on the hull blinked red.

Of course. She should have left days ago. Her gut twisted.

A familiar, wiry woman with a shaved head and a face like cracked stone leaned against the bulkhead beside her ship, tapping at a data pad. A faint smirk curved the enforcer's lips as Lena approached.

"Problem?" Lena kept her voice cool.

"You're late," the woman replied, not looking up. "Your ship's grounded. You want it back, gotta settle the balance."

Lena's jaw tightened and her pulse spiked. "How much?" Not that it mattered. Her credits were gone—every unit funneled into the crate of forbidden meds strapped to her side. Gambling for extra funds would take hours, if not days. Her mother didn't have that kind of time. Her condition was worsening. If she didn't get these supplies back to Lyra soon ...

Lena's gaze swept the bay. Options were slim. Except—

Near the far end of the bay, a sleek, rugged courier-class vessel powered down with recent arrival still written all over it. As a bonus, there was a green e-SAM attached to its hull.

Nearby, leaning against a stack of crates, deep in conversation with a mechanic, was a tall man with short-cropped dark hair, worn spacer's clothes, and a guarded, no-nonsense air. He had the unmistakable look of someone who didn't belong here either.

Lena's eyes narrowed.

She didn't know his name—but she'd caught part of the conversation when she'd passed the docking checkpoint. The mechanic had called him Reed.

Lena decided in less than a heartbeat.

Tucking the medical crate tighter under her arm, she slipped away from the Starlashed enforcer, into the crowd of dock workers, smugglers, and the usual Purgo-Max rabble. No one noticed her peel away toward the ship.

The hatch access panel glowed faint blue. Approaching it, she pulled a slim, palm-sized tool from her belt pouch and pried open the panel. Then she set to work, fingers flying over the interface. The device chirped softly as it spoofed the biometric lock—Lyran tech meeting black market ingenuity. A moment later, the hatch hissed open.

Lena slipped aboard and smacked the control to close and lock the hatch behind her.

Sliding into the pilot's seat, she powered up the unfamiliar systems. The ship hummed to life beneath her hands, responsive, well-maintained. She couldn't help but be impressed. Reed was a man who knew how to take care of his machines.

Feeding power to the thrusters, she felt the docking clamps disengaged with a satisfying hiss.

As the ship rose, she risked a glance back through the viewport. Reed had turned just in time to see his ship lifting off, and his expression had gone from confused to outright furious.

"Sorry, Reed," she muttered under her breath. "But desperate times and all that." She angled the ship skyward, fingers flying across the controls. "But I'll leave it in one piece. Maybe."

Reaching the top of the docking tower, she heard the e-SAM fall off. Then the ship was shooting above the planet's surface. Flipping the engines to full burn, she watched Purgo-Max and its tangled web of criminal factions drop away below her. Ahead lay the stars—and home.

She set the course for Lyra, promising herself that when she was done, she'd leave the ship at the Outer Fringe space station with enough credits to smooth over the theft. With luck, Reed would never need to know who stole his ship.

Outer Fringe Series

ROBIN T. POPP & GEORGIA TRIBELL

Phoenix Rising
(Robin T. Popp)

Echoes of the Fallen
(Robin T. Popp)

Rogue Star
(Georgia Tribell)

Turn the page to read an excerpt from ***Rogue Star!***

ROGUE STAR

GEORGIA TRIBELL

SWEAT SLID DOWN NERO'S back in hot, relentless streams, soaking into the inside of his flex-armor and making it cling in all the wrong places. Every movement irritated the burn between his shoulder blades. His heart thudded too loud, too fast, too hard as he fought to unlock the safe in front of him. His fingers fumbled, clumsy where they shouldn't be. A subtle tremor worked through his prosthetic arm. A reminder he wasn't his old self.

Krauk.

Nero cursed under his breath as he released the slim metal rod he had been using as a lock pick. His metal fingers flexed as he let the arm rest, soft whirring sounds purring from the joints. It had been eleven months since that hell-job went sideways and cost him his arm. Eleven months of surgeries, recalibrations, grueling therapy and guilt.

His crew had scraped together every spare credit to get him to Earth, to pay for the best doctors, the most advanced prosthetic on the market. Even with the latest cutting-edge technology and his crew's tweaking, it still didn't function like his natural limb had. And now here he was, stuck, arm shaking, locked in a high-stakes vault job and barely holding it together. He should've let Orin handle this. Hell, Trin had been right—they should have brought on someone else for jobs like this.

The pain and frustration of not being able to do his job to the best of his ability gnawed at him constantly. He needed this. *Needed* to prove he still had it. Still had *something* to give. He refused to be benched, replaced, or coddled like some broken piece of scrap tech. If he failed here, it would mean every sacrifice they'd made for him was for nothing. His crew's sacrifices still humbled him. Now, they were depending on him to crack this safe and retrieve its contents.

He blew out a frustrated breath. Refocused with renewed determination. Failure was not an option.

"Captain."

Dracke's whisper crackled through his earpiece. Nero tensed immediately on alert. His hand went to his sidearm.

"What is it?"

"A single blip appeared on the radar near your location. Then vanished. It could be something or...nothing."

Nero scanned the room with sharp eyes. Empty, quiet yet, he could feel the silent presence of danger lurking nearby.

"Get ready for extraction," he muttered, as he turned back to the safe

He took hold of the rod. His arm erupted into a tremor, sharp and intense. Gritting his teeth, he pressed the rod into place. The soft tick of the tool entering the locking mechanism gave him hope. Six down. Three to go.

By the time he had another two rods in place, pain licked up his shoulder like white-hot flames. It always hurt more near the connection points, where synthetic joined flesh, nerve to circuit. He rubbed the sore joint, teeth clenched, and reached for the last rod. Sweat beaded across his forehead. Focus. He needed this.

For his crew.

For himself.

For everything they'd sacrificed.

He tried to maneuver the last rod into place. His arm shook. The rod slipped.

Krauk.

His body jerked, barely stopping the tool from jamming into the wrong position. He'd failed. The pain in his arm was too much; he had to stop. His hand trembled again. He could feel it. He was out of time, out of strength, out of—

"Easy there, big guy."

The whispered words brushed his ear like a phantom. Nero froze, his whole body going taut. Small fingers closed over his, steadying the rod with practiced ease. Warmth pressed against his back. Soft curves. Feminine.

What the hell?

His mind tripped over itself trying to catch up. Who the *krauk* was touching him? How had she gotten past the security grid? And why was she here on the top floor of D'Nair Turbyn's five hundred story fortress on Tactac9 helping him rob one of the galaxy's most notorious crime bosses?

"Almost there." The voice whispered again, her body molding tighter to his.

Every instinct screamed to react, to strike, to defend. But his body's conflicting emotions kept him locked in place. His fight-or-flight response screamed for him to move, to protect, and to defeat this threat. The man inside him wanted to stay still and enjoy the warm feminine body pressed against his. Despite the armor, he felt every curve of her body. And stars help him, her scent of lemons and warm sunshine wrapped around him like a memory he didn't know he'd needed.

The last rod clicked into place. With a hiss, the safe opened.

The sound snapped his attention back into place. *Focus. Don't be an idiot.*

"What a beautiful sound," she murmured before stepping back.

Nero turned fast. They stood face-to-face. Too close and yet not close enough. He felt the heat radiating between them. One small move forward and they'd be touching again. He didn't budge. Stars, he wanted too though.

She almost met his gaze in height. Her armor hugged curves that said fit, lethal, and undeniably female. And damn it, some traitorous part of him liked that. Liked it *a lot*. She looked like a woman who could handle anything he gave her in a fight, in bed, on a battlefield.

No, no, no. Not the time. Not the krauking time.

He shouldn't like anything about this threat. And he sure as hell shouldn't be thinking of her in his bed. Black holes. She was a monumental risk.

Her gaze dropped to his right shoulder.

Her hand rose slowly, deliberately. Ever so gently, she brushed her fingers along the line where machine met man. Despite her tenderness, he flinched when her fingers skimmed over the tiny knotted tendons where his body never quite accepted the tech.

"The couplers are too tight," she said, her voice low and sure. "Have whoever performs your adjustments back them off by one-twelfth of a click. Then, make sure you do the required stretching and cold compresses twice a day. After a month, if any are still bothering you, repeat the process but only on the tendons still hurting. Don't over loosen though, or you'll disengage your arm and that's never a good thing."

Nero stared at her, not sure if he wanted to throttle her or kiss her.

He reached into the safe—and so did she.

Their hands brushed.

Her gaze met his, violet and full of mischief.

"Nice try." He studied her face as beautiful lavender eyes studied him. A man could lose his way and possibly his life around this woman.

"A girl's gotta do, what a girl's gotta do," she replied with a slight shrug of one elegant shoulder.

He imagined sinking his teeth into that shoulder and licking away the pain.

"Captain," Dracke's voice broke the spell weaving around them, or at least around him. "You've got company headed your way."

Her sharp inhale told him she'd gotten her own warning. Hell, maybe she'd tapped into his comm system. Either way, *krauk.*

They both pulled back, each now holding a bag of gems.

Judging by her scowl, she'd wanted it all.

So did he.

Footsteps and voices echoed from the corridor. No time.

Nero knew he could either leave with half the loot or be captured while arguing with this woman. Yeah, no way he was letting either of them be taken by D'Nair. He shoved the pouch into the leg compartment of his suit. She mirrored the motion, stashing her share with a glare. He closed the safe, yanked out the rods, and heard the lock engage.

"This way," she hissed.

He followed.

She led him to the corner where a ceiling tile had been shifted and a rope dangled down.

So that's how she got in.

Without hesitation, she clipped herself to the rope. "Grab the line above me and hang on."

Before he could ask, she stepped into him, wrapping her arms around him tight. The rope lifted.

He barely got a grip before his boots left the ground and her legs hooked around his.

"Press close; it's going to be a tight squeeze with both of us."

He did. *Too* well. His hard-on pressed into her lower stomach. There was no way she missed that.

But she said nothing. Didn't even flinch.

They slid upward, bodies locked together.

Once their feet were on the ceiling supports, she unclipped herself and bent to replace the ceiling tile. As she leaned over, her ass pressed flush against him. He grabbed her belt to steady her. Big mistake. She wiggled, whether to tease or torment, he didn't know. Either way, he gritted his teeth and endured.

The tile dropped back into place only moments before the door beneath them opened. He held on as she straightened. Then wrapped both arms about her and pulled her flush against his body. It felt like the most natural thing in the galaxy. His unexpected partner activated the screen embedded in her left arm, and together they watched as ten of D'Nair Turbyn's best grunts entered the room. Armed, armored, and stupid.

The closed vault threw them off. D'Nair hadn't hired them for their brains. They left after a cursory sweep of the room, never looking up.

"Follow me," she whispered again.

And he did. Because following that fine ass of hers over amaze of building supports in this attic was infinitely better than dying in this stars-forsaken fortified deathtrap. Her movements were light and graceful. Above them lay the rooftop of D'Nair Turbyn's five hundred story fortified building on Tactac 9. Below them were D'Nair Turbyn's men and Nero's extraction point. Extraction plan A was no longer an option; it had gone up in flames.

The woman in front of him stopped so suddenly, Nero almost stumbled into her.

"My team's compromised. Exit plan gone," she whispered over her shoulder.

Nero's gaze swept the structure. Calculating.

Options?

One, and it was risky as hell.

Krauk it.

"We're past stable backup plans," he said grimly. "Follow me."

Marlo followed when Mr. Crazy moved.

There was something in his quiet, clipped, almost calm voice that betrayed the urgency beneath his hard-edged exterior. For a man built like a tank, he moved through the maze of beams and conduits with an unsettling amount of grace. She should've taken him out the second he hesitated at the safe. Standard protocol. But the look on his face...that moment of failure, raw and unguarded, had cracked something open inside her. Before she could think better of it, she'd stepped in and touched him.

Stupid. So, so stupid, Marlo.

"Hold."

The single word froze her blood. Mr. Crazy went motionless, and Marlo followed instinct, pressing against a support beam just as the redeye of a security drone zipped past, its sensor scan brushing mere inches from her boots. She held her breath, pulse hammering against her ribs. The cold metallic tang of fear filled her mouth, sharp and unwelcome. A drop of sweat slid from her temple down to her jaw.

Her gaze flicked to him. Statue-still, his head slightly tilted, blue eyes locked on the corridor ahead. He didn't flinch.

And yet, something in her wanted to know what color his hair was beneath that skullcap of his armor. Ridiculous. She tore her gaze away as the panicked voices in her earpiece reminded her how royally *krauked* they were.

He moved, this time faster, deadlier. She matched his pace through the skeletal framework of the rooftop supports. The sudden snap of laser fire lit the shadows with brief, lethal brilliance.

Marlo ducked, heat kissing her cheek as a bolt sizzled past.

"Guard patrol behind us. Coming in hot," she shouted, no longer needing to stay quiet.

She ducked behind a beam as another bolt burned a black scar into the metal beside her. Stars, that was close.

"Thanks, but I noticed the laser fire," Mr. Crazy muttered, his tone as cold as the void of space.

Arrogant bastard.

Metal clanged under their boots as they leaped across girders, barely staying ahead of the guards. She gritted her teeth and pushed herself harder.

"Keep your head down," he barked.

"Hard to do when trying not to fall to one's death," Marlo retorted, searching for a viable exit. Another shot scorched past. Close. Too close.

Behind them, angry voices rang out. Close enough now to make the hair at the back of her neck stand on end. Fear clawed at her spine, but adrenaline rushed faster. They zigzagged through the airborne obstacle course, with no room for error. Shouts echoed behind them, muffled yet menacing, spurring them onward. Both fear and the thrill of the chase rushed through her.

"Focus, Little Thief," Mr. Crazy snapped, but there was no malice in his voice—only the shared understanding of what was at stake.

And damn it, she listened. Survival meant more than avoiding capture. It meant trusting your partner, even if he might be insane.

Up ahead, a service door, miracle of miracles, appeared out of the gloom. Mr. Crazy reached it first. No hesitation. He slammed his palm onto the reader, and for one agonizing second, it stalled before granting access with a grudging hiss.

He yanked her inside, then sealed the door. The narrow corridor smelled of old oil, recycled air and the staleness of nonuse. Still, it gave them a brief respite from the guards' relentless advance and the drone's constant firing.

She met his eyes. Respect, wariness, and stars help her...desire bloomed in her chest. Her type had never been mercenary renegades with bad attitudes, cybernetic arms and hot bodies. She usually went for stable. Predictable. Boring. Only the missionary position in bed type.

Clearly, she had a malfunction.

"Let's not make a habit of this," she muttered, the fleeting sanctuary allowing a momentary drop in her guard.

"Wouldn't dream of it," he replied, his gaze holding hers for several long seconds before he turned towards whatever uncertain fate awaited them beyond the safety of this corridor.

His fingers danced with practiced precision over another security panel, his cybernetic arm whirring faintly as he worked to override the system. Her pulse hammered in her ears; each beat a countdown to their potential capture or worse. The door's locking mechanism finally clicked, the sound barely audible above the cacophony of alarms and distant shouts that now filled the area behind them.

"Got it," he muttered, more to himself than to her as he shoved the heavy door open.

She stepped up and stopped cold.

There was no floor. Just...oh stars...air.

Her breath hitched. Beyond the threshold was the glittering sprawl of Tactac 9, stretching down into forever. Her gaze locked onto the sheer drop. The cityscape below reduced to a tapestry of lights and colors that seemed impossibly far away.

"Dead end?" she whispered, voice tight with disbelief and panic. Disappointment and terror swirled in her stomach, making her ill.

"Hardly," he replied, already moving forward. No hesitation. No Fear. He stepped onto a narrow ledge that ran the length of the tower's exterior. Then he turned, extended his hand.

"Come, Little Thief."

Marlo stood frozen. The wind howled against the side of the tower, clawing at her clothes, her hair, her sanity. The growing thunder of boots and shouts echoing like the drumbeat of death behind her left no room for fear. There was no time to hesitate. With a nod, she took his hand and stepped out onto the ledge.

The wind slammed into her like a freight hauler. She inched forward, clutching at the wall, feet testing every step, balance teetering with every shift, every gale force gust of wind. Fear threatened to render her useless. Her heart thundered as vertigo coiled low in her gut.

"Stay close," he ordered, his voice cutting through the howling windstorm that battered against them.

"Like I have a choice," she shot back, her attempt at bravado sounding weak even to her own ears.

His piercing blue eyes met hers for a moment, and something unspoken passed between them—a silent pact that they were in this together ,come what may. They clung to the side of the structure, inching along the ledge. Each step was a testament to their will to survive, to the unforeseen partnership that had formed under the direst of circumstances. Despite the chaos swirling around them, there was a steadiness to him that Marlo relied on more than she cared to admit.

"Can't say I'm enjoying the view," Marlo quipped, trying to focus on anything but the dizzying height and her rising panic.

"Focus on staying alive, Little Thief," he retorted, though his tone lacked an edge.

They pressed on. The ledge offering no quarter, no mercy. Yet amidst the danger, a thread of exhilaration wove itself into Marlo's fear. This dance with death, with destiny. It was the price one paid for living a life unbound by the rules that shackled others to the ground.

"Almost there," Mr. Crazy said.

Where the hell is there? She wanted to yell.

They reached an outcropping where the ledge widened enough, where they could both stand with ease and no fear of plummeting to one's death. He stopped. Accessed the screen embedded in his cybernetic arm and spoke to some unseen person. The words were too low for her to catch. Done, he turned to her.

Held out a hand.

This time, she didn't hesitate.

She placed her hand in his, and he immediately pulled her forward with the urgency of a man who bore the weight of both their lives in his cybernetic palm. Her fingers tightened around his as he guided her to stand in front of him so they faced one another. His movements were precise and swift as he secured her safety belt to his. The click of the metal fastener felt far too final.

Her heart pounded as she looked up at him. Icy blue eyes met hers and didn't waver.

"Get ready for a pickup," he said into his comm. "We're about to be airborne."

"What?" she yelled over the howling wind.

She had to have misheard. Surely, he wasn't going to...

"Trust me, Little Thief. I've got you."

Then he tipped them both over the edge.

www.ingramcontent.com/pod-product-compliance
Lightning Source LLC
Chambersburg PA
CBHW031156310726
48969CB00001B/99